Immedia... a pen, se... ...favorite rocker by the bedroom window and began to write...

Saturday 23 June

Heavenly Father, I don't even know what to write in these pages, except that I feel so far removed from being the kind of loving person You want me to be. Just when I thought I could reach out to Michael, Beth intruded on our lives. How can I compete for his love when I feel such distance between us?

And Lord, help me to know how to handle Katie. Lately she's more remote than ever. I feel as if I don't know her, or what she really needs in her secret heart.

And Father, I ask for the miracle of discovery, of knowing myself and those I love beyond the window dressing and shiny veneer. Give our family—each one of us—the miracle of Your love!

Books by Carole Gift Page

Love Inspired

In Search of Her Own #4
Decidedly Married #22

CAROLE GIFT PAGE

writes from the heart about contemporary issues facing adults. Considered one of America's best-loved Christian fiction writers, Carole was born and raised in Jackson, Michigan. She is the recipient of two Pacesetter awards and the C. S. Lewis Honor Book Award. Over 800 of Carole's stories, articles and poems have been published in more than 100 Christian periodicals. She is presently under contract for her fortieth book.

A frequent speaker at conferences, schools, churches and women's ministries around the country, Carole finds fulfillment in being able to share her testimony about the faithfulness of God in her life and the abundance He offers those who come to Him. Carole and her husband, Bill, have three children and live in Moreno Valley, California.

Decidedly Married
Carole Gift Page

Published by Steeple Hill Books™

STEEPLE HILL BOOKS

Steeple
Hill™

ISBN 0-373-87022-1

DECIDEDLY MARRIED

Copyright © 1998 by Carole Gift Page

Printed in U.S.A.

And you shall love the Lord your God with all your heart, with all your soul, with all your mind, and with all your strength. This is the first commandment. And the second, like it, is this: You shall love your neighbor as yourself. There is no other commandment greater than these.

—*Matthew* 22:37-40

To my husband, Bill,
who has always been there for me and made more
things possible than I had ever dreamed. I love you,
darling—decidedly!

Prologue

Memories.

Neil Diamond is singing something croony and sensuous, the melody getting under my skin, doing a job on me, turning this moment electric, unforgettable.

Memories. Dusky and fleeting as a sunset sky. But I remember that warm spring night seventeen years ago as if it were yesterday....

...The muggy, hypnotic warmth of Harry's Steakhouse. The booth cozy and dark, a familiar cave. The air sweet with perfume, tangy with garlic and charcoal, and tinged at its edge with cigarette smoke, faint and hazy and distant as the voices around us. I sit tapping my neatly clipped, pale pink fingernails on the linen tablecloth, a nervous gesture. I'm wound too tight, walking the edge, wanting to please him.

Michael.

Michael Ryan.

He raises his glass. "How about a toast?"

I touch the stem of my goblet, lift it high and hear the ring of fine crystal.

"To us." Michael speaking.

"To us." I raise the drink to my lips and sip the chill, bubbling effervescence.

But my gaze is fixed on Michael.

He sits across from me in sport shirt and slacks, bronzed and strapping, elbows on the table, hands folded, his thumb nudging his sturdy chin. He is smiling, not quite smiling, just the slightest curve in his lips. He is smiling more with his eyes—lazy, half-closed eyes, warm with amusement. Hazy blue, inviting, bedroom eyes.

I am swimming in those eyes.

Drowning in those eyes.

"I feel as if I've known you forever." He says it without moving. Without disturbing that smile.

"Three weeks," I say breathlessly.

"Three?"

"We've known each other three weeks. Don't you remember? Three weeks ago tonight Mr. Plotnik's drawing class began."

"Ah, yes. Dear Mr. Plotnik. He was in rare form tonight, wasn't he? The Southland's answer to Salvador Dali—those piercing eyes, that rare mustache, the look of genius—or insanity."

I stifle a laugh. "Don't be unkind, Michael. He's actually quite good. I've learned a lot in three weeks. Haven't you?"

"I suppose so." Michael winks and says invitingly, "But there's so much more I want to know."

He reaches across the table for my hand. His touch is warm. I feel it like an electric charge shooting up my arm, like a tickle, a tremor, the thrill of a sudden dip in the road, the tummy-turning sensation of a roller coaster ride. My heart is turning somersaults, my skin turns to goose flesh. Holding hands never felt so good.

"You're the best in the class, Julie," he says. "In every way."

My face flushes with warmth. "I am not. I'm not nearly as good as that one girl—"

"Who? Myra? Myra Mayonnaise?"

"No, silly. It's Myra Mason."

"The girl who looks like Wolf Man's sister?"

"Yes. No! Come on, she's not that bad. In fact, she's good. Talented. Her technique is flawless."

"You're prettier, with those big, mahogany brown eyes and your golden hair tousled around your face."

"What do my looks have to do with being an artist?"

"Easy. Watching you made it tolerable for me when it was my turn to pose tonight."

"Really? And here I thought you hated posing. You balked enough, until Mr. Plotnik reminded you every student has to take his turn modeling for the class or—"

"Or risk lowering his grade. I know. Why do you think I gave in?"

"So you didn't mind posing after all?"

"I said it was tolerable. That's a far cry from acceptable."

"I have to admit, you looked a bit uncomfortable sitting there in your swim trunks."

"Wouldn't you be? Sitting like a statue for an hour with everyone's eyes boring into you? I tell you, Julie, if I hadn't had you to watch, I'd have—"

"You really watched me? I thought you were joking."

Michael's voice is low, caressing, hypnotic in its intensity. "You really didn't notice? I watched your eyes moving over me, and I imagined it was your lips. I imagined—"

"Michael—really, I—"

"You're blushing. Am I embarrassing you?"

"No, Michael. It's just that you've got the wrong idea. I was looking at you as—as an artist, not—not as a woman."

He presses my hand against his lips. "The way you're looking at me now?"

"Yes—no—I mean—"

"Tell me, Julie. Do you believe in love at third sight?"

"Third?"

"Our third anniversary. You said so yourself. We met three weeks ago tonight. And we've gone out maybe half a dozen times. And yet, would you believe—?"

"Believe what, Michael?"

"Already I'm falling in love with you."

My voice is hushed, full of wonder. "How do you know it's love?"

That smile again, warmly seductive, intoxicating, breaking through my defenses. "It doesn't get any better than this, Julie—my jewel. You feel it, too. I know you do. I can see it in your eyes. It's like everything in our lives has led up to this moment."

Yes, Michael. You were right.

And everything since has led away from that moment.

From that night, seventeen years ago.

The night Katie Lynn was conceived.

Remember, Michael?

Chapter One

Today: the reality.

I'm sitting here.

Sitting here watching Oprah Winfrey on TV.

Thinking how great she looks since she lost all that weight.

Watching Oprah interview an elderly couple who were high school sweethearts and are getting married fifty years later after outliving a wife and two husbands. They're holding hands and looking at each other like there's nobody else in the world.

I'm sitting here eating the expensive candy Michael got me for my birthday—my thirty-fifth, heaven help me!—and I'm squeezing the round ones to find the chocolate cremes. Feeling guilty that I'm sitting here stuffing myself when I should be at work doing something productive. I would have been at work, if it weren't for this head cold—persistent little bugaboo.

Julie had taken all the decongestants and antihistamines she dared. And she still felt lousy.

Wish I'd gone to work, she thought. Wish I'd never found that note. Dying inside over that note.

The words of the note reeled through her mind like one of her mother's old-fashioned vinyl records with the needle stuck in a groove, playing the same refrain over and over:

"Michael,
Sorry about last night.
How about tonight?
My place.
Love, Beth."

Julie couldn't get the words out of her mind. Nor the questions. What does a woman do when she finds that kind of note in her husband's shirt pocket? Written in a feminine hand on faded blue paper. Smelling faintly of perfume. With a phone number at the bottom in her husband's scrawled hand.

What am I supposed to think?

Julie tried hard not to think about the implications of that note. The idea that Michael was meeting a woman named Beth. Tonight. At her place. That he had planned to see her last night, but...something happened. What happened? He was home last night, irritable, distracted. But home.

Julie wrapped her robe around her as if it would ward off the chill numbing her senses. I feel like one of those children who has slipped through the ice and is hanging suspended in frozen waters waiting for someone to fetch him out and thaw him back to life. I am frozen with disbelief. I am too stunned to feel pain. But even through the numbness I already know I am dying inside.

Michael, how could you do this to me? To us?

Oprah was signing off now, smiling that wonderful smile of hers. Julie mused, No matter what issues or ordeals she offers us, the world always rights itself again in her smile.

Julie could imagine Michael on Oprah's show—a poised, successful real-estate executive with his own office—sitting there on stage in his smooth, professional way, his sturdy hands gesturing expansively as he tells Oprah, "I can explain everything. Julie and I were only kids when we got married, nineteen and twenty. She was pregnant, so what can I say? I did the right thing by her."

"And how has the marriage turned out?" Oprah might ask.

"It's been an okay marriage," Michael would reply. "We've got a beautiful daughter named Katie, sweet sixteen and already strong-willed like her mother. I've got to admit, when it comes to wedded bliss, the romance department's nothing to write home about. The fireworks stopped years ago, but Julie and I are comfortable together. What more can you ask for these days?''

"But what about Beth?" Oprah's asking.

What about Beth?

I'm waiting, too, Michael. How do you explain Beth?

Michael, who in blazes is Beth!

Julie flicked off the TV and headed for the kitchen where she quickly put on the kettle. A cup of hot tea was what she needed now. It would calm her nerves and melt the cold dread gripping her heart.

When she was a child, her mother always gave her hot tea when she was sick. With a dash of cream and a spoonful of sugar. Then her mother would sit beside her and talk about her childhood, about the days when she ate vegetables from her own garden and picked apples from the tree next door, and milk still came in glass bottles with cream at the top. Sometimes in the winter the milk on the porch froze, popping the solid cream right through the cardboard cap. And sometimes her mother would suck on that icy mound of cream until her lips grew numb.

Even now, remembering the tale, Julie could almost feel her own lips turn cold. How she had loved hearing her mother's wonderful stories!

But now those days were gone.

"They don't make milk that way anymore, Mama, with cream so rich it's a delicacy," Julie said aloud. She found herself talking to her mother more and more these days, as if she were still alive and sitting across from her, carrying on an ordinary conversation. Julie couldn't seem to break the habit of pretending her mother was there, but what was the harm, if it made her feel better?

"Now everything I buy is low fat or nonfat," she went on, speaking with the casual, intimate tone she always reserved for her mother. "The stuff today tastes like the watered-down milk you poured on my cereal back when Daddy was out of work, Mama. Such long ago days. Strange. I remember nothing of those days except that watery milk. Now I pay a mint for milk like that, Mama.''

Julie poured her tea, wishing her mother was still around to share it with her. But they had buried her mother—the lovely, charming, devoted Ruth Currey—nearly a year ago. That was another truth still frozen inside Julie waiting to thaw.

I say the words in my head every day, but they never take root. They never seem real. I expect to drive through the canyon and past the lake and around the bend to the house in Crescent City where I grew up, the house just two hours away where my father lives in solitary silence, never opening his door or his heart to the likes of his only child, his wayward daughter, Julie Ryan.

Maybe he never forgave me for getting pregnant at eighteen, marrying a man he didn't know, giving up my chance for a career to put my young husband through school. Maybe he never forgave me for not dying instead of Mama. Or maybe he never forgave me for being born.

Julie took her steaming teacup upstairs to her bedroom and settled back on the sofa in her cozy retreat. As she set her tea beside her on a TV tray, she caught a glimpse of her reflection in the TV screen.

I'm wearing an old nightgown and my scuzzy robe that's soft as fleece but clouds out, adding twenty pounds to my girth. I haven't dressed all day. I tell myself it's because I'm sick. I have a cold. I have a right to lounge around and be sloppy and comfortable. Every other day I have to shimmy and wiggle into garments that make me look attractive, that befit my position as administrative assistant to the vice president of Leland-Myer Tool Company. But it's a glorified title with a beggar's pay.

I'm a glorified secretary, nothing more. But it's a life. Not like painting, of course. Nothing matches that. But it's something. At least my job gives me a satisfaction Michael doesn't offer these days.

Michael.

Oh, yes. Michael.

Julie had found the note in his shirt pocket this afternoon—she wasn't snooping, she was sorting the laundry. She sat on the sofa now and stared at it, studied it as if by memorizing every word she could somehow decipher its meaning.

Suddenly she knew what she had to do. Call that number. Like the TV commercial says, "Reach out and touch someone." She had to reach out and touch this Beth. Make sense of her words. Perhaps it was all a silly, horrible mistake. Maybe Beth was a colleague of Michael's. Maybe she was sixty and wore geriatric shoes. Maybe *Beth* was a man's last name. George Beth. John Beth. Andrew Beth.

No. The note said, "Love, Beth."

She wasn't a colleague or an old woman or a man. She was someone beautiful and desirable, someone Michael wanted to be with, would have been with, if...

"Sorry about last night. How about tonight?"

That was it. She knew she had to do it. Had to know.

She set down her teacup, got up and went over to the kingsize bed she and Michael shared. She sat down on the fluffy comforter, reached for the cordless phone on the nightstand and dialed the number. Fingers trembling. Mouth like cotton. Heart pounding like congo drums. Two rings, then the answering machine came on. A soft female voice crooned, "Hello, this is Beth. I can't come to the phone right now, but leave a message and I'll get back to you as soon as I can."

Julie racked her brain for an appropriate response: Hello, Beth, this is your lover's wife. Sorry, he won't be there tonight. He already has plans.

Without uttering a sound, Julie slammed the receiver down and covered her mouth with her hands. She was afraid she would vomit.

She returned to the sofa, sat down and sipped her tea, thinking, All I can do is wait. What time will Michael be home tonight? Will he come home at all? Is it already too late?

Julie looked over at the clock on the nightstand. Nearly three. Katie would be home soon, running up the stairs to her bedroom. Her child, her fanciful daughter, her dreamer of impossible dreams. She carries the image of my youth, Julie mused, the likeness of my mother, the steely aloofness of my father. And Michael's charm. And yet she is so totally her own person I do not know her. Behind the familiar face hides a stranger, a person of such complexity and surprise, I marvel that she came from my body, that she could possibly have been any part of me.

She denies me at every turn, Julie acknowledged darkly, her tea tepid now, tasting bitter on her tongue. In fact, if Katie could manage it she would print a disclaimer for all the world to see: "Any resemblance between my mother and myself is purely co-incidental!"

Julie stirred, pushed her teacup away, ran her fingers through her uncombed hair. When Katie walks in the door and sees me still in my robe, she will accuse me of watching soaps and eating bonbons all day. She will give me her petulant, condescending look, and she will look exactly like my father. And I will hate her for that. We will argue and exchange heated words. Sling verbal arrows back and forth, aiming for the heart.

And I will lose.

Because I am already frozen inside. I am hanging in dark waters with ice in my veins waiting to be rescued.

Will anyone come in time?

Will anyone come at all?

Chapter Two

Julie was heading for the kitchen for more tea when she heard voices outside the carved oak front door. Not loud voices: one lilting, almost singsong, punctuated by that familiar squeal of laughter that wasn't quite spontaneous. Surely it was her daughter's deliberate, girlish laugh. But the other voice was deeper, a stranger's, with a teasingly combative, seductive edge. Julie couldn't distinguish their words, only the muffled rhythm of the sounds, a light, playful cat-and-mouse quality that reminded her of the flirtatious banter of her own youth.

It must be a boy Katie likes, Julie mused, for her to be lingering on the porch with him for so long. But then she has so many friends, boys and girls, always changing, faceless, interchangeable, like strangers coming and going through a revolving door. Which one is it this time?

There was a sudden click of the doorknob. The door opened before Julie could register the fact that she was standing in the white marble foyer in her bathrobe with her honey blond hair a tangled mess, her face devoid of makeup, and her nose puffy and red from sneezing.

Still laughing, Katie sauntered in the door with a tall, strapping young man in T-shirt and jeans, his russet hair hanging down to his shoulders, a gold ring in one ear, and his bronzed arm draped over Katie's shoulder. He was laughing, too, casually, with a pleased, satisfied smirk, as if they had shared a private, even intimate, joke. When they saw Julie standing in the hallway, they stopped in their tracks, frozen momentarily. The boy dropped his arm from Katie's shoulder and flashed an apologetic half smile. Katie's eyes widened with surprise. "Mom, what are you doing home?" she asked, her tone startled, accusing.

"I live here," Julie flung back, realizing it was a dumb thing to say, the sort of answer Katie would have given her.

"But why aren't you at work?" Katie persisted, arching one feathery, finely plucked brow. Her pale pink complexion had reddened, giving her high cheekbones a rosy, self-conscious glow.

"I took the day off, Katie. I'm sick. Can't you tell?"

Katie nodded, her pouty, cranberry red lips drooping slightly. "Yeah, you look totally awful, Mom!"

"Thanks," said Julie. She could have turned the remark back on her daughter. *You look totally awful, too!* Katie stood there in a skimpy tank top and baggy jeans with gaping holes in the knees, one of her typical "ugly" outfits Julie complained about constantly, to no avail. Her long, auburn brown hair was clipped back artlessly and free-falling around her shoulders. Katie's icy blue eyes cut into Julie's soul with a single glance. She had her father's eyes—shrewd, cunning at times, unreadable, defensive; eyes containing such pure, luminous color they could steal one's breath.

"You look like you don't feel good, Mom," Katie was saying. "Did you call the doctor?"

"No. It's just a cold. Nothing to worry about." Julie could have added, I have worse things to fret over, Katie, like your father's mysterious note from some hussy named Beth and this strange boy walking into my house with his hormones raging and his octopus arms hanging all over you!

Julie fixed her gaze expectantly on the young man until his face reddened and Katie said hastily, "Oh, I forgot. Mom, this is Jesse."

"Jesse Dawson," said the tall, broad-shouldered youth. He tentatively offered Julie his hand, then quickly withdrew it when she made no move to acknowledge the gesture. His tanned, chiseled features could have been carved from granite. His jaw was set like flint, as if daring anyone to mess with him. Dark brows crouched over his smoky gray eyes. Julie had sudden visions of smoldering anger and raw passion in his gaze, but whatever secrets lurked behind his eyes, Julie already knew she wanted Katie to have nothing to do with him.

She turned to Katie and said, "Young lady, you know the rule. No boys in the house unless I'm here—or your dad."

"You are here, Mom. Besides, it's not what you think."

"Isn't it? But you brought Jesse here thinking I was still at work."

Katie's tone turned as icy as her eyes. "I swear it's not like that, Mom. Jes just dropped me off so I could change. He's taking me to youth group tonight, and I knew you wouldn't want me wearing these torn jeans to church."

"I wish you wouldn't wear those raggedy jeans anywhere! They belong in the rag bag."

"Everybody wears jeans like these," Katie protested.

Julie folded her arms and rocked back slightly on her heels. "What are you two planning to do for the next few hours until youth group starts?"

Katie shrugged. "I don't know. Just hang out. Grab a burger. Why the third degree, Mom?"

Julie might have said, Because I'm already upset. I'm afraid your father has betrayed me, and I won't risk losing you, too! Instead she ignored Katie's question and addressed Jesse. "I don't recall seeing you around church, Jesse. Are your parents members?"

"No, ma'am. My parents don't go to church," he drawled matter-of-factly. "They're dead."

Julie uncrossed her arms, feeling suddenly unnerved. "I'm sorry."

"Don't be. It happened a long time ago."

Julie groped for words. "Then where do you—I mean, who do you—?"

"I live with my grandma and little brother. Right here in Long Beach. Just off Pine."

Julie nodded stiffly. She knew the area. It was an old, deteriorating, gang-infested neighborhood of tiny rundown houses on postage-stamp-size lots—an area Michael warned her never to drive through alone, especially at night. God forbid that Katie would ever venture into such a neighborhood.

Katie pulled Jesse toward the door, as if to deliver him from Julie's obvious interrogation. "Jes, I'm going to run to my room and change. You can wait out in the car if you want."

He shrugged. "No, that's okay. Go on. I'll wait here."

"Would you like a soft drink or something?" Julie asked offhandedly. She had to admit to a certain grudging admiration of the boy; he hadn't turned tail and run.

Jesse shook his head. "No thanks. I'm not thirsty." He rubbed his palms over the thighs of his jeans. Then, hooking his thumbs on his pockets, he looked around the house with a solemn curiosity. "Nice place," he mumbled.

Following his gaze, Julie saw her home through his eyes—a bright, spacious two-story with expansive windows, thick carpets, an Italian marble fireplace and classic country French decor accented by lush, live plants and her own original oil paintings. Julie felt a rush of pride, recalling how hard she and Michael had worked to afford such an impressive home for themselves and Katie. But the feeling was followed by a prick of guilt. Jesse Dawson had never been able to live in such a house.

"Thank you." Julie tightened the sash on her robe, sighed audibly and wondered what she and the boy could find to talk about now. "Are you still in school?" she inquired.

He lowered his gaze, jutting out his lower lip. "No, I quit last year."

"You didn't graduate?"

"Naw. I was a junior."

"Really? But you had only one more year." She knew she was prying, but it was for Katie's sake. "Why didn't you stay in school?"

Jesse shrugged. "I had to work, bring in some dough."

"You couldn't wait until you finished your senior year?"

"Nope. We needed the money. Grams is too old to work. My brother, Scout, is too young."

"What do you do?" Julie asked, "I mean, where do you work?" What she really meant was, Who in their right mind would hire a high school dropout?

Jesse flashed a crooked grin. "I fix cars. I work at a little repair shop a couple of blocks from here. That's where I met Katie. She brought her car in for a tune-up."

Oh, no, a grease monkey! Julie murmured a vague reply but silently chalked up one more reason she wished Michael hadn't given Katie a car on her sixteenth birthday. He was always spoiling her, showering her with everything her heart desired. She was his beautiful little princess who could do no wrong. Why couldn't he see that he was spoiling her, giving her too much too soon? Why did Julie always have to be the "bad guy," pulling back the reins on Katie's freedom?

"I'm ready!" It was Katie's voice. She came striding down the stairs toward the foyer in a sleeveless denim top with a short plaid skirt. "Is this better, Mom?" she asked, twirling in a breezy pirouette that showed off her willowy body and long, shapely legs.

"The outfit is fine," said Julie begrudgingly, "but I didn't give you permission to spend the entire evening out with—with Jesse. We'll have dinner first—"

"But it's church, Mom. Pastor Russell is always telling us to invite people to church."

"I don't think he had dating in mind, Katie."

"Please, Mom! We'll get something to eat at a fast-food place and then go directly to church."

Julie wanted to say no, but then she would have to contend with an angry, insufferable daughter all evening. And besides, Katie and the boy wouldn't be alone; they'd be spending the evening with the youth group.

But another realization cast the deciding vote in Katie's favor. Julie would need her privacy tonight, of all nights! Somehow she had to find the courage to face Michael and confront him about this mystery woman who wrote him on blue, perfumed stationery about a secret tryst, and signed it, "Love, Beth."

Seeing the pout forming again on Katie's lips, Julie said at last, "Go on, Katie. You and Jesse go get something to eat and go to church. But I want you home right after the meeting, you hear?"

"Thanks, Mom! You're the greatest!"

But as the door slammed shut, Julie wondered if the few hours Katie was gone would give her enough time with Michael. What dark, ugly truths might she unearth with her probing? Had she already lost her happy home and just hadn't realized it? Equally disturbing, what would her daughter find when she returned home tonight? Would Katie find her parents at war with each other, their marriage in shambles?

Chapter Three

Michael phoned shortly after Katie left the house with Jesse. Julie was in the kitchen warming up a can of chicken noodle soup. She hated the stuff, except when she was sick. Grabbing the wall phone before its second ring, she spattered hot broth on her hand and uttered an exclamation of pain and frustration. But into the mouthpiece she delivered a surprisingly controlled and pleasant "Hello."

When she realized it was Michael, her heart started pounding in a way it hadn't since they were dating. Her reaction startled her. It was as if their relationship had already undergone a profound change since their parting this morning, all because of a note she had found from someone named Beth.

"Listen, Jewel, I'm glad you're home already. I'm going to be tied up tonight, so don't hold dinner, okay?"

Michael sounded distracted, harried, almost the detached, self-conscious tone people reserved for answering machines. "I'll get home as soon as I can."

"What is it?" she asked thickly. "A client?"

"Yeah," he said without missing a beat. "We're closing a deal and you know the mountains of paperwork involved. It's a headache, but what can I say?"

"'We'?" Julie repeated. "You said '*we're* closing a deal'?" Usually Michael would just say, *I'm* closing a deal.

"You know how it goes, Julie," Michael replied. "Another Realtor brought in a client for a house our office listed. We do this all the time and share the commission, you know that."

"Yes, of course," Julie conceded, feeling a trifle foolish. "Do you want me to keep something warm on the stove for you?" The rest of a can of soup? she thought bitterly.

"No, that's not necessary, hon. I'll grab a bite somewhere." His tone softened into the gentle, tender baritone that had made her heart do flipflops all those years ago. "How's Katie?"

"She went with a friend to youth group." No sense in telling him yet about the long-haired boy with the ring in his ear.

"By the way, sweetheart, you sound awful. Looks like that cold you were fighting got a real foothold."

"Yeah, it did. I stayed home from work today and played couch potato."

"Good. You can't be too careful with all the weird viruses going around these days. Better doctor yourself with that smelly stuff and get to bed early. Don't wait up for me, okay? Just take care of yourself, and I promise I'll try not to wake you when I come in."

"You think you'll be that late?" Julie asked, feeling suddenly close to tears. She was always a sucker for Michael's sweet talk. He could charm fuzz off a fly. Why did he have to use those concerned, heart-melting tones when she was all set to be infuriated with him?

"Are you okay, Jewel?" he asked. "You sound...funny—and I'm not talking about the cold now. Is something wrong?"

"What could be wrong?" she murmured without conviction. "I guess it's just—misery loves company, you know?"

"Look, I'll try to make a short evening of it, but I can't promise anything."

"Michael?" she ventured. "I was just wondering—who's the other Realtor you're working with?—on this deal, I mean."

"Nobody you'd know, sweetheart."

"Humor me, Michael. I'm curious. Which office is he from?"

"*She's* with Consolidated Realtors in Huntington Beach. They're in the book. Now I've really got to go, hon."

"What's her name, Michael?"

"Who?"

"The Realtor. In case I need to reach you."

"Are you feeling that bad, Jewel?"

"No, it's just—I assume you're meeting at her office, so I'd like to know who she is."

"Yeah, sure. Fine." Michael sounded annoyed. "Her name is Beth. Beth Chamberlin."

Julie felt as if someone had walloped her in the pit of her stomach. For an instant she couldn't catch her breath. She held the receiver away from her ear, but she could still hear Michael saying, "Did you hear me, Jewel? Julie, are you there?"

"Yes, Michael," she murmured, her voice catching. "I'm sorry. I'm feeling worse. I've got to go."

"Listen, take care of yourself, sweetheart," he said again, as if she were the only woman on his mind or in his heart. "I'll see you soon. Sleep tight."

Without another word she dropped the receiver back into its cradle, stumbled into the living room and curled up on the sofa. She felt stunned, baffled, wounded, betrayed. Beth was more than a name in a note. She was real, a real person, someone who was meeting with Michael this very evening. "Michael, sorry about last night. How about tonight? My place. Love, Beth." That wasn't the note of a colleague planning the closure of a deal; it was a woman planning an intimate tryst with a man she loved.

"What kind of a fool do you think I am, Michael?" Julie rubbed her temples. Her dull headache was quickly turning into throbbing, viselike pain. No matter how she played it, the two scenarios didn't jibe—Michael's business deal, Beth's intimate note. "Am I reading too much into this?" she asked aloud. "Or, God forbid, is Michael having an affair with some bimbo named Beth?"

The thought of Michael cheating on her left her feeling incredibly helpless and vulnerable, like someone sitting in the path of an oncoming truck. She wanted desperately to get out of the way before the careering vehicle struck, but she was powerless; her life was about to be shattered, and she couldn't fathom a way to avoid the impact.

Julie stood and paced the floor for several minutes, her mind replaying Michael's words over and over. Was there a clue she'd missed? No, nothing out of the ordinary, nothing she could get a grip on. Except Beth's note. But try as she might, she was only going in circles, retracing the same confusing details until nothing made sense.

She was exhausted, physically and emotionally. She considered going straight up to bed, as Michael had suggested. It was tempting to let slumber obliterate her pain, her questions, her confusion. Why not? She would go upstairs, swathe her throat with that greasy, pungent stuff Michael hated and tie one of his large handkerchiefs around her neck, the way her mother had always done with her father's handkerchiefs when she was a child.

Michael always teased her about her mother's homemade remedies, but he wasn't above trying them himself when he felt bad enough. And right now, more than anything in the world, Julie needed a touch of her mother's tender, loving care, even if it was only in the form of an old handkerchief smelling of camphor and menthol.

But hold on; wait a minute! What was she thinking? She didn't want Michael coming home from a date with some gorgeous blonde—for surely she would be gorgeous and surely she would be blonde—and finding his wife sleeping in her scuzzy flannels with a smelly hanky tied around her neck. No matter how lousy she felt, she would go upstairs, take a bubble bath, wash her hair, douse herself with Michael's favorite perfume and maybe even put on a touch of makeup. She would slip into her most provocative negligee, and, by George, she would be awake when Michael arrived home, no matter how late it was!

Minutes later, as she lay in her oval tub up to her neck in warm water brimming with sweet-smelling, opalescent bubbles, she allowed her body to unwind while her mind traced the rocky, bittersweet history of her marriage.

She had lived for seventeen years with the knowledge that Michael had married her because she was pregnant with his child. Some women chose to abort their unwanted babies, but not Julie. She'd never considered it for a minute; all right, maybe half a minute. But she knew instinctively that this baby—Michael's baby—was a treasure God had given her, and she would do whatever it took to nurture and protect it.

"I always wanted kids someday," Michael conceded when she told him about the baby. "Maybe not this way and not this soon, but, hey, we'll make the best of it. If it's my kid, I want to give him a good home—with two parents who love him." He managed a resigned smile. "So what do you say, Julie? We could drive to Las Vegas this weekend, tie the knot and be back in time for classes on Monday morning."

Julie agreed, relieved that the revelation of her pregnancy had gone so smoothly and that Michael had taken it so well. They would be married and their child would have a normal home. Wasn't that what she wanted?

And yet somewhere deep inside she felt a keen sense of disappointment—it was irrational, she knew—but it was there just the same. She and Michael had lost something precious, something they were just on the verge of finding. They had skipped some vital, foundational step in the larger scheme of things. Their relationship was no longer about the two of them and how they felt about each other; it was about what kind of parents they would be to their unborn child.

Julie hadn't realized until years later, perhaps not even fully until now, how much she had missed the romance and thrill of a traditional courtship. Instead of bringing her roses and whispering words of adoration in her ear, Michael had brought her ads for cribs and layettes and talked about the house they would buy and the nursery they would decorate. She had never been quite sure whether Michael was more in love with her or with the baby she was carrying. And the question that plagued her most of all: would he have loved her enough to marry her if there hadn't been a baby?

That question had haunted her all the years of her marriage, and, God help her, it still haunted her. Every time she watched

Michael and Katie playing Rook or Monopoly or tennis together or laughing and joking in the easy, comfortable way they had with each other, she couldn't help thinking, He loves her more than me. He married me so that he could have her in his life.

And now those old, nagging suspicions seemed to be confirmed. Michael had found another woman—Beth, whoever she was; some conniving witch named Beth. Maybe she would become the love of his life that Julie had never quite managed to be, for she had always felt a certain reticence with Michael, a reservation about giving herself too wholeheartedly to a man who didn't love her enough.

It was a fear—primal, unarticulated—submerged somewhere at the deepest level of her subconscious: this fear of giving herself unreservedly to a man who didn't want her. She had learned the lesson early, at her father's knee. The childhood memories had dimmed in her mind to hazy, shadowed images, like fine stationery that has yellowed with time, flimsy as butterfly wings, the ink faded to pale, indecipherable scrolls.

But, for Julie, the memories still stung. Somewhere inside, at a core that could no longer be touched, she still recognized herself—a boisterous, exuberant youngster running with girlish glee to her daddy, expecting him to swing her up in his arms and tell her he loved her. But her father had been too busy to give her a hug, too preoccupied with his own problems to play with her or read her a story, too closemouthed to tell her he loved her. Throughout her childhood, his stock-in-trade answer was, "Can't you see I'm busy, Julie? Go see your mother."

"He loves you, baby," her mother always assured her. "He just has a hard time showing it." Her mother always had an excuse for her father's lack of affection and attention. "You know how he's been since he lost his job...you know how hard he has to work to put food on the table...you know he doesn't say much, Julie—that's just his nature...you can't change him, Julie. He's not a demonstrative man, but that doesn't mean the feelings aren't there."

"Who were you kidding, Mama—you or me?" said Julie as she pulled the plug on her bath water. The bubbles were gone now, the water tepid, and she was still sneezing. "You were always making excuses for Daddy, but I stopped believing them a long time ago."

She felt the bitter irony as she wrapped herself in a thick, velvety towel. Growing up, she had dreamed of marrying a man who would give her the kind of boundless, unconditional love she had never received from her father. But the inauspicious circumstances of her relationship with Michael had ruined that possibility. She would always feel that he had married her out of a sense of duty—not because she was the one great love of his life.

And now there was this new complication: Beth.

Julie dusted herself with her most expensive body powder and slipped into a soft, clingy negligee. She took another decongestant and put on enough makeup to brighten her brown eyes and bring out the roses in her cheeks. She was running a brush through her saffron curls when she heard the door open downstairs. Her heart quickened. *Michael—he's home already!*

Then she heard Katie's voice calling up the stairs, "Mom, I'm home! Where are you?"

"Up here," Julie called back, pulling on her long, silk robe, stifling her disappointment.

Katie took the stairs two at a time and came sashaying into the bedroom looking disquietingly blissful. Her hair was mussed, her face glowed, and her glossy, cranberry red lipstick was gone—telltale signs that she and her new boyfriend of the moment had been necking. Or what did they call it these days? Making out? Macking? Playing tonsil hockey?

"Did Jesse enjoy the youth group?" Julie inquired.

"Yeah, he thought they were cool."

"Sounds like you think Jesse is pretty cool," noted Julie.

"He is. He's totally hot, Mom."

Julie shivered, but it wasn't a chill from her bath; it was prompted by the expression of rapture on her daughter's face. *I know that look,* Julie thought. *She's in too deep. She's heading for trouble and doesn't even know it.* "I hope you're not getting serious about this boy," she said, weighing her words. "You've just met him."

"What if I am?"

"You hardly even know him."

"That's not true, Mom." Katie twisted a strand of her long, burnished hair. "I've known Jesse since eighth grade. And we've been hanging out together for weeks now. He's so rad."

"Then how come you never brought him home to meet your dad and me?"

Katie shrugged. "I figured you wouldn't like him."

"Why not?"

"You know why."

"No, I don't. Tell me."

"He's not exactly the college preppie-type of guy you want me to date."

Julie inhaled deeply. If she wasn't careful, this discussion would deteriorate into a bitter clash of wills. "Katie, college isn't the issue here. Your friend Jesse told me he's not even planning to graduate from high school. What kind of future—?"

"Mom, why can't I just have fun today and let the future take care of itself?"

These were Julie's own words from so many years ago, smacking her in the face. "Because life doesn't work that way."

Katie folded her slender arms defensively. "I'm a teenager, Mom. I'm not ready to get all serious and gloomy about life like you and Dad."

"Is that how you see us?"

"Isn't it? You're always working. You never have any fun. I don't even think you guys like each other anymore."

Julie winced; she felt a sudden impulse to strike back. "That's enough, young lady. I won't have you bad-mouthing your dad and me."

"I'm not," protested Katie. "Just let me live my own life, Mom. Don't be such a control freak, okay?"

"Sure, I can let you do whatever you please, but when you get into trouble, who are you going to come running to to bail you out?"

"Please, Mom, not another one of your lectures on sex. I'm not going to get into trouble. What do you think I'm going to do—get pregnant like you did and make some guy marry me? No way, Mom!"

Julie felt the blood drain from her face. She reached out and pressed her palm against the wall to steady herself.

Katie looked stricken. "I'm sorry, Mom. You must know I've known for ages you and Dad had to get married. I'm not stupid. All I had to do was the math. You were married five months before I was born. Come on, it's no big deal."

"Go to bed, Katie. Please, it's late." Try as she might, Julie couldn't keep the hysteria out of her voice. The last thing in the world she wanted was for Katie to see how shaken she was by her thoughtless, throwaway remarks. Leave it to the young to dismiss in a few brutally candid words the deeply buried truth that had undermined Julie's marriage from the start. Julie had learned to live with her secret doubts and misgivings about Michael and their marriage. But she wasn't prepared to cope with a headstrong daughter brashly pointing out her shame in a casual conversation.

Katie reached out and touched her mother's arm—an awkward, tentative gesture. "Mom, I'm sorry. I didn't mean to blurt it out like that about you and Dad. I didn't know it would freak you out like this. I just—I don't want you being paranoid about me just because it happened to you."

"What you mean is, what right do I have to tell you to stay out of trouble when I got into trouble myself. Isn't that it?"

"No, Mom. That's not it. It's just—I know what I'm doing. I won't get hurt. I promise."

Julie stepped back and tightened the sash of her robe. The pressure in her head was ballooning, giving her a monumental headache. "I can't deal with this tonight, Katie, but we're not through talking. Do you hear me? You think you have all the answers, but you don't even know all the questions yet."

"I know more than you think, Mom. Stop worrying about me and worry about Dad for a change."

"What's that supposed to mean?"

"Nothing. It's just—you treat him like you're mad at him all the time, like he can't do anything right."

The rawness in Julie's throat took on a new burning sensation. "If I do it's—it's because he never has time for us anymore. He's so busy with everything else under the sun."

Katie's intractable expression softened and for a moment Julie saw a glimpse of the vulnerable child behind the eyes. "He has time for *me*," she said, her angular features settling into a truculent pout. With her blue eyes flashing and her chin jutting out stubbornly, she was the picture of Michael.

Julie had lost another round and felt too miserable and exhausted to protest. One thing about Katie—she would defend her dad to the death; Michael was always Mr. Wonderful in her eyes.

"I'm going to bed," Julie said in a low, grudging monotone. "I suggest you do the same, Katie."

Julie wanted to say something more, yearned to mend this unintended breach between them. But already Katie had averted her gaze, swiveled jauntily and was sashaying off to her room.

I didn't handle things right with Katie, Julie acknowledged with a heavy, sinking sensation as she slipped into bed and fluffed her pillow under her head. What's wrong with me that I always blunder in and say the wrong things? I'll do the same thing when Michael comes home, I know I will. I want to make things right between us, but I can't help it. I'll only make matters worse. What's wrong with me that I can't communicate with the people I love most?

Julie was drifting off to sleep when she heard the front door open and shut downstairs. The familiar sound brought her back to full, heart-pounding wakefulness. This time there was no question; it was Michael, home at last. After a long day of painful questions and doubts, Julie would face her husband and know the truth about this woman named Beth and she would know whether she still had a marriage worth saving.

Chapter Four

Julie slipped out of bed, put on a soft-sounding jazz CD and lit several fragrant candles on the bureau. In the muted, flickering light, the room looked romantic, inviting, as she hoped she, too, looked in her silk negligee. She knew it would be a minute or two before Michael came upstairs. He would walk around the house and check the stove and the windows and doors; he might pour himself a glass of juice and glance at the mail or scan the newspaper headlines if he hadn't already read the paper at work.

But soon—any minute now—she would hear his familiar footsteps on the stairs, and she would be here waiting. Sitting on the side of the bed looking the way he remembered her from their youth. He would come over and kiss her, and their closeness would spark old yearnings and desires. She would search his eyes and read the unspoken truths. In his arms she would feel reassured of his love for her, and they would be together again in a way they seldom were these days.

She soon heard his footfall on the stairs, and moments later he entered the room, his tall, rugged frame filling the doorway. Already he was loosening his tie and unbuttoning his shirt. He stopped a few feet from the bed and gazed quizzically at Julie. "What's going on, hon?"

She forced her voice to sound casual. "What do you mean?"

He gestured toward the candles. "The moonlight and roses bit. What gives?"

"Nothing...everything. I felt lousy all day, so I'm pampering myself tonight."

"Oh." Michael pulled off his shirt and tossed it on the sofa across from the entertainment unit, then unbuckled his belt. He had a solid chest and abdomen, and yet he possessed a graceful leanness through his waist and hips, an athlete's agility as he strode across the room to the dressing area. She heard Michael brushing his teeth at one of the twin oval sinks in the powder room, then he returned moments later in silk, maroon pajama bottoms.

He leaned over and brushed a kiss on the top of her head, then reached for the alarm clock on the bedside table. "You don't look sick, Jewel," he noted as he set the timer. "You look like you're ready to party."

"I didn't want you seeing me with my red nose and my ugly menthol hanky around my throat," she admitted.

He sat down beside her on the bed and looked directly into her eyes. She could smell the lemon scent of his aftershave, or did she detect the hint of another fragrance—another woman's perfume perhaps? "Really?" he said with a baffled chuckle. "You got fixed up like this for me?"

"You sound surprised."

"I—I guess I am. What's the occasion?"

"No occasion. It's just—well, it's been a while since we've spent some time together."

He nodded. "That it has." He studied her, as if to say, *I know there's more to it than that. What aren't you telling me?*

She waited, maintaining a small, cryptic smile, tracing his features as she often did unconsciously—the long, distinctive nose, the high forehead rising to a brush cut of thick, coal-black hair, the generous, sculpted chin that showed a five-o'clock shadow even when he had just shaved, and the thick brows arching dramatically over those insightful blue eyes.

Everything his face says comes out in his eyes, she realized.

The rest of his face is understated, the expression subtle, stony, inscrutable, as immovable as a mountain, but his eyes say it all with a deep, direct, unflinching, disarming power.

"So what's this all about, Julie?" he asked seriously.

She felt her mouth go dry. She couldn't escape those probing eyes. What was she supposed to say? I'm competing with some mystery woman named Beth in hopes that I still have a marriage to salvage? She groped for words. "It's no big deal, Michael. I knew you were closing an important deal tonight, and I just wanted to—I don't know—share the moment with you. If that sounds lame, I guess I—"

He ruffled her hair playfully. "No, it sounds very thoughtful. Thanks, Jewel."

"So tell me about it," she prompted. "How did it go?"

"Fine."

"That's it? Just *fine?*"

"You're surely not interested in the mundane details."

"Maybe I am. You said you were working with another Realtor."

"Yeah. It went like clockwork. The client's happy. We got the price we wanted, and you know how amazing that is these days."

"Then you two worked well together—you and this—*Beth?*" She struggled to say the word without an undercurrent of hostility. But the way Michael looked at her she feared she had allowed more meaning to creep into her question than she had intended.

His icy blue eyes drilled hers. "It's late. Why all the questions, Julie?"

"No reason." She looked away. Somewhere at the core of her spine she was trembling. She knew she couldn't let this moment pass without answers. If necessary, she would force the issue and make Michael tell her the truth. "It's just—I had a strange feeling about this deal tonight, this other Realtor—Beth, whoever she is—like maybe there's something more important here than you've told me." She looked at him, afraid to read the truth in his eyes. "Is there something more, Michael?"

His gaze remained steady, clear. His lips curved in a provocative half smile. "Looks like you've found me out, Jewel. You always did have good instincts about these things. How'd you know?''

"About Beth?" she asked in a small, pained voice. Was he going to force her to say the awful words aloud?

"You must have talked to someone at the office today, right? They told you?''

"No, nobody told me a thing."

"Then how did you know about us bringing Beth aboard?''

She stared at him, perplexed. If he was confessing to an affair, he had a strange way of phrasing it. "What are you talking about, Michael?''

Now he looked as baffled as she felt. "I thought you just said you knew about Beth."

She forced her voice to remain steady, controlled. "Maybe you'd better tell me yourself, Michael.''

"She's leaving Consolidated. She's accepted a position with Ryan and Associates.''

Julie waited, unmoving, her breath caught in her chest. Had she heard right? "What are you saying, Michael?''

"Good grief, Julie, is this a riddle or what? You sounded like you already knew. I'm telling you I've brought Beth Chamberlin into our camp. She's working with me now. She may be young, but she's a crackerjack agent. A real go-getter. If she's as successful with us as she was with Consolidated, we'll triple our sales in six months.''

Julie crawled under the covers and slipped over to her side of the bed. She felt dazed; her head spun. Had she been enormously mistaken about this woman named Beth and her fragrant, little blue note signed with love? Was she truly just a new colleague of Michael's? Was their interest in each other purely professional? Or was Michael a better liar than she had ever given him credit for?

"What's wrong, Julie? Hey, sweetheart, what just happened here?'' Michael climbed into bed beside her and pulled her close. His fingers moved over her face and neck to her shoulder and slipped under the spaghetti strap of her gown. "Come on, Jewel.

Aren't we going to celebrate? I know the perfect way to wrap up this evening. How about it, sweetheart?''

She pulled away and turned over, her back to him. She felt herself freezing up, her mind and body turning numb and cold and impenetrable as a glacier. *I'm sorry, Michael, I can't. I can't!*

"I thought you were ready to celebrate. What is it this time?" he demanded. "You're not in the mood anymore? What is it? Talk to me, Julie. What'd I do wrong? In the name of heaven, Julie, say something!''

At breakfast the next morning Julie sensed that Michael was still irritated with her, but he had the good grace to act as if nothing was wrong around their daughter. Katie, oblivious of any undercurrent, monopolized the conversation, raving to her dad about her new boyfriend, Jesse. "He's so cool, Daddy. He can do impressions. You should hear him do Jay Leno and Tom Hanks. And the president. He sounds just like him. You'll totally like Jesse, Daddy.''

Julie looked up from her yogurt and granola and said quietly, "He has hair past his shoulders and wears an earring in his ear, Michael.''

"Half the guys I know have long hair and wear earrings, Daddy,'' protested Katie. "That doesn't make him bad. You just don't like him, Mom, because he dropped out of school.''

"I never said I didn't like him,'' said Julie, knowing she had already lost this round.

"I'd like to meet him,'' said Michael. "Invite him over, Katie. How about Sunday? We'll throw some steaks on the grill and swap some impressions. I do a pretty convincing Robin Williams, if I do say so myself. Isn't that right, Julie?''

Ignoring the question, she stood up abruptly and started clearing the table. She had no desire to involve herself in such foolishness. *Why do you always do this to me, Michael?* she wondered with a stab of resentment. *Instead of supporting me and urging Katie to date decent, college-bound boys, you encourage her by inviting this young hooligan over to the house. You always* rubber-stamp her choices, no matter how foolish they are, and leave me looking like the bad guy!

"Where are you going, Mom?" asked Katie as Julie reached for her purse.

"Where do you think?" Julie shot back with a hint of acid in her tone. "Your dad and boyfriend do impressions. Well, I do a great disappearing act. I'm going to work." She gave them each a perfunctory kiss and was out the door before either could protest.

They have more fun anyway when it's just the two of them, she told herself as she headed for the freeway onramp. They always laugh more together than when it's the three of us. I cramp their style. Spoil their fun.

Before she settled into a pity party of one, Julie reminded herself that her husband and daughter needed her to keep some balance in their lives. I keep them on track. I bring them back down to earth so they don't soar away forever like helium-filled balloons. I give their lives stability and direction.

But somehow that knowledge didn't comfort her. She knew her husband and daughter shared a special bond she could never break through. She would always be the outsider looking in; that seemed to be the quintessence of her life.

And now she had a feeling her relationship with Michael was growing even more strained and distant. Why couldn't she respond to him the way he wanted her to last night? She had set him up. Why had she turned away, freezing him out? What was wrong with her that she couldn't surrender to the sweet abandonment of loving her husband?

She wanted to blame her problems on a stranger named Beth, but maybe the real problem was Julie's own irrational fears and feelings of inadequacy. I've got to meet this Beth, she decided. That's the only way I'll know if she's a real threat to my marriage.

After work Julie stopped by Michael's office with the pretense of suggesting a dinner date to make up for last night's fiasco. His real-estate office, Ryan and Associates, occupied a quarter of the ground floor in a modern, three-story office building in a thriving, commercial section of Long Beach. The large suite of rooms was

tastefully decorated in classic white antique furniture and uphol-
stered armchairs, accented by ornate gold-leaf mirrors, bold,
bright Cezanne prints and plush ivory carpets. It was an office
that looked and smelled of success. Michael had a knack for making everything he touched seem wonderfully luxurious and appealing; no wonder he was a natural at selling houses.

Julie walked straight back to Michael's private office with the
deliberate, self-assured stride of a woman who knew she had
every right to be here. After all, her husband owned the place.
This was in a sense her company, too. She had a stake in it, a
right to be here. That's what she told herself every time she came
in, every time she found herself feeling ill at ease in the midst of
Michael's perfectly ordered world.

Rose Gibbons, Michael's secretary and girl Friday, stopped Julie just short of his door. "Hello, Mrs. Ryan. How nice to see
you!" Rose was at least fifty, but she dressed stylishly and carried
herself like a much younger woman. She had a wonderful smile
and a way of making people feel she was genuinely interested in
them. "Your husband's out with a client, Mrs. Ryan, but he
should be back anytime. Do you want to wait in his office?"

Julie looked around, hoping to spot the new girl in Michael's
office—and maybe in his life. "Michael told me he hired a new
agent. I thought I might just say hello, welcome her to the firm,
you know?" Did her words sound as lame to Rose as they
sounded to Julie herself?

"Oh, sure, Mrs. Ryan. Miss Chamberlin has the office right
next to your husband's. Go right on in. I'm sure she'd love to
meet you."

Julie nodded and started across the wide expanse of carpet toward the cubicle next to Michael's. Sure enough, Beth Chamberlin's name was already on the carved oak door. Julie felt her
ankles weaken, and her heart skipped a beat. What was she doing
here? Spying on her husband? Trying to make something of nothing? Would this woman see through her and guess her real motive
for wanting to meet her?

Julie was about to turn, walk away, and forget the whole thing,
when Miss Chamberlin's door opened and a tall, willowy brunette

emerged carrying a stack of file folders. She met Julie's gaze and flashed a radiant smile, showing perfect white teeth.

"Miss Chamberlin?" Julie inquired.

The young woman's amber brown eyes glinted with recognition. "Yes, and you must be Michael's wife. I've seen your picture on his desk. You're Julie, right?"

"Yes, and you must be—Beth." Outwardly, Julie was smiling, but inwardly she groaned over Beth Chamberlin's classic good looks: a glowing, porcelain complexion, high cheekbones, a healthy mane of raven black hair and a perfect figure for her form-flattering silk blouse and short skirt.

"I'm so glad to meet you, Mrs. Ryan. You have a great husband. He's really taken me under his wing."

"Has he?" Julie's tone was chilly.

Beth seemed not to notice; she was still beaming. "Oh, yes, he has. I've learned so much from Michael in the short time we've been working together."

Julie winced at the cozy way Beth said *Michael*. It was the very tone she had used in her perfumed note. "But I thought you just joined the company, Miss Chamberlin."

"Yes, officially." Beth's tone was buoyant. "You see, Michael and I worked on several deals together while I was still with Consolidated. When we discovered how well we worked together, he asked me to come over here to Ryan and Associates, and of course, I couldn't say no. It's such a wonderful opportunity. Michael runs a marvelous operation. There's so much room for growth and advancement."

"And with all your energy and enthusiasm, I'm sure you'll go far," said Julie, trying not to sound snide.

Beth shifted the folders in her arms. "I hope so. I just don't want to disappoint Michael—and, of course, everyone else here."

"I'm sure you won't be a disappointment." Julie felt a churning sensation in the pit of her stomach. If she stood here another moment talking to Miss Sugar and Spice, she'd have a diabetic reaction. "I'd really better go. Please tell Michael I stopped by. I'll see him at home."

Beth's bright eyes took on a sudden, keen shrewdness. "Mrs.

Ryan, I'm looking forward to getting better acquainted in the days ahead. We have so much in common!''

Julie blinked with bewilderment. "We do?"

Beth broke into light, lyrical laughter. "Yes. We have Michael! Your husband and my colleague and mentor. He's very important to both of us."

Julie's throat constricted, leaving her with nothing more to offer than a polite nod. She took an awkward step backward, then swiveled around and strode wordlessly out of the office, her breathing ragged, her mind reeling.

As she climbed into her automobile and shakily turned the key in the ignition, she had the sensation she had just been attacked. But by what? An assault of sweetness? Youthful exuberance with a Doris Day smile? It was an irrational feeling, but she sensed the battle lines had been drawn. She was in for the fight of her life with an angel-faced beauty with the cunning of a snake.

Chapter Five

On Saturday Julie telephoned her father, Alex Currey, in Crescent City, two hours' drive from Long Beach. Since her mother's death last year Julie had telephoned her father once a week to check on him and make sure he was okay. In some ways it was an empty ritual, for Julie always had the feeling her father wished she hadn't bothered to call. It was as if he were saying, We never talked when your mother was alive...what do we have to talk about now?

Still, she phoned him every Saturday at noon, as regular as clockwork. Her questions were always the same: Are you feeling okay? Are you eating right? Have you gone anywhere? Have you seen anybody? Do you need anything?

Her father always answered with one-word, often one-syllable replies: Yes ... no ... sure ... nope ... can't ... dunno ... why? ... nothing ... nobody ... nowhere. All dead-end answers, conversation stoppers, as if he deliberately wanted to keep communication with his only daughter nonexistent.

Julie always felt dry-mouthed and tongue-tied when she called her father. No matter what she said to him, he had a way of making her feel stupid for having said it. It often took her days to recover her self-esteem after one of their conversations. That's why she limited the calls to once a week; that was all she could handle.

Not that her father was an ogre or even mean-spirited; it was just that they had always been on different wavelengths, coming at each other from separate planets, aliens of the heart forced to live together all those years under one cramped roof. She had never understood him; he had never understood her.

Alex Currey was a solemn, private man, a former aerospace engineer who had been forced to retire during the massive layoffs prompted by the recession several years ago. He still lived in the same small, stucco, frame house where Julie had been born and raised. He seemed to her as changeless, invariable and eternal as the house itself.

The only time her father's low, melancholy voice took on a lilting note was when Julie mentioned Katie. Then her father would suddenly come alive and declare in a startlingly cheery tone, "Let me talk to my girl, Katie! Tell me, what's that grand-daughter of mine up to these days, anyway?"

This time, Julie had the irresistible urge to reply, "Your darling granddaughter is dating a high school dropout with long hair and a ring in his ear. He's a grease monkey in a garage and lives on the wrong side of the tracks. That's the good news; the bad news is that he could be a gangmember or on drugs or having sex with Katie or who knows what all? And dear Michael has invited him to a family barbecue tomorrow!"

But Julie quickly edited her comments, telling her father only that Katie had a new boyfriend who was coming over for a Sunday barbecue. Why worry him? Let him think life in the Ryan household is idyllic and problem free.

And, as always, after a few minutes of abbreviated conversation, her father droned, "Well, this call is costing you money—you'd better go." Knowing this was his way of saying he had talked long enough and wanted to hang up, she always promptly ended the call without argument, but she was often tempted to say, So what? It's my money and I'll spend it the way I please. I'll talk all day if I want to!

But, of course, she never said such a thing; it was painful

enough to know her father apparently found not the slightest pleasure in talking with her. After hanging up, she was often left with
an odd melancholy feeling, as if something had been stirred up
again for the umpteenth time and not resolved; never resolved.
And what this thing was she had no idea, except that it was like
the flaring up of an old toothache; she had probed the sensitive
core of some deep-set need just enough to remind herself the pain
was still there, buried somewhere beyond reach.

Julie spent the rest of her Saturday painting watercolors—two
bright, churning seascapes taken from her own photographs of the
Pacific Ocean off Laguna Beach at sunset, and a rather prosaic
still life of garden flowers in an antique ceramic vase.

Painting was another of Julie's weekend rituals, like the phone
calls to her father. The calls were made out of a long-standing
sense of obligation, but painting sprang from Julie's deepest
yearnings to express creatively all the multilayered feelings in her
heart for which she had no words. Painting was tied to Julie's
innermost nature; it was as much a part of her as breathing, and
just as necessary.

In college she had dreamed of receiving her degree in fine art
and then studying painting in Europe for a year or two before
launching her professional career in New York, perhaps even in
New York City's Greenwich Village. She had hoped to work
possibly as an illustrator for a national magazine, or more likely
to freelance, conducting workshops and exhibiting her own one-
woman shows until she found a prestigious gallery to represent
her. She had known it would take years of dedicated hard work
to build her name and reputation as an artist, but she'd been
willing to endure whatever it took.

But that was all before Michael and Katie. Seventeen long
years ago. After learning she was pregnant and agreeing to marry
Michael, she knew his education would need to take top priority.
So she quit college and got a nine-to-five, bread-and-butter job to
pay the bills, and her art career became "the road not taken."
She had accepted her fate and taken solace in being a weekend
painter, but always at the back of her mind was the nagging question, What would I have accomplished as an artist if Michael and

I had never— She never finished the question—at least not in so many words, for it seemed somehow a betrayal of both Michael and Katie.

And if there was one thing Julie was, it was loyal. She loved her husband and daughter and couldn't imagine life without them. Surely they were more precious than any imagined career success. Seventeen years ago she had chosen the two of them, and she would make the same choice all over again, without hesitation. And yet, in spite of her commitment and loyalty to her husband and daughter, in spite of what she had given up for them, lately they both seemed to be slipping away from her...irretrievably away.

As usual on Sunday morning Julie and Michael attended services at Bethany Chapel, where they had been members for more years than Julie could recall. Katie was there in the congregation, too, sitting a few aisles away with Jesse. It was the first time she had brought him to a morning service. She was obviously ready to let the world know she had a new boyfriend.

From the corner of her eye Julie could see the two of them whispering together, Katie touching his shoulder and his hair in the intimate, possessive way women let others know they've found their man. Be careful, Katie, Julie wanted to shout. Don't throw away your future on this boy. You'll regret it for the rest of your life!

But there's nothing I can say, Julie realized. The distance between us is too great, in every way.

"She never sits with us anymore," Julie whispered to Michael, as if she expected him to offer a consoling word.

He merely gave her that look that said, What do you expect? She's a teenager!

Julie knew, of course, with or without Jesse, Katie would be sitting elsewhere with her friends; it had been years since she had sat in church with her parents. She was too old now, she would insist, practically an adult. Julie never argued with her about it. And as Michael was quick to remind her now in a confidential whisper, "You know how it is, Jewel. Teenagers don't like to be seen in public with their parents unless it's absolutely unavoidable.''

But Julie missed having her daughter beside her, their arms touching lightly as they shared a Bible during the Scripture reading; she missed hearing Katie's light, clear soprano when the congregation sang hymns and praise choruses.

But it wasn't just Katie she missed. Something else was lacking, too. Julie couldn't quite put her finger on it. Often when she left church she felt the same inexplicable sadness she felt after hanging up the phone with her father, as if she had gone through the motions but hadn't quite connected.

Where was God during church? Why did she always feel as if she were worshiping Him from afar? Surely if she were going to feel close to Him, it should be *here*.

Perhaps if I were worshiping God in some glorious, centuries-old cathedral in Europe, something wonderfully Gothic or Byzantine, like I studied in art history, I would feel God's presence. How different that would be from these modern, sterile, utilitarian church buildings.

Bethany Chapel was typical of so many in Southern California these days. The structure was fairly new, still smelled new, in fact—a sprawling stucco building, attractive in a spare, serviceable sort of way, but nothing like those exquisite European cathedrals, nor even like the little country church Julie had gone to growing up.

Her childhood church had possessed lovely stained-glass windows showing Jesus the Good Shepherd and Jesus with His disciples at the Last Supper. It was a quaint, picture-postcard church complete with a steeple and belfry. In sharp contrast, Bethany Chapel's huge all-purpose auditorium served as both sanctuary and gymnasium, and from the outside it could be mistaken for a school or even an office building. Still, it was better than the public school gymnasium they had met in for years until the money was raised to build their own facility.

Julie felt a stab of guilt as Pastor Brady fleetingly met her gaze from the pulpit. He was a genteel, middle-aged man with a witty, urbane manner, impeccable taste and flawlessly styled graying hair. He had a way of looking right through you so you were convinced he had crafted his sermon just for you. He was looking at Julie that way now. Did he realize her mind was wandering? She relaxed a little as he cleared his throat and moved his discerning eyes over the rest of the congregation. What had he said? Was he waiting for some response? Shamefacedly she realized he was halfway through his sermon and she hadn't heard a word.

In his sonorous tone he was saying, "We are going to look today at God's most significant commands to His children. These verses are found several times in both the Old and New Testaments. That shows us how vitally important God considers these instructions..."

But even as her fingers moved automatically through the rustling, tissue-thin pages to the Gospel of Mark, Julie's thoughts turned inward again, meandering, traveling to a far corner of her consciousness. She was facing an inner crisis, something she couldn't even articulate, but it had been building for days. A dark, ominous cloud had settled over her soul; the darkness encompassed Michael and Katie, her father, and even a woman named Beth and a boy named Jesse. With her mind whirling in such a maelstrom, how could Julie sit quietly and listen to mere words, even from a man of God?

And there was more.

After all these years I still sit here feeling anonymous, wearing a mask, pretending. I've seen these same people for years and yet never gotten to know them well. We go through the same routine every Sunday—entering the vestibule, smiling and saying hello, exchanging brief pleasantries, then sitting down, singing, praying, listening, getting up, going out and wishing one another a nice day or a good week. But we never go beyond the surface of one another's lives.

With a start, Julie realized something else. *God forgive me, I maintain the same facade with You, Heavenly Father—dutifully praying or reading a few verses, my time with You sandwiched among myriad other demanding activities. What does it mean? Who do I think I'm fooling?*

From a distance she heard Pastor Brady raise his voice and

declare with a solemn authority, "'And you shall love the Lord your God with all your heart, with all your soul, with all your mind and with all your strength. This is the first commandment.'"

I love you, Lord—surely I do, Julie reflected with a twinge of conscience. *Isn't that one of the givens of life, one of the things we just assume? But I admit I don't know You very well. Dear God, sometimes I wonder if I know You at all, or do I only think I know You?*

Pastor Brady was still reading. "'And the second, like it, is this: you shall love your neighbor as yourself. There is no other commandment greater than these.'"

Pastor Brady paused for a long moment, allowing his words to take root. Then he went on in his smooth baritone, "Dear friends, how well do we even *know* God and one another? Have we cut God down to our size to fit conveniently into our priorities, our time restraints, our selfish desires? Sadly, many of us have hardly scratched the surface of knowing and loving God and one another. Because of our own blindness and indifference, we are destined to remain strangers all of our lives—strangers with God, strangers with one another."

He's talking about me! Julie realized. She felt as if someone had gripped her shoulders and shaken her like a child. *He's describing me. That's exactly how I am. That's my life!*

Every relationship I have is superficial, transitory, with little meaning. I have no connections with anyone, nothing that allows me to vent the raw, unedited emotions I feel. I have no one with whom I can be totally myself. Was I ever truly myself with Michael? Or have we always worn the masks we thought the other wanted to see? Do I know Michael at all? Do I know Katie?

Startling her out of her reverie, Michael leaned over and whispered, "Are you okay, Julie? You look a little pale."

"I'm fine!" she told him, but she said it with such force that several people in the pew ahead glanced around curiously.

"I'm fine," she said again, licking her dry lips.

But she wasn't fine. Her mind was going a mile a minute, dredging up alarming thoughts and painful insights in a random, pell-mell rush.

After all these years, how can we be such strangers to one another? How can you live in the same house with someone, the same little collection of rooms, the same walls and windows and furnishings and pictures—and not know someone? How can you live together in the routine of daily life and remain strangers? How can you live together for years and hardly scratch the surface of who they are, and have no idea what they think or how they feel?

Another thought was just as dismaying.

If Pastor Brady is right, I've spent my whole life living among strangers. I knew my mother—thought I knew her, but did I really? How well have I known anyone in my life—my father, my husband, my daughter, and yes, even God? Have I even bothered to try?

Or have I accepted superficial relationships because they're easier, because they demand nothing of me? I've struggled to understand myself and I'm still light-years away from knowing who I am, what I feel and what I want. How can I know others if I'm not even sure about myself? What can I do to reach across the barriers and feel the texture and grain of another living soul?

And what if no one wants to let me in? she wondered darkly. What if remaining pleasant strangers is all anyone really wants of another person? What if everyone else is as protective of their private world as I am of mine? How do I start breaking down barriers and getting inside where someone else lives?

Is it possible others have been trying to break down my barriers, and I've never noticed? Michael? Even Katie? Have I been as impervious to the invasions of others into my life as my father has been? In the name of heaven, am I just like him?

The questions were overwhelming, terrifying, shattering. But before Julie could even begin to explore the answers, her attention was drawn back suddenly to Pastor Brady. He was saying, "Are you listening to me, my friends? This is important. This hits at the crux of all our lives."

Julie gave the sagacious man in the pulpit her full attention. He had touched a raw nerve and she needed to know what healing balm he was going to offer.

"My friends," he said, his deep, resonant voice growing buoyant with hope, "I challenge each of you to let yourself fall in love with Jesus...get to know Him as you would your most intimate friend. Make Him a vital part of your daily life. Don't leave Him in the pages of your Bible or in the walls of your church. Let Him come alive in your heart. Let His Spirit breathe and speak in the hidden rooms of your mind. Let Him move in you and change the very landscape of your soul."

Chapter Six

At the barbecue that afternoon Julie couldn't get Pastor Brady's words out of her mind. She thought about them as she marinated the steaks for the grill...as she boiled potatoes and eggs for the potato salad...and as she stirred catsup into the baked beans and made frosty pitchers of pink lemonade. "Love the Lord your God with all your heart, mind, soul, and strength...." But how did one love God that way? It was a mystery. Beyond Julie's comprehension. "Fall in love with Jesus...let Him change the very landscape of your soul...."

But how? It sounded so perfect, but so unattainable. Could such love really change her? Change the very landscape of her soul? Would she be different if she let God into the hidden rooms of her heart? She already believed in Him. Wasn't that enough?

And just as puzzling and paradoxical was God's command to love your neighbor as yourself. It was a cliché, a vague and irrational idea. Did it mean the intimate circle of one's life—one's family and friends—or everyone she came in contact with? The admonition seemed overwhelming, paralyzing. How did one love like that?

Certainly Julie had no energy or motivation to think about loving people beyond her own family. She wasn't even sure she loved her husband and daughter the way God intended. Her emotions changed so often and were colored by disappointment, exhaustion and irritability. Love was mingled with so many other feelings.

Julie had supposed she would feel more loving and hopeful after the pastor's message this morning, but instead, she felt fretful, peevish, overwrought. In fact, at the moment she was having a hard time being civil to Katie's boyfriend as he draped his arm over Katie's shoulders at the family barbecue.

"Katie, I could use your help in the kitchen," Julie snapped, her eyes narrowing on Jesse.

He must have got the message, because he released Katie and stepped back, looking sheepish. His long brown hair was tied back in a ponytail and the afternoon sun glinted off his gold earring. He was wearing his usual T-shirt and baggy trousers and those ugly steel-toed army boots. How can girls these days find such sloppy attire attractive? Julie wondered, as she strode into the house, her pulse racing.

Katie followed several steps behind, moping, dragging her feet. In the kitchen she leaned against the wall and crossed her arms, her eyes reproachful, her glossy red lips pursed petulantly. She was wearing shorts and a tank top that revealed too much of her budding figure. "Okay, Mom, what do you want me to do?" she asked, more a challenge than a question.

"To start with," said Julie, "you can tell Jesse to stop pawing you like some lovesick Romeo."

Katie straightened her slender frame and jutted out her chin. "He wasn't pawing me, Mom. He's just affectionate. Is there anything wrong with that?"

"If he's like this in public, what do you two do in private?"

Katie's mouth curled mockingly. "Nothing you wouldn't do, Mom."

Julie raised her hand reflexively, but stopped herself just short of slapping Katie's cheek. "That's enough, young lady. If you want to entertain your boyfriend in this house, you'd better show some respect."

"You didn't invite Jesse over. Dad did!"

"That doesn't matter. He's here, and I'm trying to make the best of it. I could use a little help from you."

"I know you don't like him," said Katie. "He knows it, too."

Julie sighed. This wasn't going the way she had intended. "I just don't think he's right for you, Katie. Don't you understand? I'm concerned because I care about you."

"If you care about me so much, be nice to my friends. Treat Jesse like a person, not like some mongrel dog you can't wait to shoo out of the yard."

"Believe me, I'm trying to be nice to Jesse, but you two don't make it easy." Julie handed Katie the platter of marinated steaks. "Take these out to your dad, will you? Then come back and help me carry the rest of the food out to the picnic table."

Balancing the tray, Katie pushed open the screen door with her shoulder and edged out onto the porch. "Jesse and I will *both* come back and carry out the food."

Julie closed her eyes for a long minute and whispered, "Help me, God. You tell me to love others, but sometimes I have a hard time even *liking* them!"

Considering Julie's jarring confrontation with Katie in the kitchen, the meal itself went surprisingly well. Michael was in wonderful spirits as he barbecued the steaks. He told one joke after another and even persuaded a reticent Jesse to do several of his impressions of popular comedians and public figures. He was actually quite good, and Katie was obviously enraptured by both men.

Julie had to admit she was feeling better, too, less stressed out, more optimistic. Maybe she had been unfair to Jesse, judging him too quickly, condemning his relationship with Katie. Maybe there was nothing to it. Maybe it was a passing fling, one of those teenage romances that were here today, gone tomorrow. Perhaps if she bided her time and kept her doubts to herself, Katie would tire of this ragamuffin, streetwise kid and find some college-bound young man of her caliber.

Julie watched Jesse as he consumed his third helping of steak and potato salad. His manners were adequate, but he ate like there was no tomorrow. Didn't his family feed him at home? But who were his family? That's right, Julie remembered. He had told her his parents were dead; he lived with his grandmother.

When Julie brought out a huge strawberry shortcake brimming with whipped cream, Jesse's eyes nearly bulged out of their sockets. She gave him an especially large helping and felt a ripple of gratification when he thanked her profusely. Even Katie looked pleased by Julie's spontaneous generosity. "It's great, Mom," she said. "Totally great."

"You can have all you want," said Julie, "as long as you promise to help with the dishes."

"We'll both help," offered Jesse.

"It'll be a cinch," Katie told him. "We just rinse them off and load them in the dishwasher."

Jesse grinned. "At my house, *I'm* the dishwasher."

"You must be quite a help to your grandmother," said Julie.

Jesse nodded. "I'm all she's got, except for my little brother, Scout, but he's just a kid, you know?"

"I'm sure you must try to be a good example to him and keep him out of trouble." Julie really meant, Please reassure me you stay out of trouble, for Katie's sake!

"I try to keep Scout on the right track," said Jesse, "but sometimes trouble has a way of finding him."

Katie hugged Jesse's arm possessively. "Come on, Jes. Let's go do those dishes. Then maybe we can take a swim."

Jesse's eyes moved to the oval swimming pool several yards beyond the picnic table. "That's cool, babe. That's one radical pool!"

"If you forgot your trunks, you can borrow a pair of mine," said Michael as he scraped the grill. The pungent, charcoal smell filled the air.

"Thanks," said Jesse. "I don't swim much. Too busy working."

Michael set his blackened barbecue utensils on the cedar picnic table, grabbed a terry cloth towel and wiped the charcoal smudges from his hands. "Well, Jesse, if you ever want to earn some extra money, I could use some help."

"Working on your car?"

"No, on a house I'm renovating. It's my hobby. I buy old fixer-uppers and fix them up."

"Sounds like a lot of work," said Jesse.

Michael tossed the towel on the table and sat down on a corner of the narrow cedar bench beside Julie. "It is a lot of work, but I like it. I've turned some real losers into beauties, haven't I, Julie?"

She waved a fly away from the half-eaten potato salad. "Yes, Michael, you've worked miracles," she said wearily. "Some of those places I wouldn't have touched with a ten-foot pole."

"And I sold them for good money, didn't I, Jewel? I even surprised you, didn't I?"

She nodded reluctantly. She hated in any way encouraging or validating Michael's obsession with old houses. Over the years he had spent countless hours tearing out old drywall, shoring up broken beams, painting, plastering and fixing leaky plumbing in dilapidated ruins a more timid soul would have bulldozed on the spot.

"Sure, I'd be glad to help you sometime," said Jesse, "but I don't know much about construction."

"That's okay. I'll teach you what you need to know. I have a feeling you'll be a natural."

Katie tugged on Jesse's arm. "If we're going swimming after a while, we'd better hit the dishes now."

As Katie and Jesse carried dirty dishes into the house, Michael moved over closer to Julie and pulled her against him. His tanned face and arms glistened with a sheen of perspiration; she could smell a mixture of charbroiled tenderloin and spicy aftershave on his skin. She felt a ripple of pleasure at his closeness, even here with the two of them squeezed together at this rough-hewn picnic table. He murmured against her ear, "It's been a nice barbecue, hasn't it, sweetheart?"

"Very nice," she agreed. No sense telling him about the earlier clash with Katie in the kitchen. After all, she and Katie had apparently worked out an unspoken truce and all seemed forgiven. As long as I'm nice to Jesse, we'll all get along.

"You don't sound very convincing," said Michael. "Are you still worried about Katie getting too involved with this boy?"

"Aren't you, Michael?"

"He seems nice enough."

"We don't know anything about him."

"He seems crazy about Katie."

"That's what worries me. Where are they headed? She has a wonderful future. I just hope he doesn't mess it up for her."

Michael's blue eyes darkened. "Like I did with you?"

She pulled away and stared at him. "That's not what I meant, and you know it!"

"It's what I heard," he replied, releasing her. He moved off the bench and began gathering the last of the dishes and utensils. She stood and helped him, but they both worked in an uncomfortable silence, until she heard the shrill ring of a phone nearby.

Michael reached into the pocket of his sport shirt and pulled out his cellular phone; he carried it with him everywhere. Julie was surprised he didn't take it with him to bed. She hated that phone; it was like an umbilical cord connecting him forever to his work. It meant interrupted plans, broken dates, shortchanged family times.

Julie heard Michael say, "Oh, really? They're in town just for today? Right, the Emerson place would suit them very well. Yes, I have all the stats. It's a custom home with a spacious floor plan on over an acre of land. Vaulted ceilings, skylights, French doors, a bonus room, island kitchen, fireplace in the master suite, huge balcony... Right. A swimming pool, spa, gazebo, circular drive, the works."

Excitement glinted in Michael's eyes as he rushed on. "It's an amazing property with the perfect price for just the right buyer—someone with loads of money to spend. So you think these people fill the bill? That eager, huh? Sure, I could meet you there. Give me a half hour."

Michael pressed the Call button and slipped the slim phone back into his pocket, then gave Julie an apologetic smile. "Business," he said. "I'm sorry, hon. I've got to go."

"A big deal to close?" she inquired coldly.

"It could be."

"And this person on the phone couldn't handle it without you?"

"You said it, Jewel. It's a big deal, lots of money involved. I own Ryan and Associates. The client wants the benefit of my experience and expertise in the negotiations."

"Who was on the phone?" asked Julie, her tone vitriolic.

Michael was already striding toward the house. "Does it matter?"

"It matters to me."

"It was just one of our agents."

"Who?"

"The new one, for crying out loud!"

"That woman you just brought in? Beth somebody? Is that who you're meeting?"

Michael looked back at her, his eyes flashing exasperation. "Yes, I'm meeting Beth Chamberlin. So what? Give me a break, Jewel. You know I need to work on Sundays sometimes. Stop acting like it's the end of the world!"

Chapter Seven

Julie was living on a high-tension wire, or at least that's how she felt in the days that followed the Sunday barbecue. She was walking a tightrope between desiring to demonstrate godly, unconditional love to her family and at the same time wanting to strike out at them in anger for falling so far short of her expectations.

Perhaps she was most disappointed with herself, for she knew there was nothing within her that resembled the sort of love her pastor had described. What was wrong with her that she couldn't summon that kind of love for the people she was most closely connected to—her husband, her daughter, her father? They were all linked by marriage or by blood, and yet sometimes she didn't feel connected, not emotionally, not the way she should feel. She felt bound, tied, trapped at times, as if the yoke were too great, the responsibilities too heavy.

At times Julie wondered why God would even bother to tell His children to love Him and others so profoundly, in the gritty real world of flawed human hearts? Even the thought of trying to measure up to God's standards left Julie feeling more discouraged than before. Perhaps that was why she so seldom scratched the surface of her faith; she knew she would be depressed by what she found.

And surely God understood that her life was too busy, too demanding, too overwhelming to worry about issues that apparently had no answers. After all, her daily routine was exhausting. Long hours at the office were consumed with idle, tedious, mind-numbing work; evenings at home were filled with cooking, cleaning, laundry, paying bills and collapsing before the television set for an hour of video pablum before bed.

Katie was rarely home these days, choosing to spend her evenings at the library—pray to God that's where she was!—or out somewhere with Jesse. Many evenings she came home late, too late, leaving Julie dreading an accident as she anxiously watched the clock and listened for the sound of a car or the ringing of the phone.

Michael, too, was seldom home, his evenings filled with appointments to show houses when he wasn't off renovating one of his own squalid fixer-uppers.

Julie had a feeling many of Michael's so-called appointments involved Beth; whether professionally or personally, she couldn't be sure. But several times when Julie played her answering machine she heard messages from Beth telling Michael she would meet him at this or that property at such and such a time. It all sounded so innocent. Was it? Or were the two of them playing the scam of the century on Julie?

Why don't you just come right out and ask him about Beth? she asked herself over and over. She knew she should; surely she couldn't continue on like this, living with these terrible suspicions, not knowing whether she still had a marriage. But as difficult as it was living with the uncertainties, the truth might be even more painful. If Michael admitted he was having an affair, what then? A whole new series of choices would confront Julie. Should she forgive him? Would he want to be forgiven? Or would he want a divorce? And would she give him one?

On and on the questions might go, leaving her life shattered, ruined. No, she couldn't cope with such issues yet. She wasn't strong enough. It was all she could do to deal with the simple, surface issues of life, like what to fix for dinner or how much to pay on her credit card balance this month.

The nights were the most painful, for just when Julie wanted desperately to turn to Michael for confirmation of his love, when she yearned for the warmth and comfort of his arms and his kisses, she found herself pulling away, closing him out, turning a cold shoulder. How could she make love to a man—how could she give herself to a man—who could be betraying her in the cruelest of ways?

Worst of all, she couldn't bring herself to answer him when he demanded, "What's wrong, Julie? What gives? You act like I'm untouchable. What have I done to make you treat me this way?"

And when she made no reply, his anger would flare and he would punch his pillow or throw his covers aside and swing his legs out of bed and stomp out of the room. She would hear him slamming doors in other parts of the house or banging utensils in the kitchen. Often she would be asleep before he would steal back into bed an hour or half hour later, and sometimes she merely pretended to be asleep so that she wouldn't have to deal with his anger and her own heartache.

Several weeks passed this way. Dreary, monotonous days merged together, indistinguishable, and fell away, shifting, desolate, and elusive as beach sand. One afternoon, as Julie drove home from work, she looked around, startled by how quickly spring's warm, sunny days had turned into the hot, glaring, sun-baked days of summer. California's climate changed only by degrees—warm, dry winters became hot, airless summers, but most of the time the weather was fairly pleasant, unremarkable, interchangeably overcast or sunny.

Much like Julie's life. Except that these days were much more overcast than sunny. As usual, Michael was remote, Julie distant, Katie rarely home.

"Some family we've got," Julie said aloud as she pulled into the driveway of their sprawling, custom-built two-story. "We live in the same house, under the same roof, and yet we all go our separate ways. Our lives never touch anymore. Dear God, what's wrong with us? Or is everybody like us?"

What did the poem say? "No man is an island..." But these days everyone was an island—distant, solitary, unreachable.

Julie parked her car and crossed her arms on the steering wheel. She was feeling stressed out as usual, her emotions blunted, her spirits deadened. Life wasn't supposed to be this way. She knew it, but she had no idea how to change it—or herself.

"Lord, we need a miracle around here," she whispered, "a touch of Your love, something from You to draw us together and help us love one another the way You want us to love." She felt tears sting her eyes. "And, dear God, please help me to love You more, too. I know I don't give You much of my time these days. I'm sorry. Help me to do better."

That evening, while Michael showed a client a house and Katie was out with Jesse, Julie sat curled on the sofa in the cozy retreat just off their bedroom and read her Bible for the first time in days, the verses in Psalm 36 speaking poignantly to her heart.

How precious is Your loving kindness, O God!
Therefore the children of men put their trust
Under the shadow of Your wings....
For with You is the fountain of life;
In Your light we see light.

Julie read the words over and over. They described the way she yearned to feel about God and her own home and family. But were such lofty emotions possible only in Scripture? Or could she experience such satisfaction and pleasure in her everyday life with her family?

"Lord, is this the miracle I asked for this afternoon? Will You break through the hardness of my heart and help me love Katie and Michael the way You want me to?"

Even as she prayed, she felt a pervasive warmth rippling over her, a growing sense of well-being. Yes, life was going to get better in the Ryan household, she was sure of it! She and Michael and Katie would grow closer than they had ever been. Somehow, God would give her His miracle!

When Michael arrived home later that evening, Julie was waiting for him, dressed in her most alluring peignoir. She went eagerly into his arms and turned her face up to his with a welcoming smile. He stared at her for a long moment in baffled surprise, then kissed her soundly.

"What's going on, Jewel?" he asked as she pressed her cheek against his solid chest.

She looked up and gave him a slight pout. "What do you mean? Can't a wife give her husband a little kiss?"

He chuckled. "Doll baby, there was nothing little about that kiss. You haven't greeted me like that since—to tell you the truth, I can't remember when."

She slowly loosened his tie and unbuttoned the top button of his shirt. "I know, darling, and I'm sorry. It's been way too long." She felt suddenly as if she were acting out a scene in some tawdry movie—the glamorous seductress tempting the unsuspecting boy next door, or some other sleazy, half-baked plot. "Michael, I'd like to make it up to you," she said softly. "Do you remember how it used to be, when we were first married?" This was crazy. She even *sounded* like an actor reciting lines from a play. But if this was what it took to win Michael back, to convince him she loved him...

He pulled his tie off from around his neck and tossed it on the bed with an exasperated sigh. "There's nothing I'd like better, Julie, than a little romantic romp with my wife, but this just isn't you. Come on. What gives?"

She sat down on the bed and ran her palm over the silky-smooth sheet. "Don't analyze everything, Michael. You're spoiling the mood."

He removed his cuff links and pulled off his shirt. The furrow of doubt in his brow was already giving way to a crinkly smile. "You win, Jewel. Heaven forbid that I'd spoil such a rare, wonderful mood." He sat down beside her and drew her against him, kissing her hair, her earlobe, her neck. "But I'd still like to know what inspired it. I'd like to bottle it and save it for a rainy day.''

"Why a rainy day?"

"Rainy, sunny, twice on Sunday, I don't care. I just don't want to let magic like this get away."

She closed her eyes dreamily. "It's been here all along, Michael. Maybe you just haven't noticed."

"Oh, I would have noticed. Where has this spicy little coquette been hiding?"

"Really, Michael!" she chided. It didn't seem appropriate now to quote from Pastor Brady's sermon on love, so she said simply, "I'm not some steamy vamp. You're my husband! I want us to be closer."

"So do I, Jewel." He kissed her tenderly—a slow, warm, inviting kiss—then glanced toward the door. "Where's Katie?"

"Out with Jesse. Where else?"

"Then it's just the two of us?"

"For at least another hour."

"Perfect," he said, guiding her head down on the pillow, his face above hers. "Now where were we?"

The telephone jangled on the bedside table, shattering what would have been a very delectable kiss. "Don't answer it," said Michael.

"We've got to," she replied. "It could be Katie."

He sat back. "If it's not an emergency, hang up."

"I promise." She rolled over, grabbed the receiver and said a clipped hello.

There was a long moment of silence, then a woman's voice broke from the other end, sounding muffled, distraught and vaguely familiar. "Is Michael there?"

"Yes, who's calling please?"

The woman spoke over a choking sob. "It's Beth. Beth Chamberlin."

The roof of Julie's mouth went dry. Without a word she handed the receiver to Michael.

"Yes, Beth? What's wrong?" He stood up and turned his back to Julie. "For crying out loud, how did he know where to find you? Did you call the police? All right, I understand. Listen, make sure the doors are locked. I'll be there as soon as I can."

He slammed the receiver into its cradle and flung on his shirt, hurriedly buttoning it as he strode toward the door.

"Where are you going?" demanded Julie.

Michael stopped and stared at her, as if suddenly realizing how suspicious his rapid departure looked. "I—Beth needs my help."

Julie pushed back her tousled curls distractedly. "Beth—your new associate? Why on earth would she call you here at this time of night?"

Michael finished buttoning his shirt. "It's a long story, Julie. One I don't have time for right now."

Julie clasped his arm. "Don't go."

"I have to." Michael pivoted and headed for the hallway.

Impulsively Julie grabbed the knit shirt and pair of jeans she had stepped out of earlier, and pulled them on. "Wait, Michael! I'm coming with you."

"Hurry!" he called back.

Michael and Julie maintained a stony silence during the ten-minute drive to the Ocean View Apartments on Atlantic where Beth lived. During the drive, Julie couldn't bring herself to utter a sound. Michael seemed intensely, disquietingly preoccupied, and she was too angry, too stunned, and too mortified to disturb him. It was bad enough that her most intimate moments with her husband had been interrupted by a woman who could be Michael's paramour. And, like an insane person, Julie had insisted on going with Michael to rescue his damsel in distress.

I'm pathetic! she thought darkly.

What would they find? Was the emergency real? Was Beth in imminent danger? Or had her call been merely a ploy to get Michael out of the house and into her arms?

Michael was already pulling up beside the curb in front of a sprawling apartment complex surrounded by palm trees and bougainvillea. He jumped out and raced ahead of Julie across a grassy expanse to a first-floor apartment on the left. Julie noted with dismay that he seemed to know exactly where to go.

Julie stepped back into the shadows as Michael hammered on Beth's door. "Let me in, Beth. It's me, Michael!"

Immediately the door opened and Beth flew into his arms. "Thank God!" she said, repeating the words several times as she burrowed her face against his neck and wept.

At last Julie stepped out of the shadows. Beth must have heard the rustling noise, for she looked up suddenly, her eyes wide as saucers, and made a little gasping sound.

Michael held Beth at arm's length, his palms still supportively under her elbows. "You remember my wife Julie, don't you, Beth? She wanted to come along, to—to..." He faltered a moment, then said forcefully, "We want to help out any way we can."

Beth rocked on her heels momentarily, then gestured for the two of them to come in. "Please, sit down," she said in a soft, shaky voice. "The sofa, anywhere. Make yourselves at home." She gazed around, her hands moving in a helpless flutter. "I have some coffee—it may be cold—I could warm it up. I'm sorry. I'm not thinking too clearly right now."

"No, no coffee. We're fine," said Julie. She felt an unexpected wave of sympathy for the slim, flustered brunette. She was a shadow of the confident, professional, impeccably dressed woman Julie had met weeks before in Michael's office. This woman, wearing no makeup, her expression hardened and her long dark hair mussed and unattended, looked like a ragamuffin in a gray tank top and faded denim overalls.

Julie and Michael sat down at opposite ends of the long periwinkle blue sofa. Beth sat down cross-legged on the love seat opposite them, a guarded, teary-eyed waif, barefoot, all arms and legs, her fingers fidgeting nervously. It struck Julie that this girl didn't look much older than Katie, although certainly Beth had to be in her mid-twenties.

"I feel so foolish," Beth was saying. "I never should have called you."

Julie wanted to agree wholeheartedly, but she held back her biting remarks. Instead she gazed around the room with feigned interest. The apartment was small but tastefully decorated in a classic, contemporary style. It had a generic, anonymous quality to it, as if the apartment might have come furnished, with all the other apartments in the complex boasting the same basic decor. There was little to distinguish it as a place where someone had put down roots or added her own unique stamp.

"So Roger was here," said Michael, looking at Beth, his tone solemn.

Julie looked at the two of them and knew she was missing something. "Roger who?" she inquired.

"My ex-husband," said Beth. "He was here tonight." She choked back a sob.

Michael picked up the story while Beth reached for a tissue. "Beth moved to Southern California last year to get away from an abusive ex-husband. But now he's found her and is stirring up trouble." Michael looked back at Beth and asked with concern, "Did he hurt you?"

Beth averted her gaze. Her fingers went instinctively to the side of her face. She rubbed her cheekbone, and Julie could see now that her skin was discolored, a faint circle of purple and red. "I'm okay," she said in a small voice. She was lying and they all knew it.

"He hit you, didn't he?" said Michael, his voice resonant with sudden, swift anger. He was on the edge of his seat, as if about to attack some invisible assailant.

"He slapped me, but I started screaming, and he got scared and left."

"But he'll be back. That's what you're afraid of, isn't it?"

She looked away, refusing to answer.

"Did you call the police?" asked Julie. Surely that was the most reasonable course of action.

"No, I can't turn him in," said Beth. "Roger's been in trouble before. They'd send him back to prison for years. He could never survive another prison term."

Michael stood and crossed the room to the window and looked out. His tone held a raw agitation. "I'm not sure you'll survive if he remains free, Beth."

"There must be someone you can call for help," said Julie. "Family, friends, colleagues?"

Beth looked directly at her, her gaze unflinching, her deep umber eyes almost defiant. "No, no one... Only Michael."

Julie recoiled slightly. Beth had just sent her an unmistakable message: *Be forewarned. I've got my eye on your man!* Surely Julie hadn't read her wrong, had she?

"We should get going soon," said Julie, standing uncertainly. "Katie will be coming home anytime, and we need to be there, Michael."

He nodded, but he didn't look convinced. "Let me take a glance around the place to make sure everything's okay—the doors and windows locked—before we go. And, Beth, you get a restraining order to keep Roger away, you hear me?"

Beth looked up solemnly at Michael. "Yes, I hear you, and I know you're right. I'll do whatever you say, Michael."

Beth's tone sounded entirely too cozy and familiar for Julie's peace of mind. She watched Michael as he tried the windows and closed the miniblinds. *This girl means something special to you, Michael. I can see it in your eyes, in the way you're behaving, and in the way she looks at you. Do you love her, Michael? Is that it? Are you in love with Beth Chamberlin?*

"I'll check the kitchen windows and the back door," said Michael, "and before we leave I'll walk around outside and make sure everything's okay."

"Oh, Michael, I knew I could count on you."

When Michael was out of the room, Beth looked at Julie and smiled wanly. Beth was a pretty girl even without makeup. She had a fresh, clean-scrubbed look and an intelligent warmth in her eyes. Julie could see how Michael could be attracted to her, infatuated, flattered by her obvious devotion to him. But was he willing to risk his marriage for this girl?

Julie realized suddenly that Beth was talking to her, leaning forward as if imparting a secret, her voice soft and warmly confidential. Even Julie could be charmed by that voice and that smile, taken in, fooled by those dark, soulful eyes. "You don't know how lucky you are to have such a wonderful husband, Mrs. Ryan," Beth was saying. "You just don't know how lucky!"

Chapter Eight

For days after Beth's untimely phone call and their impromptu visit to her apartment, Julie struggled with misgivings over Michael's growing attachment to his new colleague. Julie knew her doubts and suspicions were casting a dark cloud over her entire life, but she felt helpless to dispel them. Nor could she bring herself to confront Michael. What if she were wrong? Michael might never forgive her for doubting his integrity.

One Saturday morning Julie decided to direct her nervous energy into cleaning the house from top to bottom. Every room would be spick-and-span by the time Michael arrived home that evening. While cleaning the spare bedroom she came upon an old leather-bound journal she had purchased during college and never written in. Looking at it, slowly turning the crisp, blank pages, Julie had an idea. *I should keep a prayer journal. It will help me keep my focus on God and on learning to love Him and others with Christlike love.*

Immediately she reached for a pen, settled into her favorite rocker by the window in her bedroom retreat, and began to write.

Saturday, June 23

Heavenly Father, I don't even know what to write in these pages, except that I feel so far removed from being the kind of loving, giving person You want me to be. Ever since Pastor Brady's sermon on love weeks ago, I've longed to be able to love You with all my heart, mind, soul and strength, and to love others as myself. But in my daily life those words seem like an impossible dream.

Just when I thought I could break out of my shell and reach out to Michael the way a wife should, Beth intruded on our lives in a way that frightens me. She's so needy and vulnerable in ways I could never be, and I can see that Michael likes that. He likes feeling needed and being flattered and fussed over. Maybe he doesn't even realize it, but Beth's drawing him into her web, seizing pieces of his heart little by little, and if I try to stop her, Michael will think I'm being unsympathetic and mean-spirited.

Lord, just when I trusted You to give our family a miracle of love, You've made things even more difficult for us. Help me to know what to do about Michael and Beth. Lord, I don't want to lose Michael, but how can I compete with Beth for his love when I feel such a distance between us?

And, Lord, help me to know how to handle Katie and her boyfriend Jesse. They're getting too serious, I know, and shutting the rest of the world out, but she turns a deaf ear when I tell her to date other boys. Lately she's sullen and withdrawn. She won't talk to me; she's more remote than ever. I feel as if I don't know her. I know the plastic facade she wants me to see, but I can't read the tender texture and terrain of her soul—what motivates her, what she really needs in her secret heart, the deep, shrouded paths her mind travels.

Now I'm back to that terrible, bitter truth, Lord: I don't know anyone with the kind of deep, insightful knowledge I believe You created us to have about one another, the kind of discerning wisdom born of pure, absolute love. Does anyone possess such love? How do I attain it, Father—I, who am so filled with myself I can hardly see anyone else?

I confess. I have this habit, Lord, of standing in front of a mirror and staring at my reflection, trying to see through to the person behind the skin and bone. I ask myself, who is this woman in the mirror, this person who looks back at me, solemn and

*unblinking? I live in her body, but what do I know of her? I search
for clues, I make assumptions, I function in the everyday world
in her skin, and yet there are so many facets of this person I do
not know or understand. How can I know the others in my life if
I am still trying to understand myself?*

*Maybe it all starts with You, God. I can't know myself and I
can't know others the way You intended until I know You, a deep,
profound, sacrificial knowing, until I've scratched the surface of
omnipotence and caught a glimpse of who You are.*

Give me that glimpse, Lord.

*And, Father, I ask for the miracle of discovery, of knowing
myself and those I love beyond the window dressing and shiny
veneer. Give our family—each one of us—a miracle of Your love!*

Julie felt better after writing in her journal, as if a burden had
been lifted and something resolved. Surely she was on the right
track. God would see that she was serious about wanting to love
her family more, and He would answer her prayer. It was just a
matter of time.

''Now I'd better get this house cleaned before Michael and
Katie get home,'' she said aloud. ''Maybe the three of us can go
out to dinner together tonight, if I can pry my daughter away
from Jesse for a few hours.''

Julie felt a sweet ripple of euphoria, thinking about the three
of them dining together at some posh restaurant or even at a fast-
food joint; the place didn't matter. It was being together that
counted. They needed some quality time, a pleasant evening out,
a chance to talk and share what was happening in their lives.

Julie's mind was so absorbed with the evening's potential that
she was hardly aware of the task at hand, one so distasteful she
usually reserved it for Michael—emptying the trash. She went
from room to room dumping the contents of the waste baskets
into a large plastic garbage bag; she would let Michael carry the
bag out to the trash can.

She opened the door to Katie's room—a mysterious, cluttered
sanctuary Julie invaded only to deposit clean clothes or remove
trash. Otherwise it was Katie's private domain, its walls papered
with photographs, posters and an odd assortment of teenage mem-

orabilia. Julie couldn't imagine living amidst such chaos and clutter—clothing piled on dressers, jeans and shirts draped over the
bedpost, CDs, videotapes, magazines and makeup in disarray on
the desk beside her personal computer. Katie had everything a
young girl could ask for—her own television, VCR, and stereo
system. And she didn't take care of any of it!

She has too much! Julie told herself firmly. How is Katie ever
going to learn to appreciate anything when everything is handed
to her? But tell Michael that. He would shower his little princess
with even more of the world's baubles, if Julie allowed him to.
Face it, they would never agree on how to raise Katie.

"You spoil her, Michael!" she often told him.

"And you, Julie, would deprive our only daughter of what I've
worked so hard to provide!"

Long ago they had arrived at a stalemate. Neither was willing
to budge. So, in Katie's eyes, Michael was always the good guy
and Julie the bad. Just once, Julie wished she could come across
as the beneficent, understanding parent.

"Not in this lifetime," she said aloud as she reached for Katie's
waste basket. Her hand accidently sideswiped the plastic container
and it tipped over, its contents spilling onto the plush teal blue
carpet.

"Oh, great!" Julie grumbled under her breath. It would be just
her luck that some discarded lotion or cologne or powder would
stain the rug. She knelt down and gingerly scooped the litter back
into the basket—discarded tissues, candy wrappers, crumpled
notebook paper, and—what was this?—a small, shiny white box.
The words caught Julie's attention and instantly sent a knifelike
shock through her. "Pregnancy Test."

She dropped the plastic garbage bag and stood up, holding the
small box in both hands, staring at it, as if trying to make sense
of it. Why was this in Katie's trash?

Surely it belonged to one of Katie's girlfriends. Perhaps one of
the girls at school had brought it over, too afraid to take the test
in her own home. But Julie realized immediately the fallacy in
such thinking. Katie rarely had girlfriends over these days; she
spent all her free time with Jesse.

The test was Katie's.

Katie had brought home a pregnancy test because she was afraid she might be pregnant.

"Dear Lord, no," Julie whispered, her heart pounding fiercely against her ribs. Her wrists felt weak, her fingers stiff and awkward as she fumbled to open the box. She had to know the test results. "Please, God, don't let it be!"

She managed at last to seize the little white stick that would show positive or negative. She stared long and hard at it, her mind refusing to comprehend what she saw. There was a plus sign in the tiny window.

Julie sank down on Katie's bed. She couldn't force her mind beyond this present moment, couldn't make her arms and legs function. Her thoughts kept short-circuiting. She sat unmoving for a very long time, taking ragged breaths through her mouth that left her throat tight and dry.

Katie can't be pregnant. She wouldn't let this happen. We've talked about sex, about waiting, about her future. She knows what happened to me. She's too smart to let it happen to her, too!

But if it's true, what will Michael do? He'll blame me, just as he blamed me for Katie!

In a daze Julie closed the little white box and took it to her room and set it on the bathroom counter. She picked up the cordless phone and called Michael. "Come home, Michael, please," she said when she heard his voice.

"What's up?"

"I can't talk about it over the phone. Just come home. Now!"

"I'm out the door."

Julie sat down on the sofa in her bedroom retreat and waited, wondering how she would tell Michael that his little girl was pregnant. Or maybe it was all a ghastly mistake. Maybe she should have waited and confronted Katie first, before involving Michael. Surely Katie would have a perfectly good explanation for having a positive pregnancy test in her trash.

No, there was only one explanation, and Julie didn't have the strength to confront Katie alone.

It seemed that hours had passed by the time Julie heard Michael's car in the driveway, but no, it had actually been less than fifteen minutes. She waited, her hands clammy, her head pounding, as the door clicked open downstairs. She heard Michael enter the marble foyer and call her name, his tone filled with urgency.

"I'm up here, Michael," she called back, her voice betraying her distress. She listened to the sound of Michael's footfall on the stairs, wishing she had never phoned him. She should have let the situation ride until she was better prepared to handle it. But it was too late now. Michael was already bounding into the room, his tie askew, his jacket flaring open, his eyes the piercing-hot blue of a gas flame.

"What's wrong? Are you sick?"

"No."

"Is it Katie? Your father? Did someone die?"

"No, Michael. I mean, yes, it is Katie."

"What happened? Where is she?"

"Where else? Out with Jesse."

Michael expelled a relieved breath. "I thought there'd been an accident. For crying out loud, Julie, why'd you call me home like this? You scared the life out of me."

She wanted to say, Forget it, Michael. I made a mistake. Go back to work. But she couldn't. "I was cleaning today, Michael, collecting the trash…"

"The trash?" He looked at her, baffled.

She massaged her hands. Why were her fingers like icicles? "I was in Katie's room. The waste basket spilled over, and I—I found a pregnancy test."

Michael removed his jacket and tossed it over the sofa arm. "A pregnancy test? In Katie's room?"

She nodded.

"You think it was Katie's?" Michael ran his fingers through his ebony black hair. "It could be anybody's—one of her girlfriend's."

"Who, Michael? Who's even been here lately?"

"Katie wouldn't—"

Julie met his gaze as if to ask, Wouldn't she?

"So you think Katie's been fooling around? With Jesse? Great Scot, I'll ground her till she's thirty, if I have to."

A pent-up sob tore from Julie's throat. "It's too late."

"Too late?"

"The test was positive."

"You're telling me Katie's pregnant?" He sat down beside Julie and put his head in his hands. "No. It can't be. She's only sixteen, still a baby herself."

"I don't want to believe it, either, Michael. I don't know what to think."

"You haven't asked her?"

"No. I called you. I thought we should talk to her together."

Michael stood and paced the floor. "It has to be a mistake." He made a sound low in his throat, like laughter, only hard and bitter. "Or maybe this is God's idea of a practical joke. Yeah, sure, that's it. I got you pregnant—now it's my kid's turn. What goes around comes around. Like mother, like daughter!"

"Stop it, Michael. We've got to stay calm, for Katie's sake."

"Stay calm? Come off it, Jewel. I get the picture here, real sharp and clear. This is payback time. It's that whole sins-of-the-father bit. We messed up our lives, and now Katie messes up hers, and what do you want to bet, her kid will blow it, too, someday!"

Sudden, white-hot anger flashed behind Julie's eyes. She sprang at Michael, her clenched fists pummeling his muscled chest. "Don't you dare start your little pity party with me!" she shrieked. "How many years do I have to suffer guilt for getting pregnant with Katie? You'll never let me forget, will you?"

Michael seized her wrists and held them firm. "Don't you think I live with the guilt, too? We're both to blame, me more than you. And now Katie—"

Julie heard a door open and shut downstairs. "Quiet, Michael. She's home!"

Michael released Julie's wrists, only to gather her awkwardly into his arms. They clung to each other in a loose embrace, their bodies tense, girding themselves for a battle neither wanted to face.

After a long, nerve-racking moment Julie broke free and went out to the hallway and called down, "Katie? Come upstairs please."

Katie took her sweet time trudging up the stairs. She ambled into the bedroom in her usual tank top and cutoff jeans, all gangly arms and legs, her long, sun-washed hair pulled back artlessly with a barrette. Her luminous, eggshell white skin showed a spattering of freckles across her cheeks and nose.

She's been out in the sun too long without her sunscreen, thought Julie. But that was the least of their worries.

Or is it the rosy glow of pregnancy?

"What'd you want, Mom?" Katie asked, her full, glossy lips drawn down in an insolent pout. As her gaze moved to her father, her unreadable blue eyes widened in surprise. "Dad, what are you doing home this early?"

"Your mom called me," he said, tight-lipped.

"What's wrong? Is it Grandpa? Did he—"

"No, it's not Grandpa," said Julie.

"Sit down, Katie. We need to talk," said Michael.

She held her ground. "What is this—a Big Three conference—you two against me? Come on. What's the big deal?"

"Sit down and you'll find out," Michael told her, his tone brusque.

Hold your temper, Michael, Julie warned silently. If you lose it now, we could lose Katie for good!

With an offhand shrug, Katie eased into the rocker and curled her long legs under her, while Julie and Michael took the sofa. The moment felt heavy, unnatural, even ominous. Julie sensed already that nothing good was going to come out of this encounter. Katie was closing in on herself, drawing the curtains, barricading the doors. Julie could see her eyes glazing over with a detached skepticism, a stony aloofness. There was no way they were going to pry any secrets out of this girl today.

"Katie," Julie began tentatively, feeling as if some fragile part of herself were at stake, "your dad and I are very concerned about you—"

"Is this about Jesse again? If it is, Mom, I told you—"

"It's more than Jesse," said Julie, a little breathless now, as if she herself were on trial.

"For crying out loud, let's get to the point here," said Michael. "Katie, your mom found a pregnancy test in your room."

Katie blanched, her eyes blinking rapidly and her lips parting with a slight quiver. Even as the color drained from her skin, the astonishment in her face quickly hardened into defiance. She looked stonily at Julie. "You were snooping in my room, Mom?"

Julie's stomach clenched, forcing a bitter taste into her throat. How had this turned into an attack on her? "No, I wasn't snooping," she replied. "I was emptying the waste basket—because you didn't."

"The test was positive," said Michael. "What do you know about it, Katie?"

Katie shrugged, her face deliberately blank, a frigid mask firmly in place. "Nothing. I don't know how it got there. Maybe one of my friends—"

"Then it's not yours?" coaxed Michael.

Katie's eyes narrowed. "Really, Dad! How can you even think—"

"Then you're not pregnant, Katie?" said Julie, sounding too eager. "Is that what you're telling us?" *Please, God, let it be so. Let it all be a dreadful mistake. Let her have a perfectly logical explanation so we can end this interrogation and get on with our lives.*

Katie stood abruptly, tossing her tawny hair back as if the matter were settled, and wiped her palms on her cutoffs. "Listen, can I go now? I've got stuff to do."

Julie stood shakily, facing her daughter. "You didn't answer me, Katie. Are you pregnant?"

Katie pivoted, avoiding Julie's gaze. "You're both way off the wall. This is totally stupid. I'm outta here."

Michael sprang forward and gripped Katie's arm. "You're going nowhere until we've told you you can go. Now sit down so we can finish our talk."

Katie curled back into the rocker, turning sideways and drawing her legs up against her chest. She rested her cheek against her knees, her face to the wall, her long wheat-colored hair cascading over her shoulder. She looked fragile and breakable as a china doll.

"All right, Katie girl," said Michael slowly, "talk to us. Your mom and I are here for you. We just want to help."

Katie kept her face to the wall.

"Katie, please," Michael prodded. "We've got to know. Are you in trouble? Did Jesse get you pregnant?"

The silence was electrifying. A foreboding prickled in Julie's stomach. She knew what transpired in these next few moments could rip the delicate fabric of her family to shreds.

Michael went to Katie and pulled her up from the rocker, his grip firm, yet gentle where his large, tanned hands clasped her thin upper arms. "Look at me, Katie," he demanded, the words erupting with thinly controlled anguish. "It's me, your dad. Talk to me. In the name of heaven, tell me if it's true!"

Katie looked stricken, like a fawn caught in the blinding white orbs of an oncoming car. Julie knew that rank, breath-stopping terror that came when you realized you had placed yourself in the path of devastation and your life would never be the same.

"If you're pregnant, Katie, it's not the end of the world," said Julie. "You'll survive. We'll all survive."

"Your mother's right," said Michael. "But we can't help you until we know the truth."

Something shifted in Katie's expression. The protective mask shattered and fell away. Beneath it was a child's frightened face, soft, pliant, needy. She flung herself into her father's arms and sobbed convulsively. "Oh, Daddy, I'm sorry!" she wailed, huge tears streaming down her cheeks. "I'm so sorry!"

Chapter Nine

They talked for what seemed hours—Julie, Michael and Katie—going round and round in bewildering circles, running into daunting, head-throbbing dead ends. The facts were undeniable: Katie was two months pregnant; it was Jesse's child. What they were going to do with those facts was anybody's guess.

Michael teetered back and forth between paternal empathy and malignant anger. One moment he was saying, "We'll take care of you, sweetheart, don't worry, it's going to be okay." And the next minute he was bellowing, "How could you do it, Katie? How in blazes could you let that scumbag jerk put his filthy hands on you!"

Julie could feel the situation deteriorating. When Katie responded with only morose silence, Michael warned her grimly, "Getting pregnant isn't the worst thing that can happen when you have sex these days, you know. There's AIDS and a dozen other horrific STDs. When you play with fire, Katie, you get burned. Did you stop to think about such things when that punk took you to bed? Did you, Katie? Answer me!"

Katie jumped up, her hair flying around her head like cornsilk in the wind, and shouted, "No, Daddy, I thought about how much I loved him, the same way Mom loved you!"

The tendons in Michael's flushed neck constricted and bulged. "We're not talking about your mother and me, young lady. We're talking about you and Jesse."

Katie stared back, her own face ruddy and glistening, her eyes unblinking. "You're teed off with me for doing the exact same thing you did! Don't give me your sermons, Daddy—I know the truth. I wasn't supposed to happen either. I was a mistake just like my baby!"

"*You* weren't the mistake, honey," Julie assured her quickly before Michael hurled his own retort. "Yes, your dad and I made a mistake, but we always loved you and wanted you, from the day you were born."

Michael nodded wearily. "Your mother's right, Katie. There was never any question about our loving you."

As they lapsed into an uneasy silence, Julie realized they had reached a painful stalemate. She looked at Michael. "Let the matter rest. Let's go to bed. Things will look clearer—we'll be calmer—in the morning."

But morning didn't make the situation any better. When Julie and Michael were dressed and ready to leave for church, Katie told them she wasn't going; she had morning sickness. For the first time Julie learned Katie had been suffering from morning sickness for over a month. Why hadn't she noticed? Was she too busy getting ready and rushing off to work each day?

After church—and a sermon Julie was too preoccupied to remember a word of—she and Michael returned home to find Katie still in her bathrobe, sitting on the floor before the TV, watching cartoons and eating cheese puffs and peanut butter cookies.

Something's wrong with this picture, Julie thought darkly. This girl with a baby in her tummy is still a baby herself!

Michael told her irritably, "Turn off the cartoons and put away the junk food. I want you to get on the phone and call Jesse over here. He needs to be in on this discussion about your—your future."

"He already knows about the baby," said Katie, making no effort to budge.

"And what did he say?" asked Michael, seething now.

"He says whatever I decide is fine with him."

"And what does that mean?" Julie wanted to know.

Katie shrugged and turned her eyes back to the television set, where a cartoon bear was chasing two chipmunks through a field of yellow daisies.

"Get that boy over here, Katie," Michael insisted through clenched teeth.

She looked up at him and jutted out her lower lip; she could match her father's stubbornness without skipping a beat. "No, Daddy. I won't call him. You'll just yell at him."

"I may do more than yell," Michael shot back, pummeling his fist against his palm. But when he saw Katie's eyes well with tears, he raised his hands helplessly and heaved a sigh of resignation. "All right, Katie, we'll talk to Jesse later. But I hope you're giving some serious thought to what you're going to do with a baby," he told her solemnly. "You'll be starting your senior year in the fall. Pushing a baby carriage around campus can cramp a girl's style real fast."

"It's not your problem, Daddy," Katie said, sniffing noisily. She kept her wet eyes riveted fiercely on the cartoon chipmunks and bear frolicking in the daisy field. "It's not your problem either, Mom. Don't worry. Jesse and I will figure something out."

"Well, if you're thinking of marrying that boy," said Michael, "you're going to have a hard time raising a kid on the minimum wage Jesse makes at that garage."

Katie scooted closer to the television set and turned up the volume. They had stopped talking, but the air still crackled with tension.

Julie had a feeling there would be no further conversation on the subject today.

"I know one thing," she told Michael privately that night as she lay in his arms, "I'm taking Katie to my obstetrician tomorrow to make sure everything's okay. A sixteen-year-old having a baby can be dangerous. Her body isn't ready to handle the trauma of childbirth. So many things could go wrong. I couldn't bear to think of anything happening to her, Michael."

"She'll be fine," he said, without conviction.

"At least I was almost nineteen when I had Katie," Julie said as an afterthought. "But it was still hard—the hardest thing I ever had to do."

Later, after Michael had drifted off to sleep, Julie stared up into the darkness, tears brimming her eyes, and whispered, "God, where were You this weekend when everything in our lives was falling apart? *Where were You?*"

She let the question hang in the velvety silence for a long moment. Then she rolled over and hugged her pillow, and the thought came to her like a blast of cold water, After all that's happened, why did I wait until now to think of God? Maybe He wasn't ignoring me—I was forgetting Him!

On Monday morning Julie dreaded going to work; she hated leaving Katie alone in the house all day to brood over her condition. Even more worrisome, Katie would probably invite Jesse over to commiserate with her.

Julie's anger flared. Jesse was the last person Julie wanted making himself at home in her house. Hadn't he taken enough already—this teenage reprobate who had stolen her daughter's purity? Her entire future?

At noon Julie drove home for lunch. She could have grabbed a salad as usual at the little homestyle restaurant near her office, but she wanted to check on Katie without having to admit that's what she was doing. But as soon as she opened the door and stepped into the foyer, she sensed no one was there. She called Katie's name, then hurried upstairs to her room. She opened the door without knocking, and her eyes moved quickly over the room with its myriad posters, stuffed animals and cluttered furnishings. Surprisingly the bed was neatly made with Katie's favorite childhood baby doll ensconced between the throw pillows.

But Katie was gone.

When Julie's gaze swept over the room a second time, she spotted the note propped on the bedside table. She crossed the room and seized the folded notebook paper, opened it with awkward fingers and scanned the scrawled message in Katie's familiar script.

Dear Mom and Dad,
I'm sorry I disappointed you. I talked to Jesse and we're going to fix things the only way we know how. He has some money saved and he's making the arrangements and driving me, so I'll be okay. Don't worry. And please don't try to stop me. I know this is how it has to be. When I get home tonight it'll all be over. Life can be normal again, and you won't have to be upset. Please forgive me and I hope you still love me.

Your daughter, Katie

Julie sank down on Katie's bed, her knees weak and trembling, as if she had been rocked by a seismic shock. She felt light-headed, incredulous. "Dear God, what have we done? Have we driven her to this?"

She reached for the phone, knowing instinctively she had to stop Katie, no matter what. She could never live with herself if Katie sacrificed her child for the sake of harmony in the family.

When she got Michael on the line, she said decisively, "Come home, Michael! Hurry! It's Katie. We've got more trouble!"

When he arrived home fifteen minutes later, she had already gone through the yellow pages and circled all the women's health clinics in the vicinity. She grabbed her purse, tucked the thick phone book under her arm and pushed Michael back out the door.

"What's going on?" he quizzed as she climbed into the car beside him and fastened her seat belt.

"I'll tell you. Just drive."

"Where are we going?"

She studied the listings in the open book on her lap. "To a clinic on Carson."

Michael sounded dubious. "What clinic?"

Through several labored breaths she blurted out the story and haltingly read Katie's note.

"She's gone to get an abortion?"

Julie fought back tears. "What else could it mean?"

"She wouldn't do that. She knows how we feel about the sanctity of life."

"Does she? Did we ever say one word to her last night that made her feel we cared about her baby? We were too busy trying to resolve the mess she'd gotten herself into."

Michael ground his jaw. "Okay, we didn't handle things very well, but for her to do this without consulting us first—"

"It's too late for excuses or hindsight or second guesses," said Julie. "We've got to find her before she—"

"But how? Do you have any idea where she went?"

"No. We've just got to pray we find the right place."

Michael looked at her, the muscles in his face tense as rubber bands. "That's like searching for a needle in a haystack, Jewel. We'll never find her in time."

"Yes, we will," she said, almost reverently, like a prayer, a vow. "Make a left on Carson. The first clinic should be a few blocks down, on the right."

Minutes later Michael pulled up beside the medical office—a nondescript, two-story, white stucco building with gray wood trim. According to the metal-framed sign on the wall of the outer lobby, the building housed a dental office and several other medical specialties in addition to the women's clinic.

"The clinic's right here on the first floor," Julie told Michael. "Let me go in alone, okay?"

He nodded. "I'll wait in the car."

Her pulse quickened as she entered the small waiting room with its bleached white walls and orange chrome-and-vinyl chairs. Several women of various ages and ethnic backgrounds sat reading, several in advanced stages of pregnancy. Julie approached the reception desk and inquired politely, "Do you have a patient here named Katie Lynn or Kaitlyn Ryan?"

A slim, middle-aged woman with short, ash brown hair and wire-rim glasses smiled back at her and said, "I'm sorry, but we're not allowed to divulge the names of our clients."

"But you don't understand," said Julie, her heart pounding faster. "I'm her mother. She came here for an abortion, because she thinks that's the only answer. I have to let her know that's not so. I have to stop her!"

"I'm sorry, ma'am, but we must respect the confidentiality of our patients. There's nothing I can do for you."

"Maybe she's not even here," said Julie shrilly. "She could be at another clinic. If she isn't here, just tell me, so I can check the others. Please!"

The woman shook her head. "I'm sorry."

Julie fought an impulse to reach across the desk and grab the appointment book from the receptionist's hands. She resisted the urge to shout for all the room to hear, *Don't you understand? This is a matter of life or death! I could lose my grandchild. I could lose my daughter because of your asinine protocol!*

But the woman might call the police and accuse Julie of harassing her. They could cart her off to jail and that would be the end of her search for Katie. No, she had to stay calm, had to stay in control.

For a long moment Julie remained standing at the desk, waiting, as if dogged persistence might change the receptionist's mind. But the woman had already blithely turned her attention to some paperwork on her desk and seemed oblivious now of Julie's presence.

Julie returned to Michael's car with a deep sigh of discouragement. As he pulled out into the street, he looked over at her and said, "So no sign of Katie there?"

"They wouldn't tell me a thing. It'll be that way everywhere, won't it, Michael? Everywhere we go will be a dead end. We'll never find Katie in time."

"We'll do what we can, Jewel. That's all we can do."

As Julie had expected, the other clinics refused to give out any information. Finally Julie resorted to taking out a wallet photo of Katie and asking patients in the waiting room if they had seen this young girl. No one had.

By the middle of the afternoon Julie realized her chances of finding Katie were practically nil; the clinics would be closing in a few short hours. What Katie had planned to do was probably already done.

"Where to now?" asked Michael as they drove along Pacific Coast Highway. She knew he was humoring her. He didn't hold out much hope that they'd find Katie now, and even if they did, it would be too late.

"If only we knew where she was!" Julie lamented, a sob growing like an egg in her throat. "Dear God, please help us find Katie!"

"Are you sure she didn't leave the address somewhere in her room?" Michael suggested, grasping at straws for her sake. "Maybe we should go home and look."

"I don't think so," said Julie bleakly. "In her note she said Jesse was making the arrangements."

"Then we should find Jesse."

"Don't you understand? He's with her, Michael."

"Then maybe he left the address at his house. Maybe his family knows something."

"We don't even know his family. Didn't he say he just has a grandmother?"

"Where does she live?"

"In Long Beach, near Signal Hill, I think."

"What's her name?"

"I don't know. Dawson, I suppose, if she's the paternal grandmother." Julie realized suddenly how little they knew about this boy Katie was so devoted to. "We never took the time to find out things about him, Michael," she said with regret. "We kept thinking she would tire of him or he would just go away."

"Look for Dawson in the phone book," said Michael.

"There's a Gladys Dawson on Willow. It's just off Atlantic. She could be the one."

"Right. I'm on my way."

Michael drove through a maze of narrow streets in a deteriorating neighborhood of weathered, cracker-box houses on postage-stamp-size lots. Finally he pulled over to the curb in front of a modest white frame bungalow with a sagging porch the length of the house.

"This is it," he said, turning off the ignition.

Julie gazed around uncertainly at the shabby surroundings and unkempt yards and wondered if they had made a mistake coming here. What would they tell this woman they didn't even know?

Your grandson got our daughter pregnant, and now we're trying to keep them from making an even bigger mistake?

In a neighboring yard, several grimy, ragamuffin children played catch with a red rubber ball. Several others, mainly girls, sat impassively on broken porch steps watching with solemn, insolent eyes. On the corner a group of teenage boys stood together, smoking and talking confidentially, moving and maneuvering with the limber, jaunty grace of young stallions. They wore T-shirts, low-slung baggy pants and what looked like combat boots. Some had ponytails; others wore backward caps tight on their heads so that tufts of hair stuck through above their foreheads.

"I bet those kids are drug pushers," Julie told Michael with a shiver of alarm. "Do you think we're safe here?"

"Safe enough," he replied, getting out. "Come on. Let's go meet this Gladys Dawson."

A squat, sixtyish woman in a faded, flower-print housedress answered the door. Shiny, marble black eyes shone like beacons in an unremarkable face of blunt, doughy features. Her wispy, gray-brown hair was tied back in a loose bun and she wore rimless spectacles just below the wide bridge of her nose.

"Mrs. Dawson?" said Michael in his most formal voice. "Do you have a grandson named Jesse Dawson?"

Her dark eyes flashed with sudden concern. "Yes, I do. Has something happened—"

"No, I'm sure he's fine," Michael assured her, "but we'd like to find him. We believe he's with our daughter, Katie Lynn—or Kaitlyn—Ryan."

The stout woman broke into a generous grin. "You're Katie's parents? Well, I'll be! Please come in!"

"You know Katie?" Julie asked in surprise as they entered the clean, cramped living room where heavy drapes made the light scant and the shadows long.

"Oh, sure, I know Katie." She patted a spot on the small, worn davenport and gestured for them to sit down. "I know Katie like one of my own. Jesse brings her over to visit regular as clockwork. A real nice girl."

Julie and Michael exchanged glances. So this was where Katie was spending so much of her time! It didn't seem like the sort of place she would seek out—their self-absorbed, strong-willed daughter, who took for granted the luxuries with which her parents had surrounded her.

"I'd offer you some iced tea," said the woman, "but my ice box isn't working so good lately."

"Thanks anyway, Mrs. Dawson," said Michael. "We're fine. But we do have something important to talk to you about." As simply and briefly as possible, he filled her in on the situation with Katie and Jesse. The woman's eyes widened in dismay when Michael told her Katie was pregnant. "We want to find them before it's too late," he explained, "and we thought you might have some idea where they are."

"Oh, glory be, I don't have the slightest notion," she said with a sigh, "but you go look in Jesse's room. Maybe he wrote something down."

"Thank you, Mrs. Dawson," said Michael.

"Come with me," said Gladys. But as they started down the narrow hallway the front door opened and a younger, smaller version of Jesse ambled in, swinging a broken bat in one hand.

"This here is Jesse's little brother, Scout," said Gladys. "Scout, these folks are Katie's parents, Mr. and Mrs. Ryan."

"Hi," the boy said with an impish shrug. "Man, Katie's cool. Totally cool." Scout was a lean, gangly youngster, about twelve, more angular through the face and chest than Jesse, but boyishly appealing beneath the dirt and grime. His smile lit up the room.

"Got any idea where that brother of yours is?" asked Gladys.

"Nope," said Scout, rubbing a dirt smudge from his cheek.

Gladys reached over and helped him with the smudge. "Why aren't you out playing ball?"

"The big guys chased us away."

"You tell them to leave you be. There's a whole big world to play in and plenty of room for everybody."

Scout grimaced. "If I say that, they'll bash my head in."

Gladys shook her head wearily. "No place for a boy to play anymore, without trouble coming his way." She raised her hand

and gestured for Julie and Michael to follow her down the hall. "This is Scout and Jesse's room," she said. "Feel free to take a look."

Julie entered gingerly, conscious that she was trespassing, invading someone's private space. The room was uncomfortably small—four walls with two narrow beds crammed in, a spindly dresser between the beds and a card table with two folding chairs serving as a desk. Photos of sleek sports cars and rugged football players were tacked randomly to the wall, along with snapshots of Katie over one bed.

Julie didn't feel right touching the belongings of two boys she hardly knew, but her eyes roved anxiously over scattered papers on the card table for any clue of Katie's whereabouts. After a moment her eyes caught a scrawled address and phone number on a note pad. "That could be it," she told Michael.

"Bingo!" he said, seizing the paper. "It's a medical facility over on Bellflower. Look, beneath the phone number he's written another number."

"Two-fifteen," said Julie. "That must be the appointment time."

"Let's go," said Michael. "It's already three-thirty!"

With a hasty goodbye to Gladys, they left the Dawson house and headed for the clinic on Bellflower. Fifteen minutes later, with his brakes squealing, Michael pulled into the parking lot. Julie jumped from the automobile before Michael had even turned off the ignition. She sprinted across the pavement, her stacked heels clacking noisily, and burst into the waiting room of the sprawling, single-story office, breathless. Several women glanced up impassively, then returned to their magazines. Julie scanned every face, praying one of them would be Katie's, but they were all the faces of strangers.

Julie took long strides across the carpeted room to the mahogany check-in desk, and before the receptionist even looked up, she blurted, "Excuse me, miss, I need some help."

The young girl looked up with obvious disinterest and drawled, "You got an appointment?" She was in her early twenties, had bleached hair the color and texture of cotton candy, and wore shiny, pearl white lipstick and long artificial fingernails painted in various shades of pastel.

Julie was trembling now, with a mixture of rage and desperation. Her voice wavering, she said, "I don't have an appointment, but my daughter, Kaitlyn Ryan, was scheduled for an abortion at two-fifteen. I would like to see her, please."

"Take a seat," said the girl. "If she's here, she should be done pretty soon. You her ride home?"

"I don't want to take a seat," said Julie, ignoring the question. "I want to go back wherever my daughter is and talk to her—now!"

"Sorry, nobody's allowed back there except the patients." Examining one long, pale blue nail, the girl added, "Sometimes their partners come with them, of course, but they wait in another room during the procedure."

"You don't understand," Julie implored, her voice rising. "I can't wait until the procedure's over. I'm here to stop my daughter's abortion!"

The girl pursed her glossy lips. "I'm sorry, ma'am. That's not your decision to make now, is it!"

Julie gripped the edge of the desk and swayed slightly. *Please God, help me!* she cried inwardly. From the corner of her eye she saw Michael enter the waiting room and stride toward her. When he reached her side, she sank against him and clutched his arm frantically. "She's here, Michael, I'm sure of it, but they won't let me see her."

Michael tried reasoning with the girl, too, to no avail.

As Michael and the girl talked, Julie considered making a break past the reception desk and running down the hallway, going door to door and looking in, calling for Katie. But no, she would never get away with it. Someone would stop her and probably even arrest her, and she would be of no use to Katie in jail.

But another idea occurred to her. If Katie were somewhere in one of those suites, behind one of those closed doors, she might hear her name being called. Julie drew in a deep breath, cupped her hands to her mouth, and shouted, "Katie Ryan, are you here? Katie Ryan, can you hear me?"

Everyone stared dumbfounded at Julie, including the white-lipped receptionist with the cotton-candy hair. "You can't do that," she told Julie indignantly.

"I just did." Julie raised her voice another decibel and called Katie's name again.

A tall man in a white lab coat—a doctor or technician perhaps—emerged from one of the rooms and approached Julie, shaking his head. "What's all the commotion?" he demanded.

Michael stepped forward and said, "We're looking for our daughter."

The man stared Michael down, his bristly brows narrowing over suspicious eyes. "I suggest you go sit down, sir, and if she's here she'll be out shortly."

"That's not good enough," said Michael. Julie could see the thread of his pulse throbbing at his temple. He cupped his mouth and started shouting for Katie, too.

"Call the police, Miss Baer," said the doctor.

Before she could pick up the phone, a door opened down the hall and Jesse Dawson came striding out, his face ghost white. "Mr. and Mrs. Ryan," he said, "how did you know we were—"

"Where's Katie?" demanded Michael.

"Come with me."

"You can't go down there," the doctor protested.

"Watch me!" said Michael.

Julie and Michael followed Jesse down the hall to the third door on the right, nearly running, even as Miss Baer and the lab-coated man called after them. As soon as they entered the stark, sterile room smelling of antiseptics, Julie's gaze focused on Katie sitting like a woebegone child on a utility bed, her long legs dangling over the side. She was wearing a shapeless, white hospital gown, her long, amber hair spilling over her shoulders, her pale blue eyes reflecting pools of desolation.

"Oh, Katie!" Julie uttered brokenly. Everyone and everything else faded into the background as she ran to her daughter and gathered her into her arms.

"Mom, I'm sorry, I'm so sorry," Katie cried, breaking into huge, convulsive sobs. In Julie's arms she felt like a little child

again as her slender frame shook and her arms clung frantically
to Julie's neck.

Memories flooded back of all the times Katie as a child had
run to Julie with a skinned knee or a scratch on her arm. Julie
had always been able to mend the hurts and offer comfort. But
now as she held her inconsolable daughter in her arms, all she
could think was, *Dear God, I'm too late! Too late!*

Chapter Ten

"Take me home, Daddy. Please take me home!" Katie begged as Michael embraced her.

"I will, baby," he said with a catch in his voice. "Your mom and I are taking you home right now." He smoothed back her hair and looked directly into her face. "You're going to be okay, honey. You've got to believe that. Your mom and I will do everything we can to help you get over this."

Michael glanced over at Jesse who stood by the door, his chin on his chest and his thumbs hooked on his jeans as he traced linoleum squares with the toe of one well-aged sneaker. "I think you should go on home and give Katie some time alone," said Michael. "She's upset enough already."

"No, Daddy. Please, I want him here."

Julie clasped Katie's hand. "If only you'd talked to us about this, honey. If only you and Jesse hadn't taken things into your own hands! We could have worked things out—"

Katie hiccupped another sob. "You and Dad were so upset, Mom. I just wanted to make our lives go back the way they were."

"None of us can do that," said Julie tearfully, pressing Katie's hand against her cheek. "We tried to stop you. Your dad and I

tried to get here in time, but we didn't know where you were.
I'm so sorry we couldn't save you. I'm sorry we couldn't save
your baby—''

Katie wiped the tears from her cheek, her penciled brows knit-
ting in perplexity. ''What are you talking about, Mom?''

Julie looked back, puzzled. ''I'm talking about the abortion.
I'm sorry we couldn't stop—''

''I didn't have it,'' said Katie, sniffing.

''What?'' said Michael sharply.

''I couldn't, Dad. I just couldn't.''

Julie's heart raced. ''You didn't have the abortion?''

''No, Mom.'' Julie sniffed again. ''Are you mad?''

A sound of relief burst from Julie's throat. ''Mad? Are you
kidding? I never wanted that for you!''

Michael leaned closer, massaging Katie's neck. ''Tell us what
happened, sweetheart.''

She hugged herself to keep from shivering. ''I—I was lying on
a hard table in another room, my feet in those awful metal stir-
rups. I was so scared, my legs wouldn't stop trembling. And this
man—he kept telling me to lie still and it would all be over soon.
I kept saying, 'Doctor, you're going to hurt me,' and he said, no,
it wouldn't hurt if I'd be a big girl and lie still.''

Katie drew in a shuddering breath. ''But I could tell he was
just saying that. He wasn't paying any attention to me...he just
kept fingering his instrument tray. And then he started toward me
and said, 'Just relax. This won't hurt.' But I knew better. I knew
what was happening was going to hurt for the rest of my life. I
started feeling real panicky, like a scream was building inside me.
I thought, this must be what being raped is like. I wanted to get
up and run, but I couldn't move.''

''Oh, Katie,'' Julie soothed. ''My poor baby!''

Katie's voice quavered. ''I kept thinking, there's this little life
growing inside me, and it's mine—it's part of me. It's there separate from me, different from me, even though I can't see or touch
it.

''And I thought, this man is going to kill my baby, and he

doesn't know me. He doesn't even care about me or my baby. And I started bawling, real loud and hard.''

"Katie girl," said Michael, "it's over, honey. You don't have to talk about it now. Let's just go home."

"No, Daddy. I can't leave it in my head all bottled up. I've got to say it, and maybe it'll go away. The doctor told me to stop crying, but I couldn't. I told him I wanted to go home. His face reddened and he swore. He told me to go and not come back until I made up my mind what I wanted. So I climbed off the table, and they told me to sit in this room until I calmed down so Jesse could take me home.''

Michael pulled Katie against his chest and massaged the back of her neck. Perspiration dotted his forehead and upper lip. "You did the right thing, honey," he told Katie gently. "Thank God you're okay! You and the baby.''

"Michael," said Julie, "we should go out now and let Katie get dressed.''

He nodded. "Then we'll all go home."

Katie looked at Jesse. "You're coming too, aren't you?"

He was still toeing the linoleum, one shoulder against the wall. "I better not. Maybe later."

In the car heading home Julie sat in the back seat with Katie, holding her hand, as if she were a child again needing a mother's touch. Julie wasn't sure who was more upset. Katie, surely, but Julie herself felt nearly as ravaged, as unsettled. They had rescued their daughter and their grandchild, but now what? Where did they go from here?

Katie was still taking deep, ragged breaths that made her shoulders shudder, and her eyes were focused somewhere outside the window. She kept twisting a strand of her long shiny hair around her index finger, so tight she was in danger of cutting off the circulation. Julie had no idea what was going on now in her daughter's head.

Shortly after they arrived home, Michael telephoned Jesse's grandmother and suggested the two families get together and talk. "She invited the three of us over next Saturday afternoon," Michael told Julie after hanging up the receiver.

"I won't go," Katie told him. "I can't face anyone ever again, especially Jesse's grandma."

"You're going," said Michael. "Your mom and I will be there with you. You know we love you, whatever happens."

But when they pulled up in front of Gladys Dawson's little bungalow on Saturday afternoon, Katie wasn't the only one feeling reluctant. Conflicting feelings tossed in Julie's heart. She and Michael had come to work out a reasonable plan for Katie and Jesse and their unborn baby, but what options did they really have? What answers could a teenage boy with a minimum-wage job and his widowed grandmother provide?

Jesse's grandmother welcomed the Ryans as if they were already family, her arms open wide, her smile genuine, her tiny house smelling of freshly baked bread. Gladys cut the warm, golden brown loaf into thick slices and served it with her own homemade strawberry preserves, along with a sparkling pitcher of sun tea.

They sat around the small red Formica table and ate while a radio droned country music in the background. Julie's eyes moved around the kitchen, noting the ceramic red-hen cookie jar and matching canisters on the linoleum counter and the hardware-store calendar and Norman Rockwell prints hiding a fine network of cracks in the walls. The room was muggy, except for a slight breeze coming through the screen door and ruffling the chintz curtains at the window over the sink.

Gladys sat fanning herself with a paper Japanese fan, her faded housedress sticking to her skin at the hollow of her throat. "It was too warm a day to be baking bread," she conceded, "but Jesse loves my homemade bread, and I figured you folks would like it, too."

"My mother baked bread when I was small," said Julie. "I still remember that toasty aroma wafting into my bedroom. I'd climb out of bed and sneak to the kitchen and beg for a warm, crusty slice."

"And she'd always give in, wouldn't she?" said Gladys, chuckling. "That's how mamas are."

Julie nodded, feeling a sudden tightness in her throat. As vivid as the memory was, that's all it was—a memory, fleeting, elusive. When had she stopped being the child, loved and protected by her mother? Julie was the mother now, and soon, all too soon, her daughter would be the mother. How did things change so swiftly?

As Julie and Michael sat at the table with Jesse's grandmother, Katie and Jesse paced the room, restless as young colts, eager to break away, to be done with this painful, disquieting conversation.

Michael shifted uneasily in his chair. "Mrs. Dawson, we need to discuss Katie and Jesse and the baby. What steps to take…"

Gladys pinched a crust of bread between her thumb and forefinger. "All I know is my Jesse's too young to get married."

"So is Katie," Michael agreed. "Besides, two wrongs don't make a right."

"If marriage is out of the question," said Julie, "what are our other options? Adoption?"

"No," cried Katie, leaning over the table. "No one's going to make me give my baby away! It's mine, and I'll take care of it."

"Honey, we're just trying to consider all the alternatives," said Julie.

"You talk about us like we're not even here," Katie countered. "Like Jesse and I have nothing to say about what happens. If we want to get married, we'll get married!"

"Is that what you want, Jesse?" asked Gladys.

Jesse stared at the floor. "Whatever Katie wants."

"Katie?" asked Julie. "Do you want to marry Jesse?"

Katie stepped back and rubbed her arm distractedly. "I don't know. Not now, but maybe someday. I just want things to be like they were."

"Things will never be like they were," said Michael.

"Maybe someday you children can marry for the right reasons," said Gladys.

Julie nodded. "I think it's best they wait until after the baby's born to decide what to do."

"But I won't give my baby away," said Katie. "You didn't give *me* away, Mom."

"No, but your dad and I were older. We were in a position to get married. It was still a struggle, but—'' She let her words die away. She didn't want to talk about the hard road she and Michael had traveled, were still traveling, in fact.

Michael drummed his fingers on the table. "Frankly, I think it would be best if Jesse and Katie stopped seeing each other."

"No," Katie exclaimed. "Jesse's still my boyfriend, and I love him!"

Jesse found his voice at last, snapping out of his moody silence. "I want to be with Katie when she has the baby. And—and I want my name on the birth certificate." He looked urgently around the table, a patina of sweat glistening on his forehead. "Just so you all know—I'm going to support my kid, even if I have to work double shifts at the garage."

"You can't, Jesse," protested his grandmother. "You're exhausted now."

"I have an idea," said Michael. "If you want more work, Jesse, I could use some help with the houses I'm renovating. You interested?"

Jesse shrugged. "You'd want me around?"

"I think we could get along."

"I don't know anything about fixing up houses. If I did, this place wouldn't be such a rundown rattrap."

"I can teach you all you need to know. If you've got a strong back and a willingness to learn, you'll do okay."

Jesse's interest perked. "What would I have to do?"

"Help put up drywall, pound a few nails, paint, work on some plumbing. Maybe some electrical work. I'll show you what to do."

Jesse looked at his grandmother and she nodded. "Sounds good to me, boy. You'd be learning a good trade."

"And *I'll* be getting some much-needed help," said Michael, warming to the idea. "So far I haven't been able to persuade Julie to wield a hammer or try her hand with a saw."

"I'm more the paintbrush type," Julie replied. "The paint-a-picture-not-a-wall type."

Jesse looked at Katie, his face flushed. "Katie, what do you think? If I helped your dad, I could support my kid pretty good after all.''

Late that evening, as Julie undressed, she looked over at Michael, sitting on the side of the bed setting the alarm. She went over and sat beside him, studying the way the lamplight transformed his handsome features into a silhouette of golden bronze against deep-velvet ebony.

''You handled things well today with Jesse and his grandmother,'' she told him as she massaged his bare shoulder. ''And with Katie, too. You've been supportive since this whole nightmare began. I don't know how I could have coped without you. I would have been a basket case.''

''I just did what had to be done, Jewel,'' he replied, slipping his arm around her and drawing her close.

''And offering Jesse a job helping you with the houses, that was a compassionate thing to do. Most men would have punched him in the nose. I wish I could feel as generous.''

''To tell you the truth, I don't feel so generous, either. At first I wanted to punch Jesse's lights out. Wring his lecherous little neck. But when I looked into his eyes all I saw was this really frightened kid. I felt sorry for him. He's as overwhelmed as any of us. I figure the best way to help Katie is to help the boy she loves.'' He looked gently at Julie and added, ''Besides, I was that boy once.''

''And I was that girl,'' she acknowledged, her tone bittersweet. ''But it's still so different with Katie. We were adults. She's still a child.''

''Not for long.''

Julie rested her head on his sturdy shoulder. ''No, not for long.'' She trembled and Michael ran his hand over her bare arm as if to warm her, even though the room was sultry with June's early summer heat. ''I'm still numb,'' she murmured distractedly. ''It's not real to me yet—our little Katie expecting a baby.''

Michael kneaded her upper arm, her shoulder, her neck. ''Me too, sweetheart. But we've got to be strong for Katie. It's going to take a lot of patience—''

"And a lot of love and prayer," she added. "I just pray I'm up to it, Michael. Sometimes I feel like I'm starting to connect with Katie. Other times I feel like we're worse than strangers."

"She's going to need us. The three of us have to pull together like never before."

"I like the sound of that, Michael."

"And I like the feel of you in my arms," he whispered.

She looked up and met his gaze. It was as sultry and hot as the night. He lowered his head to hers until their lips were nearly touching. "Katie's not the only one around here who could use a little extra TLC."

"TLC?" she repeated in her most tantalizing voice.

"You know. Good, old-fashioned...tender...loving...care..." His words were muffled against her lips and lost at last in the passion of their kiss.

Chapter Eleven

On Sunday morning, while faint streamers of darkness still stippled the sky, Julie woke with a mixture of hope and restlessness. She had never really believed the old bromide that it was always darkest before the dawn, but maybe something good would come out of Katie's crisis pregnancy, a blessing in disguise, for she and Michael had been closer last night than they had been in months.

And yet she realized that they had come together out of their separate neediness, both trying to grasp something from the other, something they couldn't put into words. Even during their most intimate moments they had been silent, their minds worlds apart.

Still, she felt more confident of Michael, of his love. But she had a discomfiting feeling their family would be tested to the breaking point during the months to come. As they steered Katie through the ups and downs of her pregnancy, there would be people to face, with their disapproving stares and probing questions, and there would still be the hard decisions to make. Should Katie keep her baby or give it up? If she kept it, should she marry Jesse or raise her child alone? At best, the road ahead would be painful for all concerned; at worst, their family might not come through intact.

With the first rays of golden sunlight, while Michael still slumbered, the sheet twisted around his left leg like stripes on a barber pole, Julie rose, bathed and dressed for church. Then quietly she took out her prayer journal and sat down at the small French writing desk in her bedroom retreat and scrawled out her thoughts.

Lord, just when I think I know You, You do something so startling and unexpected I realize I hardly know You at all. I asked You to help me know and love You and my family better, and now You've thrown something so big and overwhelming at us— Katie's unplanned pregnancy—that it will force all three of us to know and love one another better if we're even to survive as a family. Maybe this is Your way of answering my prayer, but honestly, it seems more like a dirty trick.

I don't want my love for Katie tested this way; I'm not sure I'm up for it; I don't know if I can cope with the shock, the sudden disruption in our lives, and the wildly, unpredictable demands of a pregnant teenager.

Lord, when I said I wanted to know my daughter better, I never wanted to know something this painful about her. I guess I really just wanted the two of us to have fun together and feel closer, like sisters or convivial friends. I didn't want to be suddenly immersed, drowning, in the deep, hard, unsolvable problems of her life. I didn't want to feel this aching sense of loss, as if I were grieving a death.

But perhaps in a way I am. I grieve not just the loss of Katie's innocence, but of my innocence, too. I never thought this would be my child. I had such a different life in mind for her; and now those dreams are gone, and the person I thought she was is someone else; and maybe I'm someone else, too. It's as if her loss and shame are mine, or as if I am living my own guilt and shame all over again in her. Sometimes I want to shake her and tell her what a fool she was; other times I want to hug her and rock her like a baby in my arms; but mostly I just want to cry—for her, for myself, for all of us.

Dear Father, I have such a long way to go to be an example of Your love! Am I behaving like a sick child who begs for candy and complains when she's given a spoonful of medicine? Are You giving me what You know is for my own good? For my family's good? If so, help me to see it that way, too. Help me to accept what seems abhorrent to me—my baby having a baby.

In spite of everything, help Michael and me to continue growing closer. Please watch over Katie through these trying days. And bless this tiny, unseen child who has caught us unawares and is wending its mysterious and disquieting way into our lives.

Later, on the way home from church, Michael drummed his fingertips on the steering wheel the way he always did when he was about to say something Julie might not agree with. "Sweetheart, if you don't mind," he began tentatively, "I thought I'd spend the afternoon working on the house over on Lakeview. I've already asked Jesse to come with me—he seems eager to learn the ropes. Anyway, if we can get in some good daylight hours, I think the house will be ready to show by next weekend."

Julie's hopes for the afternoon dissolved. "I thought we could spend the day together doing something fun," she said, hiding her disappointment under a flat monotone.

"How about tonight?" Michael suggested. "After the evening service we could go out, grab a burger and maybe even take a drive along the ocean."

She was too angry to be placated, but she managed a modest, "Sure, Michael, whatever you say. I'm sure I'll find something to keep me busy this afternoon."

"Why don't you do some painting? You're always complaining that you don't have time to paint. Now's your chance."

She nodded. Michael had a point. It seemed like ages since she'd held a paintbrush in her hand. Maybe she could even get Katie to pose for a quick watercolor portrait. Sure...capture that rosy glow of motherhood in her cheeks, she thought darkly.

But Katie had no interest in posing for anything. She draped herself over the sofa and wailed loudly about how miserable she felt. "Oh, Mom, I'm so sick to my stomach! I'm dying! This is the pits!" Then she paced the floor, rubbing her stomach with the flat of her palms, her face as pale as skim milk. "I'm going to be sick, I know I am," she moaned over and over, all but demanding that Julie give her her fair share of "tea and sympathy."

Finally Katie stalked to the kitchen, grabbed a box of saltines and a glass of ginger ale, and said, "I'm going up to my room and watch TV—anything to get my mind off this misery."

For a moment Julie gazed around the empty living room, peeved with both Katie and Michael. At last, summoning all her creative impulses, she went upstairs to the spare room, dragged her easel from the closet, tacked a sheet of stiff, grainy watercolor paper to her drawing board and squeezed tubes of watercolor onto her palette, making a bright little rainbow of pure, liquid pigment.

She mixed dabs of raw umber and ultramarine blue with several drops of water and spread the smudgy brown wash over the paper in broad, generous strokes until only small patches of white remained. She tried a landscape with violet mountains and rugged, spiky blue spruce and a meandering stream with lots of rocks and brush. But halfway into the painting she realized it wasn't working; her heart wasn't in it, so she set it aside and cleaned her brushes and palette with a slow, listless monotony.

She thought about Michael a few miles away working so passionately and diligently to restore an old house someone had left in shambles. What drove him? What motivated him? How could he generate such ardor and enthusiasm for some grimy, dilapidated hovel?

She had always taken a perverse pride in letting Michael know how contemptuous she was of his houses, as if even discussing them or showing interest was beneath her dignity. After all, she and Michael and Katie lived in a luxurious, custom-built home with every modern convenience. Why should they waste their time or break their backs cleaning and rebuilding someone else's ramshackle house?

Michael didn't see it that way. He thrived on the challenge of transforming filthy, broken-down hovels into immaculate show places. No matter how hard Julie had tried over the years, she had never been able to get Michael's penchant for renovating buildings out of his blood. This was one area of their lives where they would always be world's apart.

A thought came to her suddenly like a prayer, as wispy and elusive—and just as profound. Why not enter Michael's world and share with him what he delights in? What better way to keep God's commandment of love?

The idea took root. She knew immediately what she was supposed to do: go to the house where Michael was working and join him, help him with his tasks. Get her own hands dirty, if necessary. Wield that hammer he said she would never pick up. Get excited about what excited him!

Before her eagerness had a chance to subside, Julie ran to her room and changed into a pair of ragged jeans and one of Michael's old work shirts. Then she stopped by Katie's room to tell her she was going to go help Michael with the house. "Want to go with me?" she asked.

Katie stared at her as if she had sprouted two heads. "You're going to help Dad with one of his grungy houses? What gives, Mom? You hate Dad's houses—you're always telling me they take too much of his time."

Julie nodded. Michael's houses were an odd, unlikely mistress, a time-consuming preoccupation she'd always resented. But maybe she'd been approaching the situation all wrong. "Maybe it's time I showed your father how loving and supportive I can be by helping him renovate his architectural monstrosities. How about it, Katie? Why not come watch the fun?"

Katie turned her gaze back to the television set. "Are you kidding, Mom? I'd rather watch a 'Lucy' rerun!"

Julie smiled ironically. "Who knows? I may *look* like Lucy when I try my hand with a hammer."

Later, as Julie drove down Lakeview Lane to Michael's property, she felt pleased with herself. She was doing a selfless, generous thing, putting Michael's interests above her own. And surely he would be pleasantly surprised by her sudden interest in his work. He would see that she was putting him first.

After all, she could still be at home painting, doing what she loved, instead of driving out to a house that had been owned by strangers and perhaps still contained their dirt and clutter. Surely it would never occur to Michael to sit down and paint a landscape with her, even though he had taken that college art class seventeen years ago and had actually been quite good, a little primitive perhaps, yet strong and bold. But she couldn't imagine him now sitting at an easel beside her and actually painting.

Then again, she wasn't sure she could see herself hammering nails into studs or sawing two-by-fours. But, for Michael's sake, she was willing to give it that old college try.

With her mind so preoccupied, she hardly realized she had pulled into the driveway of the house on Lakeview Lane. It wasn't a bad house—quite large, in fact, a two-story colonial with a wide porch and ornamental gables. It obviously needed a good coat of paint and lots of repairs. The wood fence was broken and slats were missing in several places, the shutters were splintered, and the grass was dry and parched and riddled with weeds.

Julie automatically mixed the colors in her mind, an unconscious habit left over from her college art classes. The grass, instead of a verdant green, was yellow ochre with a smidgen of burnt sienna blended in.

As Julie pulled to a stop behind Michael's car, she noticed another automobile beside his. It wasn't Jesse's old jalopy, but a shiny sports car, an expensive foreign model.

Who's here? she wondered. Maybe someone interested in buying the house?

As she walked up the sidewalk to the porch she spotted Jesse sanding the wood by the door where thin strips of old paint were peeling off like apple skins. Jesse looked up and smiled faintly when he saw her and rubbed the sweat from his forehead with the back of his hand.

"Looks like my husband's got you working hard," she said.

"Yeah, but he works twice as hard as I do."

"Is he inside?" she asked, reaching for the doorknob.

"Yeah, he's in there with that lady friend of his."

"Lady friend?" Julie felt a twinge like a rubber band stretched and released between her ribs; not physical pain, but something worse, an alarm sounding, a sense of foreboding.

She went inside, her sneakers soundless on the worn carpet. She was torn between wanting to make a sound and wanting to take Michael by surprise. What did she expect to find—Michael and some woman in a passionate embrace? Had she lost that much trust in her husband?

She could hear voices coming from the kitchen—familiar, light, even jovial. Michael was saying something in a jaunty, lilting tone, but the words were muffled, indistinct. Then Julie heard a woman's voice and knew immediately that it was Beth Chamberlin.

Closer now, she could hear every word bell clear. Beth was saying, "Oh, Michael, no one makes me laugh the way you do!"

"Then we're even," said Michael, "because nobody laughs at my jokes like you do."

Julie hung back, her first impulse to wheel around and run back outside before Michael even knew she was there. But a deep, primal instinct took over, self-preservation perhaps—a mixture of anger, indignation and the steely determination to claim and defend what was hers.

She stepped into the roomy, fifties-style kitchen with her chin high and a brittle smile in place. Michael and Beth stood facing each other, about a foot apart, both leaning against the whitewashed pine cabinet. They were laughing in the casual, easy way of good friends. Or lovers.

Beth was wearing a powder blue shorts outfit that brought out her natural, clean-scrubbed good looks. The sleeveless blouse was tied at the waist, revealing a provocative ribbon of bare midriff. Her legs were tanned and shapely, and she wore leather sandals that showed fire engine red toenails.

Julie had the jolting sensation she was intruding on a private, even intimate moment, as if they were the couple and she the interloper. "Hello, Michael," she said, trying to inject a light, breezy tone. Then she turned her gaze to Beth and said, dripping irony, "Why, hello, Beth. I didn't expect to see you here."

They stared at Julie with surprise bordering on astonishment, then sprang apart, putting a safe distance between themselves. Michael recovered first and said brightly, with a slightly baffled note, "Julie, honey, what are you doing here?"

"I came to help," she said, setting her purse on the linoleum counter top. "Is that why you're here, too, Beth?" she inquired politely. "Are you helping Michael resurrect this gloomy old place?"

"No," Beth said, brushing a wave of shiny black hair back from her forehead. "I just dropped by to tell Michael about a client who might be interested in buying this house—if the price is right."

Julie forced a smile. "Really? A buyer? That sounds like quite an opportunity, Michael, wouldn't you say?"

"Depends on the price," he said unevenly. Sweat, like tiny glistening crystals, beaded on his tanned forehead and upper lip. He moved his hand back and forth over the edge of the counter, a random, nervous gesture she knew very well.

But Beth was still buoyant, her voice soft and breathy, like a young girl speaking excitedly about her best beau. "If I could afford it, I'd buy this house myself," she said. "It's so cute and quaint. It has Michael's own unique stamp on it, don't you think so, Mrs. Ryan?"

"I never thought of it that way before," Julie admitted, "but I suppose you're right. Michael does have his own unique style."

"It shows in everything he does," said Beth, "whether he's closing a deal or redesigning a room in one of his houses."

"Goodness, you sound like quite a fan," said Julie thickly.

"I am. I'm Michael's biggest fan. He's taught me everything I know about the business."

"I wouldn't say that," said Michael uneasily.

"No, Michael, let her talk. It's fascinating to see my husband through another woman's eyes. It gives me a whole new appreciation of you."

"See, Michael?" said Beth, absently twisting a strand of coal black hair curling around her collar. "Wives like to hear good things about their husbands."

"Speaking of husbands," said Julie, "have you heard anything from yours? I remember you were so upset that night you phoned Michael and asked him to come over."

"Oh, I was," Beth agreed. "I was a basket case. I'm still a nervous wreck, thinking I hear that man pulling in the driveway or knocking on the door. Sometimes I think I see him in a car behind me on the freeway or walking up another aisle in the supermarket, but then he's gone, and I figure it's just me, getting spooked over nothing.''

"Beth got a restraining order against her ex-husband," said Michael, getting to the point. "We hope it'll do the trick."

We? Michael sees himself as part of Beth's dilemma! "It must be a very stressful situation," Julie noted.

"Yes. When Roger calls, we get into it over the phone, screaming like a couple of banshees. But so far he hasn't come banging down my door, thank heaven, knock on wood!"

"It's nice you have Michael to help you," said Julie, cringing at her own cattiness. But Beth seemed not to notice.

"Oh, I am so thankful!" Clutching her handbag to her side, Beth said, "Well, I'd better run along now, Michael. I've got some shopping to do. It was good seeing you again, Mrs. Ryan."

"Julie."

"Yes. All right. Julie." Beth looked quickly at Michael. She swayed a little, as if not quite sure whether to advance toward him or to back away. At last she shrugged and said, "Bye, Michael. I'll see you at the office tomorrow."

He nodded. "Tell our prospective buyer—"

"I'll tell him the house will be ready..."

"By next weekend. If all goes as planned."

"Next weekend. I'll tell him."

Julie waited until she heard Beth's car pull out of the driveway, then she looked Michael directly in the eye. Her hands trembled slightly, and her throat felt dry as cardboard, but she forced out the words, "That girl has a crush on you, Michael."

His face drained of color. "What are you talking about?"

"She has a schoolgirl crush. It's enormous! Can't you see it?"

Michael turned his attention to the ornamental molding on one wall. "You're imagining things, Julie. Besides, she's hardly a schoolgirl."

"You're right. She has a certain callow sophistication about her that some men might find appealing. But she's still a girl, not even ten years older than Katie."

"So what?"

"So I know what I see. She's devoted to you, Michael. Like a little groupie. Did it ever occur to you that you might be leading her on, without meaning to?"

Michael craned his neck around, his eyes a smoldering blue-gray. "Julie, are you suggesting something's going on between Beth and me?"

Julie felt herself backing down, her combativeness shrinking like a balloon losing air. She didn't want to know the truth, not if it held the power to destroy her. "Can't—can't you see? Beth is a very needy and vulnerable girl."

"I'm well aware of that. I'm just trying to be her friend."

Julie searched Michael's face. Was he blind or deliberately obtuse? Flustered, peeved, she groped for the precise words to convey her concern. "There are *friends,* and then there are friends. I'd hate to see her get the wrong idea about you."

Michael turned and rubbed his palms on his jeans. "Don't worry, I can handle Beth. She's not a problem. Now tell me, why did you come out here."

For a moment Julie couldn't remember why she had come. What had seemed like such a good idea an hour ago now seemed a fiasco. "I told you," she murmured solemnly. "I want to help."

"Since when?"

Julie shook her head. "I was just trying to do something nice. If you don't want my help—"

He stepped forward and grabbed her arm. "Wait. I do. It's just—you never cease to amaze me, Jewel."

She looked around and sighed. "Where should I start?"

"Wherever you want." He pointed to the ceiling. "I'm working on the cornice moldings, nailing the trim. I have only a few more strips to go, and it'll be ready to paint."

"It looks good."

"Thanks."

"How is Jesse working out?" she asked, changing the subject.

"Jesse?"

"Yes, how's Jesse?" she repeated irritably, silently chastising herself for being such a wimp. For crying out loud, she had the backbone of a jellyfish. She had danced around the subject of

Beth, even daring to imply the unthinkable, but now she was dropping the ball, all because she was too chicken to pursue the emotion-charged issue of Michael's supposed infidelity!

"Jesse's doing okay. He has a lot to learn, but he's a hard worker. But I have to admit, every time I think of him and Katie together, I want to box his ears."

"I feel the same way." She wanted to add, "When I see you and Beth together." But no, she with the heart of a coward remained mute. She stood listening to Michael talk about Katie and Jesse when she wanted nothing more than to throttle Michael. She heard herself saying, "For Katie's sake, we all have to get along," and she wanted to gag.

"I know you're right," said Michael. "And I'm trying hard to keep an open mind about Jesse, but it's not easy."

"He seems happy to be helping you." Inwardly she kicked herself again. Why in the world was she doing this to herself—talking banalities about Jesse when Beth Chamberlin was uppermost in her mind?

Michael flashed a tentative smile. "What about you, Julie?"

She stared at him. "What about me?" Did he somehow guess the questions about Beth roiling in her head?

Michael lightly ran his palm over her bare arm. "You said you want to give me a hand. So how do you want to help out?"

"I told you," she said, dry-mouthed. She was drowning in her own seething, barely suppressed fury. "I'll help wherever I'm needed."

He turned his gaze to the kitchen, glancing around from floor to ceiling and back again, and said finally, "The cabinets could use a little lemon oil." He looked back at her and beamed a quizzical smile—the kind that started deep in his eyes and flitted like dazzling electricity to the corners of his mouth. He reached out impulsively and brushed a stray blond curl from her forehead. "How about it, sweetheart? Are you game?"

She sighed, her anger cresting, resignation setting in. The moment of confrontation had passed. Michael looked vulnerable and boyishly appealing standing with his bottle of lemon oil, waiting for her reply. She took the bottle and said, "Polish a few cabinets, huh? Sounds easy enough."

He handed her a rag—one of his old T-shirts. "You're really serious about helping me?"

"I said I was."

He was still grinning. "I don't know what to say."

She managed a grudging mite of a grin herself. "How about 'thanks'?"

Chapter Twelve

The languid, sun-bleached days of summer drifted by with a strange, surreal quality—long, mundane days of office work followed by evenings of cooking and cleaning, and weekends painting pictures when Julie could squeeze in the time. For the moment, life was deceptively tranquil. Katie, her morning sickness subsiding, enrolled in summer school to offset the classes she would miss when the baby came after the first of the year. Jesse started a savings account with the money he earned from the garage and his weekend construction work for Michael. Michael's real-estate office was experiencing their biggest boom since the economic recession several years before. And Beth Chamberlin was his number-one sales person!

In spite of the seeming monotony of her circumstances, Julie was aware that her life was changing in sweeping, substantial ways. Her mother had been dead for over a year now, and yet Julie hadn't been able to comprehend her loss in the deepest parts of her mind. Each time she thought of her mother dying, she was astonished again, as if just learning the news. She wondered when she would begin to believe it enough so the shock wouldn't hit her afresh each time.

But her mother's death was only one enormous change confronting Julie. Just as hard to fathom was Katie becoming a mother. Already her reedy body was rounding out, the angles softening, her flesh blossoming like lush fruit. Katie was losing the smooth, pliant, wide-eyed look of a child. Her pale blue eyes contained a melancholy cast, an aura of disenchantment. She insisted she was in love with Jesse and they both wanted this baby, but at times Julie noticed a remote sadness in Katie's eyes, a yearning perhaps to recapture her days of freedom and innocence.

Julie wanted to talk with Katie, reassure her, answer her questions and share her concerns, but Katie kept to herself and said little. If Julie had questioned how well she knew Katie before, Katie was even more of a mystery now. The only time Katie seemed to come out of her shell was when their family visited Jesse's grandmother. As the months passed, it was becoming something of a family ritual. Every week or so Gladys Dawson would invite Julie, Michael and Katie to dinner at her tiny Long Beach bungalow. She would serve her old-fashioned meat loaf or spaghetti or fried chicken and mashed potatoes.

Each time Julie insisted on bringing something—a roast or a salad or dessert—but Mrs. Dawson always declined her offers. So Julie began taking little bags of groceries and just leaving them on the counter—fresh fruit and vegetables, canned goods and dairy products. Gladys always insisted she didn't need such generous gifts, but before long Julie would notice the elderly woman carefully placing the items on her pantry shelf.

Whenever Julie suggested that Gladys, Jesse and Jesse's brother, Scout, come to *her* home for dinner, Mrs. Dawson always dismissed the idea with a tolerant little smile, explaining that she didn't like to leave her house alone, considering how the neighborhood had deteriorated in recent years. Julie's imagination flared with the funny, fleeting image of Gladys Dawson wielding a heavy iron skillet and warning vagrants and vandals alike to skedaddle off her property if they valued their lives. The old woman was so plucky, gritty and discerning, Julie found herself feeling an unspoken connection with her.

Gladys was nothing like Julie's mother, of course, and yet in some essential, indescribable way, they were alike—strong, nurturing women who remained stoic and unflappable in the face of immense obstacles and disappointments. Maybe that was why Julie enjoyed Gladys Dawson's company so much: she was a woman Julie hoped to be like one day. It was a strange and unexpected alliance they had formed—these two very dissimilar families thrown together by something that never should have happened but which now united them with the promise of hope and new life.

Each time they drove through the Signal Hill area to the Dawson bungalow, Julie felt uneasy and even a bit guilty as she surveyed the shabby houses with their narrow, seedy yards. Why was it some people had so little and others, like herself, had so much? But what stirred her most were the solemn-faced children who sat listlessly on sagging porch steps or dodged traffic to play ball in the crowded streets.

"It's a shame these children don't have somewhere to play," Julie told Michael one Sunday afternoon in mid-August as they approached Gladys Dawson's street.

"They need a recreation center," he replied, pulling up to the curb beside a clogged gutter, "but no one has the funds to build one. There's so much vandalism in this part of town, I imagine the city has all it can handle keeping up with basic police and fire-protection services."

"But maybe there wouldn't be so much vandalism if the kids had something to do," said Julie as they walked up the uneven sidewalk to the small porch. She noticed a little girl in tank top and shorts watching her with wide, dark eyes from the neighboring yard. Something in the girl's face imbedded itself in Julie's heart; mentally she traced her fragile features, her forlorn, all-bare-arms-and-legs gesture, her wispy, small-boned frame. If I could just capture her on canvas, Julie mused. If I could only make people feel what I feel now looking at her.

"You're right, Julie," Michael was saying. "It's a catch-22 situation. God knows what anyone can do about it."

Julie looked questioningly at him. It took her a moment to retrace their conversation and make sense of his words. As he knocked on the Dawsons' door, she whispered, "Look at that little girl next door. Doesn't she just make your heart melt?"

He nodded. "It makes you feel like we should pack up half the neighborhood and take them home."

Julie took a sweeping glance up and down the street. Michael was right. This was a neighborhood of diminished hopes and abandoned dreams. "I wish there was some way we could help," she murmured.

Michael frowned. "Right now we've got more than we can handle with Katie and her baby."

Julie's preoccupation with the little neighbor girl ebbed as Gladys opened the door and welcomed them inside. Katie and Jesse were already there, setting the table for dinner. "I've put the youngsters to work," Gladys told Julie, "so there's nothing left for us to do, except sit down with a glass of sun tea and relax."

"That sounds good to me," said Julie.

"You ladies sit down and I'll get the glasses," said Michael, heading for the tiny kitchen.

Gladys wiped her hands on her apron and sank down on the nubby maroon davenport. "That's might nice of you, Mr. Ryan."

Julie laughed. "I wish I could get him to do that at home."

"Well, a little sweet talk never hurts," said Gladys with a wink.

"You preach it, Mrs. Dawson," said Michael, chuckling.

A half hour later, when they were about to sit down to eat, Gladys asked Jesse, "Where's your brother?"

Jesse shrugged. "Out playing, I guess."

"Well, you go find him and tell him it's suppertime."

"If he's out playing, he won't want me dragging him home just to eat."

"You go find him," said Gladys. "If there's one thing I know about my boys, they like to eat."

Jesse crossed the room and pushed open the screen door. "I'll go, but don't start without us."

"I'll go with you," said Katie, absently smoothing her palms over the slight bulge of her abdomen that stretched her T-shirt tight.

Jesse held the door open for her. "Okay, but we're going to have to move fast, girl. I bet you can't keep up, now that you're walking for two."

"Oh, yeah?" Katie challenged, tossing her long blond hair jauntily. "You just watch me, mister."

The two were gone no more than five minutes when Julie heard Jesse running toward the house shouting, his voice shrill with panic. "Grams! Get help! Scout's hurt!"

Gladys bustled to the door, her face blanching, her hands raised in alarm. "Where is he, Jesse?"

"In the old warehouse down the block. He's hurt bad, Grams!"

"Where's Katie?" cried Julie.

"Staying with Scout. He's bleeding bad."

Michael sprinted to the door. "Call 911, Mrs. Dawson. You both stay here. I'll go."

"I'm coming, too," said Julie.

He glanced back dubiously. "All right, come on!"

They broke into a run, following Jesse down the street to an old building in the next block—a dark, dingy edifice made of cement and corrugated steel. A broken sign over the door read, Apex Furniture, except that several letters were missing, so the sign seemed to read, Ape Fun ture.

"Scout's inside," said Jesse.

Michael pulled open the heavy, creaking door, and they entered the cavernous building. It smelled of wood shavings and turpentine mixed with must, dust and grime. There were other more odious smells as well—rotting garbage, urine, sour wine. Julie squinted through the dusky twilight until her eyes adjusted to the shadows. Every inch of wall space was covered with graffiti. "Where are they?" she asked.

"This way," said Jesse, sidestepping mounds of decaying trash.

When they had walked another thirty feet, Julie spotted Katie and the boy, the two of them crouched together, hardly more than shadows against the building's hazy milieu. "Katie!" Running to them now, Julie saw that Scout lay sprawled unmoving on the cement floor, his head cradled in Katie's lap. Katie sat bent over him, sobbing, holding her long hair like a cloth against the boy's bloody scalp.

Michael knelt down, felt the boy's pulse and gently looked him over, careful not to move him. "Help is coming," he told Katie. Then he put his hand over the boy's motionless fingers. "Just hold on, Scout. You'll be okay. Don't give up."

"I bet those pig-faced punks from the Tribe did this," said Jesse, pounding his fist against his palm. Even Julie had heard of the Tribe, a gang with members throughout the area. "I'll kill them!"

"Go outside, Jesse," Michael told him. "Watch for the ambulance and show them where to come."

A half hour later, outside the hospital emergency room where doctors worked on Scout, Michael and Jesse paced the floor while Julie sat on a green vinyl couch with Katie and Gladys Dawson. Julie tried flipping through a magazine, but her eyes couldn't settle on the pictures or make sense of the words. Silently she prayed for this boy she hardly knew, who was in a fluky way part of her own family circle now.

After what seemed forever, a physician emerged, pulling off transparent plastic gloves. He greeted them with a professional blend of formality and courtesy and said, "The boy suffered a mild concussion and a deep scalp laceration, but after a few well-placed stitches and a day or two of bed rest, he should be as good as new."

"You're sure, Doctor?" Gladys pressed, her wrinkled cheeks wet with tears.

"Positive, Mrs—"

"Dawson. Gladys Dawson. Scout's my grandson. His parents are dead."

"Well, Mrs. Dawson, we'll take it from here. You go home and get some rest."

"I don't have insurance," she said timorously, as if the doctor might change his mind and not treat the boy after all.

Michael turned to the physician and said confidentially, "I'll give you my name and address. Perhaps I can help with the bills."

"I can't let you do that, Mr. Ryan," said Gladys. "It's too much."

"Mrs. Dawson, we're family now, remember?"

Jesse stepped forward and held out his hand to Michael. "Thanks, Mr. Ryan. You saved my brother's life. I won't ever forget it."

Michael squeezed Jesse's shoulder. "You just take good care of my daughter and we're even."

Julie glanced over at Katie. She sat huddled against the wall, rocking slightly, her arms across her middle. Her hair, T-shirt and cutoffs were spattered with Scout's blood.

"Are you okay, honey?" Julie asked. "Do you want me to try to find something for you to change into?"

"Yeah, Mom, anything, please." Katie's eyes were red from crying, and her mascara was smudged, giving her huge, sad owl's eyes. "I was so scared," she said shakily. "I thought Scout was dead. I sat there holding him, and he didn't move. He just kept bleeding and bleeding. I was sure he was going to die in my arms."

"You were very brave, darling," said Julie, slipping her arm around her daughter. "You did just the right thing for Scout."

Katie sank against Julie, her head on her chest, a child again. "I couldn't let him die, Mom. Grams died last year, and it still hurts. I couldn't stand to have anyone else I love die."

Julie felt tears sting her own eyes. "I know, baby," she said, resting her head on Katie's. "I feel the same way."

Another hour passed before Scout was taken to a private room and Jesse and his grandmother were allowed to see him. After several minutes Jesse returned to the waiting room and told Katie, "He's awake, but he's groggy. He talked a little. He said it was kids from the Tribe who hurt him. They beat him up for invading their turf. They say the warehouse is their territory."

"But it's not," Katie protested. "It's private property."

"Yeah, tell them that. Those bullies have got half the kids in the neighborhood scared out of their wits."

"Jesse, you listen to me," said Gladys. "We don't think about bad things tonight. We think only about Scout being okay. We thank God for that."

During the days following Scout's injury, Julie found herself thinking often of the little sad-faced girl next door to Gladys, and of the other needy children in the neighborhood, including Scout, who, praise God, was on the mend now. But the faces of those youngsters kept coming back in Julie's memory, like the melody of a song that wouldn't go away. At last, almost in self defense, Julie took out her watercolors, set up her easel, and began to paint the children who had invaded her mind and heart.

When she had half a dozen paintings completed, she showed them to Michael, silently hoping he liked them as much as she did. But she wasn't prepared for the force of his reaction.

"They're the best thing you've ever done, Jewel," he exclaimed with surprising fervor. "You've captured something in their faces that stirs the emotions. You've made a statement about their lives and their resiliency in the face of insurmountable obstacles."

Julie drew in a deep breath, pleased, amazed. "You see all that in these paintings, Michael? Are you sure you're not just being kind, or just seeing what you want to see?"

Michael gave her one of his piercing glances. "In all these years, have I ever given you empty flattery or undeserved praise for your paintings?"

She shrugged. "Usually you don't say much of anything."

"Right. You do fine work. I've always respected your talent, but these go beyond anything you've done before. I'm not sure why. But the images communicate real emotion."

"You know, I felt that way, too, Michael," she said, his excitement igniting her own. "When I was painting these children, I felt a power and a compulsion I've never experienced before. All the feelings that have built up over the summer—my concern and heartache over Katie and Jesse's predicament and this unexpected compassion I've felt for the needy families in Gladys Dawson's neighborhood—it's like I've caught a glimpse of something I never saw before, and I had to get it on canvas, so other people would feel what I'm feeling when I look at those faces.''

"They will," said Michael, his arm circling her shoulder. He led her over to the sofa and they sat down, facing the row of unframed paintings. He studied them for another minute, then said eagerly, "When people look at these works, I know they'll experience exactly what you're feeling, because I sense it, too."

"You really think so?"

"I know so. In fact, I might hang some of these in the office."

"Your real estate office?"

"Why not? So other people can appreciate them too."

"I hadn't thought of hanging them anywhere."

"Well, you should. Maybe we could even contact some local dealers or art galleries—"

She stared blankly at him. "You're not serious."

"Sure I am. Maybe they'd be interested in displaying your work. It's worth a try."

"You really think a professional gallery would accept these?"

"They're better than most of the paintings I've seen hanging in museums." He drummed his fingers lightly on her arm, the wheels of his mind obviously still spinning. "You know, Jewel, you could do a whole exhibit on a single theme. Call it, uh, I don't know, maybe *Children of the Streets.* Or *Dauntless Waifs,* or—or *Poverty's Children,* or maybe none of those, but something powerful, dramatic."

Julie laughed. "I can't believe it, Michael. Where do you come up with these things? You're amazing! You've got it all planned out."

"Why not? I know good stuff when I see it." He paused and let his eyes sweep over her, slowly, appreciatively. His voice took on an intimate tone. "And I see good stuff right now, sweetheart. Painting must agree with you. I haven't seen you look this vibrant in months."

She nudged him playfully, secretly pleased. "Oh, Michael, you old tease."

He bent his head and whispered in her ear, "No, darling, you're the tease."

"Maybe a little teasing is good for the soul," she replied lightly. She relaxed her head on his shoulder, recognizing this moment as one of those rare times the two of them were in sync, their hearts beating together, their bodies deliciously close, their minds instinctively playing off one another, naturally fueling the other's energies with encouragement and support.

Why did these precious occasions come so seldom? No one could plan them or anticipate them; they simply happened, like double rainbows or shooting stars. She looked up at her husband, studying the stalwart cut of his jaw, the faint stubble of his beard, the intense ocean blue of his eyes.

"I love you, Michael," she whispered.

His embrace tightened. "I love you, too, Jewel." He paused a long moment, then said, "You know, this week while you've been busy with your paintings, I've been busy with something, too."

She looked up at him. "Something besides the real-estate office and your houses?"

"Yes. I've been doing some investigating—"

"Really? What sort of—?"

"I checked the county tax records to see who owns that deserted warehouse where Scout was attacked."

"Why would you do that?"

"I was just curious."

"And what did you find out?"

"I learned Apex Furniture went belly-up, so the property went back to the bank. The usual foreclosure. What's interesting is that they've listed it for a song. Dirt cheap."

"And no takers?"

"Just one."

"Who?"

"Me."

Julie stared hard at him. "Michael, you didn't!"

He twisted one of her curls around his finger. "Sorry, Jewel."

She pulled away and looked him square in the face, her eyes narrowing. "Michael Ryan, is this the reason you were so complimentary about my paintings?"

"No, sweetheart, I swear! I love your paintings."

"And you hope I'll love that decrepit old warehouse you couldn't resist?"

Michael sat forward and rubbed his hands together. "Don't rush to judgment, Jewel. Wait'll you hear what I've got planned."

She folded her arms across her chest. "It better be good."

"It is. This past week I kept thinking about Jesse and Scout and the kids in their neighborhood not having a decent place to play. And it came to me—maybe I can turn the warehouse into a neighborhood youth center."

"A youth center?" Julie searched his eyes questioningly. "Michael, that would be an enormous undertaking. Do you think you could turn that tumble-down mausoleum into a youth center?"

He sat back and spread his arms along the back of the sofa. "Sure, I'll get Jesse and his friends to help me. Jesse himself told me a lot of the guys don't want to belong to the gang, but there's nothing else for them, so they join by default. I want to offer them another choice."

"That's an admirable goal, but you're not a youth leader," Julie conceded. "Something like that would need a full-time, or at least a part-time staff."

Michael nodded. "I've already talked to Pastor Brady. He says there are a lot of people in our church who would like to be involved in ministry, but they can't go to a foreign field or stand in the pulpit. But they could take a few hours each week to work with a bunch of kids who need some guidance and direction and old-fashioned love."

Julie looked deep into Michael's eyes and said softly, "I never thought I'd hear you talking this way—about ministry, about building youth centers and helping kids—"

"Then you approve?"

"Honestly, I don't know how I feel, Michael. I'm blown away. I'd love to see the kids have a place of their own to grow and play and learn, but I always figured it was up to the city to build it."

"Jewel, if we wait for some governmental agency to do it, it will never get done."

"But can we really do it, Michael?"

"We can do anything God calls us to do. Isn't that what you're always telling me?"

She smiled. "I never thought you'd devote yourself to anything besides selling and restoring houses."

"I guess it all began with Katie," he acknowledged quietly. "Katie getting pregnant made me realize how easily kids can get off track. I thought I'd hate Jesse for what he did, but, to tell you the truth, working with him and teaching him the trade has made me care about him. And once I cared about him, I started caring for the rest of the kids in his neighborhood."

"I care about them, too," said Julie, "but building them a center, that's such a big project. We need to be sure it's God telling us to do it."

"I'm sure, Jewel. Scout getting hurt was the topper," said Michael. "It crystallized everything for me. It's as if God used all these negative circumstances to make me see a way I could bring good out of the bad."

"That's how I felt about my paintings," said Julie. "God was showing me how I could make something beautiful out of something tragic."

They were both silent for a long minute, studying the paintings. At last Michael said, "It looks like God was telling us the same thing in very different ways."

"It's a little scary, isn't it?" said Julie, slipping her hand into Michael's. They lapsed into silence again, but the quiet in her mind was broken by several stunning insights. She and Michael were both reaching out beyond themselves, doing things and making choices on the basis of their passions, not just because it was good business or reasonable or even convenient. They were stretching their imaginations and expanding their boundaries.

But where would these new choices take them?

Chapter Thirteen

On the first Saturday of September, after clearing away the breakfast dishes and putting a load of laundry in the washer, Julie managed to steal away to her bedroom retreat, where she curled up in her rocker and began writing in her prayer journal for the first time in days.

Lord, life is so busy lately that it seems I hardly have time to talk with You, and yet I'm aware of Your working in every facet of our lives. You've watched over our Katie even though she's strayed from Your best for her. I'm afraid she started her senior year of high school with a decidedly rounder belly than most of her classmates. Hard to believe she's five months along! Fortunately, she earned enough credits in summer school so she'll be able to graduate with her class next June. She and Jesse are sounding more like prospective parents all the time—discussing names, shopping for baby paraphernalia, scrupulously saving their pennies. They're even planning to take a Lamaze class in a month or two, with Jesse as her coach.

Yesterday Michael signed the final papers to buy the warehouse, and he's already lined up a dozen of Jesse's friends to help with the renovation. He says it shouldn't require a major overhaul. The work will be more superficial and cosmetic than structural—a lot of cleaning, scrubbing, painting, and putting up new drywall in places. It's all work the boys should be able to handle with Michael's supervision. Honestly, I haven't seen Michael so excited about anything in ages.

But I understand how he feels. I feel the same way about my painting, especially since I started this new watercolor series I'm calling Poverty's Children. *Michael has hung several of the paintings in his office and he's already received dozens of compliments which he has kindly passed along to me. Even Beth seems genuinely moved by the paintings and has inquired about buying one. I only wish I had more time to paint, but with my job and the housework and giving Katie extra attention, I feel like I'm running in circles and never quite finished with anything at all.*

One bit of exciting news. Michael has contacted a former client about my paintings—a man he sold a house to last year. The man, Rolland Cains, owns a rather prestigious art gallery over on Atlantic, and he has agreed to display my paintings. He says, and let me see if I can quote him exactly, "Julie Ryan's works demonstrate not only exceptional artistic merit—they also contain a poignant and affecting social message the community needs to be aware of."

Mr. Cains says he may even be able to connect me with a New York agent who might be willing to represent my work. It sounds like a dream come true, but, Lord, I know all things are possible with You.

Last Sunday Pastor Brady talked about how important it is that we get our spiritual and emotional satisfaction from Jesus; that we fill up on His love so we can shower that love on others. Lord, I'm still working on the message about loving You and others with all my heart, mind and soul. Sometimes I think I'm getting it—I'm in touch with You in such a way that what others do doesn't really matter, and I can ride above life's petty jealousies and frustrations. But just when I think I've got it all figured out, something happens to remind me I'm still a long way from where You want me to be.

But I'm serious about this, Lord. I want Your love to revolutionize my life so that others can tell I've been with You. I know that means spending time in Your presence and letting Your Spirit live through me. Help me to remember I can't live the Christian life in my own strength. That's why You gave us Your Spirit to live inside us and do it through us—if only we'll let Him be in charge! Heavenly Father, do whatever You must to teach me compassion—Your pure, unconditional love!

On Monday evening, two days later, Julie wondered if she would live to regret asking God to teach her unconditional love. She and Michael were supposed to meet at his office after work and have dinner together at a local steak house to celebrate the acceptance of her paintings by the Cains Gallery.

But when Julie arrived at his office, one of the secretaries told her he had been called away on an emergency. No, it wasn't a family emergency, the girl assured Julie, and actually, it wasn't a work-related emergency, either. In fact, the girl had no idea what sort of emergency it was; just that Mr. Ryan received a phone call and had to leave immediately and he would be in touch as soon as possible.

Julie's next question stuck in her mouth like dry peanut butter. "Where is Beth Chamberlin? Is she still here in the office?"

"Oh, no," replied the secretary, a pretty blonde with a Barbie-doll face and a soft, breathy voice to match. "Ms. Chamberlin called in sick today."

Julie recoiled as if she'd been struck. She knew she shouldn't put two and two together—or maybe it was one and one!—when she didn't have all the facts. She had no reason to be suspicious of Michael and Beth. After all these months she still had no proof they were seeing each other.

And yet she knew in her deepest soul they were together, that if she drove by Beth's apartment, she would see Michael's car out front, and if she knocked on Beth's door, she would find Michael inside.

With her entire frame trembling, she drove straight to Beth's, and sure enough, Michael's car was parked in front just as she had suspected. Her heart pounding wildly, she parked right behind him and forced herself to get out of the car and walk up the steps to Beth's door. She had no idea what she was going to do or say, but after months of not knowing, she vowed this would be the showdown, once and for all. If Michael and Beth were having an affair, she wanted to know. Not knowing was killing her. The truth, however appalling, couldn't be any worse than these constant doubts haunting her.

From the porch she could see through the window, not well, but faintly. The curtains were a filmy, see-through material, and there was a light on inside—a table lamp in the living room that gave off a dim, rosy cast, just bright enough to illuminate the furnishings.

In the fraction of a second that Julie stared inside that window, she caught a glimpse of Beth in some sort of robe, long, a pale, velvety blue, her ebony hair flowing around her shoulders, framing her ivory face. And as Julie watched, still no more than a second, she saw Michael, her Michael, take Beth tenderly into his arms and hold her close.

The image of their embrace blurred as Julie's eyes welled with tears. She pivoted sharply and darted back down the steps, nearly stumbling, holding her mouth as if she might vomit. She climbed back into her car, started the ignition, and swerved away from the curb, as if she were the one afraid of being caught. She drove straight home, weeping blindly, uttering every oath she could imagine, her insides crawling with such loathing for Michael and his paramour, she wondered if she could survive such raw, suffocating hatred.

As much as she hated Michael, she hated herself even more for not having the courage to confront him and Beth. Why had she run? Why hadn't she hammered on that door and demanded they let her in? Why hadn't she looked them both in the eyes and insisted on the truth? If they were in love, why didn't they let her know, so she could stop living a lie and pick up the shattered pieces of her life and move on?

When Julie arrived home she went straight to her room, shut the door and curled up on her bed like a snail, hugging her pillow. Her thoughts tumbled like shards of colored glass in a kaleidoscope. Michael and Beth. Beth and Michael. Together. Embracing. Just as the image started to wane, she resurrected it and felt the shock jar her senses again. She kept replaying the scene in her mind like a videotape—Beth and Michael—hit Rewind, Play, then Rewind and Play again, and again, as if in replaying their embrace she might begin to make sense of it.

After a while her pulse slowed and the image of Michael and Beth seemed less shocking. She began to wonder if she had imagined it. Had she really driven to Beth's and seen the two of them through the window? Was anything real? Could she trust her own mind?

Suddenly she realized she wasn't thinking about Michael anymore. The image in her mind had changed. It was her mother's face, and the pain she was feeling now was for her mother. Her mother was dead and that fact seemed no more real than the image of Michael and Beth. Only the pain was real, erupting from some secret, central core of her being, and rising over her like flood waters, immersing her in smothering darkness. She opened her mouth to let out a scream, but there was no sound, only sharp, shuddering grief. Her mother was gone. Michael was gone. She heaved great, dry sobs into her pillow.

After a long while she lay on her back and stared into the darkness. "Dear God," she whispered, "how could I ever think I could love with Your love, when all I feel now is anger, resentment and loss? I don't even know who I'm grieving for anymore—my mother, my husband or myself."

A short time later Julie heard the door downstairs open and Michael's footsteps on the stairs. Alarm edged out the pain. She didn't want Michael seeing her like this. She sat up quickly and dried her eyes and blew her nose.

He came in the door and stopped a moment, his tall silhouette framed by the doorway. She caught the scent of his spicy aftershave. "Julie, I'm sorry about tonight," he said, his tone forced, unnatural. "Listen, I know it's late, but we could still go out and grab a bite to eat if you're up for it. How about it, sweetheart?" He reached over and turned on the light switch. "Hey, Jewel, what are you doing sitting here in the dark?"

She turned her face away. "Nothing. Don't—"

He approached the bedside. "Are you sick?"

"No, I'm just—feeling sad."

"So you're not in the mood to go out." When she didn't reply, he murmured to himself, "Okay, so I guess that means we're staying in." He shrugged off his jacket and loosened his tie. "Did something happen today?"

"No," she said again. "Don't worry about it, Michael. I'm fine."

"You look like you've been crying."

"I—I was thinking about...my mother." It was true, just not the whole truth.

Michael sat down beside her and unbuttoned his shirt with slow, weary fingers. She stole a glance at him and noticed for the first time how haggard he looked. "Julie, it's been over a year since your mother died," he said, as if that made a difference.

"So what's a year?" she challenged. Her sinuses ached, heavy with unshed tears. "Regardless of what they say, Michael, time isn't the great healer."

"I just meant—"

"I know what you meant. Don't tell me I should get over it. I may never get over it."

He reached over and massaged the back of her neck. "I thought you were doing better. You've been so excited lately about your painting."

"I was doing better," she retorted, "until—"

"Until what? What's wrong, Jewel? Tell me."

She stiffened her back and her neck muscles tightened. "Man, you're tight as a drum," said Michael. "I guess you had one lousy day, huh?" After a minute he sat forward, his hands on his knees, and shook his head wearily. "To tell you the truth, it's been a wild, crazy night for me, too."

"I don't want to hear about it," she told him sharply.

He studied her with a frown. "Man, you really are out of sorts, sweetheart!"

"Don't start on me, Michael," she countered.

"I know what this is about," he said. "You're mad about tonight, right?"

She looked at him, startled. Had he somehow seen her outside Beth's window?

"You're mad because I couldn't make dinner. I'm sorry, Julie. It couldn't be helped. Didn't my secretary Rose tell you I was called away unexpectedly?"

"I didn't see Rose. I talked with one of the other girls. And yes, she told me," said Julie thickly.

"Aren't you even going to ask me where I went?"

She bit her lip to keep back a sob. "I don't want to know."

"I went to Beth's," he said matter-of-factly. He moved his hands to her shoulders and swiveled her around to face him. "There was an emergency, Julie. I had to go."

She steeled herself. Was he really going to try to make an excuse after what she'd seen? "What sort of emergency?" she asked skeptically.

Michael's voice was uneven, edgy. "Beth stayed home sick today. But she called late this afternoon. All hysterical. Her ex-husband violated the restraining order and showed up drunk and brandishing a gun. The police took him away. Beth wasn't hurt physically, but the whole experience devastated her."

Julie could summon only one question. "Since when did you become Beth's protector, Michael?"

His expression turned stony. "Come off it, Julie. She's our friend. She has no one else to turn to."

"She's *your* friend, Michael, not mine."

Michael shook his head. "Julie, where's all that talk about Christian love?"

"It's not Christian love I'm worried about, Michael," she shot back.

His jaw dropped. "You're doing it again, Julie. Making insinuations about Beth and me. What's got into you, anyway?"

She considered blurting out the question, "Michael, are you in love with Beth?" But she knew how he would respond. He would pretend to be shocked, just as he was doing now. Then he would dismiss the question with great indignation, and she would still be left wondering.

"Did you hear me, Julie? Where are you getting these hare-brained ideas?"

She remained silent. She couldn't tell him she followed him to Beth's and saw them embracing, because then he would know she didn't trust him, and she'd feel humiliated for chasing after him like a crazy jealous wife.

"Beth was beside herself, Julie, ready to crack. She called me and I went over and tried to comfort her, and that's all there is to it." His voice grew ragged. "And I don't know why on earth I have to defend myself to my own wife, like a criminal or something. You've got to stop this, Julie, or we're not even going to have a marriage anymore."

Julie sat staring at her hands; they seemed disconnected from her somehow, as if she might try to move her fingers and find she had no power over them, the way she had no power over this moment and these circumstances. She was drowning, and Michael didn't even know, couldn't even see it. She was being swallowed up by events that had taken on a life of their own and they were devouring her, inch by inch, piece by piece. Maybe she was wrong about Beth and Michael. Maybe her whole view of reality was distorted, out of whack.

Even God seemed distant now when she needed Him most. Why wasn't He fixing their lives when she had asked Him just this morning for help? Where was He and what was He doing when everything was falling apart?

Chapter Fourteen

The next day Julie read the police report in the newspaper. Just as Michael had told her, Beth's ex-husband had been arrested for harassing her at her home and threatening her with a gun. He had been jailed and would be standing trial on several counts, including a weapons charge and violation of the restraining order.

In light of these facts, Julie began to wonder if she had completely misjudged what she had seen at Beth's home. Everything Michael had told her made sense now. Even the incriminating embrace was evidently only an innocent attempt to bestow comfort. Of course Michael would want to be supportive of a friend and colleague under such dire circumstances.

And yet a niggling doubt remained in Julie's mind. What if her original instincts were right? What if the threat posed by Beth's ex-husband was just an excuse for the two of them to be together? As long as even a sliver of mistrust lingered in Julie's thoughts, she couldn't bring herself to open her heart and her arms unreservedly to her husband. She found herself holding back, pulling away, allowing long periods of silence to hang between them like an invisible shroud.

For days the tension bristled between them, a prickly undercurrent of anger that generated a fury of its own. Michael seemed to have no idea why Julie had developed a subtly hostile attitude toward him. His bafflement grew into irritation and finally a barely contained rage. But the more Michael demanded to know what was bothering her and why she was behaving like such a shrew, the wider their emotional distance grew.

In her prayer journal that week, Julie wrote:

I'm depressed, Lord, plain and simple. I feel lousy and resentful. I don't want to have anything to do with Michael or with You, or even with Katie, who seems to think an expectant mother should be coddled and pampered like an ailing child. No one ever pampered me, and I'm not about to start with her!

Father God, I'm becoming a realist, maybe even a pessimist. How I ever thought I could love You and my family with pure, godly love is beyond me. What I'm feeling lately is anything but love. I'm learning a painful lesson very well—no flawed human being can love the way You do. It's not in me, no matter how good my intentions are, no matter how hard I try.

In fact, I'm mucking around in the Slough of Despond these days. I feel like, What's the use? I'm frustrated with Michael and Katie and, most of all, with myself. I guess I expected more of myself, but I can't seem to rise above petty jealousies and minor irritations. Why can't I be more generous, trusting, patient and magnanimous with those I love?

Lord, I throw myself on Your mercy. I'm falling so far short of Your standards. If Your love for me were as fickle and feeble as my love for Michael and Katie, I'd be the lost sheep still wandering in the wilderness. Show me the secret of loving as You love!

It was the following weekend before Julie felt the atmosphere in her home returning to a semblance of normalcy. Her anger at Michael had dissipated to a tiny nugget of doubt buried in the inmost recesses of her consciousness. She had nearly convinced herself of her own pinheaded foolishness.

Just as she was debating how to mend their precarious relationship, the phone rang. It was an anonymous, formal-sounding voice from the hospital in Crescent City. ''Mrs. Ryan—Julie

Ryan—is your father's name Alex Currey and does he live at 102 Hyacinth Lane?''

"Yes, that's my father," she said, the panic already mushrooming inside her. "What happened? Is he okay?"

The woman went on in her smoothly professional voice. "I'm sorry to inform you, Mrs. Ryan, that your father was admitted to the hospital earlier this evening with a possible heart attack. He didn't want his family notified, but we persuaded him to give us the name of his closest relative. He mentioned you—"

Julie broke in. "Is he going to be all right?"

"The doctor is running a battery of tests, Mrs. Ryan. We should know more by morning. Your father is resting comfortably at the moment, but the doctor suggests you come at your earliest convenience."

"I'm on my way," said Julie. Already she was racking her brain, wondering who she would get to come stay with Katie for a few days. Michael could pinch hit part of the time, but they would need someone to spell him—not Jesse, of course, but maybe his grandmother. Was she up to such a task? There was no way to know until Julie broached the subject with Gladys Dawson.

As she called Michael on her cell phone, Julie threw some clothes and toiletries into an overnight bag and prayed she wouldn't have to be gone long. Maybe her father's condition would improve sufficiently so that she would have to stay only a few days. And, if necessary, she could make a daily commute to the hospital; the traffic would be horrific but it wasn't that great a distance.

Just what I need, Lord, she mouthed silently. *One more complication in my life! Does everything have to fall apart at once? Couldn't I solve one problem before the next one hits?*

Immediately she felt a stab of guilt. How could she be so selfish as to think only of herself when her father could be dying?

When Michael came on the line, she told him breathlessly what had happened and announced that she would be making the drive to the hospital tonight, as soon as she had thrown a few things together. "Would you call my work on Monday morning and tell them I may be gone a few days? If they give you any static, remind them I have some vacation time coming."

"Sure, I'll call them. No problem."

"And you'll need to find someone to spell you with Katie— maybe Jesse's grandmother for a day or two, if she doesn't consider it an imposition."

"Don't worry, I'll check with her. Listen, do you want me to come with you, Jewel?" Michael asked, sounding genuinely concerned.

"I'd love that," she admitted, "but you need to be here for Katie. I'll be fine. Maybe it's just a false alarm."

"I'll be praying for that," said Michael. "You be careful, Julie, and give your dad my love." The tenderness in his voice wrenched her heart. She had spent so much time lately being angry with Michael, but at this moment all she could feel was an unexpected rush of love for him.

"I know how tough it's going to be for you, Jewel," he continued. "But maybe you and your dad can both get past the old tension and animosity—"

Julie wanted to say, You mean like you and I have done, Michael—or failed to do? Fat chance I can make amends with my father when I haven't fully reconciled this temporary estrangement with you!

"Julie? Did you hear me? Maybe you and your father can—"

"I heard you," she replied, her tone too abrupt. "Michael, I'd better go. I want to get there before—" She was going to say, Before it's too late. But she let the words die in her throat. She refused to give voice to the deep, unspoken fear that her father might die.

The two-hour drive to Crescent City took almost three hours on the commuter-clogged freeway heading out of Long Beach. Even at nine at night, traffic moved at a snail's pace. It was moments like this that made Julie wonder why she and Michael hadn't moved years ago to Nebraska or Outer Mongolia or some other place where no one had ever heard of smog, bumper-to-bumper automobiles and wall-to-wall people!

At last Julie passed the familiar landmarks of her hometown—the homey mom and pop restaurants, the old post office, the turn-of-the-century Victorian homes along Main Street that had been turned into medical and real estate offices. She drove straight to Crescent City General Hospital on the north side of town—a massive three-story stucco and steel structure with expansive windows and fluted columns across its unadorned classic facade.

She parked in the dimly lit parking lot and quickly crossed the dark expanse of concrete, clutching her purse tightly against her side. She relaxed a little. This wasn't Long Beach; the crime rate here had always been low. She entered the hospital lobby—a white, Spartan, high-ceilinged room with a gray tile floor and miniblinds on the windows. At the information desk, she inquired about her father, Alex Currey. The nurse gave her a room number in the cardiac-care unit, then added, "I'm sorry, but visiting hours are over for the evening."

"The doctor sent for me," said Julie. The nurse gave her a polite nod, and Julie continued on her way, taking the elevator to the third floor. She made her way down the long, echoing corridor to the cardiac-care unit and passed through the double doors. She hated the heavy, antiseptic smell of hospitals—a mixture of disinfectant and ammonia and that pervasive, indefinable odor of illness and infirmity.

When she arrived at her father's room, she stopped dead in her tracks, a wave of panic engulfing her. She had come this far, but the prospect of taking the last few steps to his bedside filled her with abject terror. What would she find? Would he be the father she remembered, or someone she hardly recognized? Had she come to help him recover—or to say a final goodbye?

Drawing a deep breath, she slipped gingerly through the half-open doorway and blinked against the stuffy, medicinal-smelling darkness. One dim light cast its meager rays across the single hospital bed with its raised guardrails. A shadowy figure lay motionless under a ghostly white sheet. Flanking the bed was an array of forbidding equipment with blinking lights, pulsing beeps and snakelike tubes that fed into mysterious, unseen orifices.

Julie stole to the head of the bed, breathless, her heart pounding, and stared down at the frail occupant—a pale, wizened old man with white hair and prominent features like her dad's. But certainly this wasn't he—the strapping, vigorous, big-boned man she knew, so overbearing and unapproachable, more godlike than flawed human being. This poor, broken man was little more than a caricature of her strong, steel-willed father. The mouth gaped open unnaturally, the jaw lay slack, and oxygen tubes threaded from flaring, vein-riddled nostrils. Only the eyes looked familiar as they opened halfway and gazed up at her, unfocused, a glazed, watery blue-green.

"Daddy?" she whispered, her voice catching.

His chapped lips moved with effort to form the word, "Ruth?" *Mama's name!*

"No, Daddy, it's me, Julie. How are you feeling?"

His eyes closed and his chest heaved and shuddered until at last his breathing took on a slow, steady rhythm. Julie pulled a straight-back chair over by the bed and sat down. She reached through the guardrail and rested her palm lightly on his large, mottled hand, being careful not to disturb the IV needle that fed into his purplish, paper-thin skin.

She sat that way for a long time, her back aching and her legs growing numb, not wishing to disturb her father's slumber but desiring to offer whatever meager comfort she could give. Did he know she was there? Would he care? Watching him, her thoughts ran rampant, summoning dusky snapshots of memory—her father coming and going, slipping in and out of the house like a flitting shadow; her father's handsome face looking solemn and inscrutable as he read the newspaper or watched TV; her father, so close and yet so far away, his innermost thoughts and feelings as concealed from her as if they had been locked all his life in a strong box. And he had never once given her the key!

Julie lost track of time, but after a half hour or so a nurse entered the room, making evening rounds. She looked at Julie in surprise, then offered a gentle smile.

Softly Julie said, "I'm Julie Ryan. I'm his daughter."

"As you can see, your father's resting comfortably," said the nurse, moving briskly around the bed, checking both the patient and the monitors. "You might as well go get some rest too, Mrs. Ryan. Come back in the morning and I'm sure he'll be happy to see you."

"When can I speak with his doctor?"

"He'll be by first thing in the morning. About seven."

"Good. I'll be here."

Weariness washed over Julie as she made the ten-minute drive from the hospital to her parents' home on Hyacinth Lane. It was nearly midnight and, except for the sallow beams of random streetlights, the street was as dark and still as a tomb. In spite of the shadows, Julie knew every inch of this timeworn neighborhood. This was home. Decades of memories—both joyful and melancholy—had imprinted themselves on her soul.

Julie parked in the sloping driveway and walked up the familiar sidewalk, remembering instinctively where all the cracks were. In her mind rang the girlish chant, "Step on a crack, break your mother's back!" Only Julie's mother was gone now, buried. She wouldn't be opening the door, welcoming Julie home, offering her special comfort and nuggets of wisdom.

Julie climbed the narrow steps to the covered porch with its latticework trim and old oak swing. How many hours had she spent rocking on that creaky swing, counting stars and forging dreams, yearning to know what the world beyond her porch was like? Now there were times when she would give a queen's ransom to escape that chaotic, all-consuming world.

She dug into her purse—yes, she still had her old house key—unlocked the door and opened it gingerly. What did she expect to find—the memories of Childhood Past? She stepped inside and reached automatically for the wall switch. The room blossomed with light, bringing into focus the fifties-style furniture—floral-print, slipcovered sofas and chairs, Early American tables with ceramic bell-jar lamps, and nubby flatweave area rugs scattered over gleaming hardwood floors.

And of course, the walls boasted Julie's own ghastly paint-by-number renderings her mother had lovingly framed when Julie was still a child exploring her artistic potential. More than once Julie had begged her mother to discard those primitive eyesores and replace them with her professional artwork. Her mother had partly complied, crowding in a few of the polished works beside the gaudy number paintings.

Julie paused and caught the rich scent of cedar from her mother's hope chest, and the delicate fragrance of rose-petal potpourri filling crystal bowls on the mantel and buffet. Everything of her mother's was here as it had always been, as if Julie had stepped "through the looking glass" into the past.

Only the people were missing.

Julie had the eerie sensation she had stumbled into the wrong time dimension. If only she were standing on this spot two years ago or five or ten or even twenty, these silent, gloomy rooms would spring to life. Voices and laughter would echo in the air like the rustle of autumn leaves or the patter of spring showers. And cherished faces would break into smiles like shimmering rainbows and weep tears of joy like golden dewdrops caught by the sun.

But the people were gone and the empty rooms groaned with their absence.

They still live in my memory, Julie argued silently. She wandered from room to room savoring the sights, sounds and smells of yesterday. In her former bedroom she sat on her iron hoop bed and ran her palms luxuriously over the downy comforter. She looked out the window she had gazed through thousands of times before and traced again the knowing, ageless face of the Man in the Moon. She fingered the familiar curios and baubles on her knickknack shelves, making them her own again.

For over an hour she roamed the home she knew better than the sworls of her own palm—this house from which she had wanted desperately to escape as a girl. But she hadn't escaped. Even now this house was part of her very fiber, the warp and woof of her being. It was in her blood, etched in every brain cell. She saw herself in every corner and doorway, in every hallway and window and mirror.

Julie slept fitfully that night, tossing and turning and reaching viscerally for Michael, who was not there. Several times she woke with a start and lay holding her breath in the darkness listening for sounds of another era. The house felt enormous, its shadows almost palpable, its silences magnified by the reverberant emptiness of its rooms.

What irony that she should be back here in her childhood room, alone, surrounded by memories, when she had tried so hard to distance herself from the past. But now, lying in her own bed, she knew she had never really left this place. She carried it with her, bottled up in a secret place she had nearly forgotten.

After her mother's funeral she had come back to this house with her father, and suddenly the silences she had tolerated before burgeoned to unbearable levels. She could not stay in the same house with someone so impassive and inert, who moved soundlessly from room to room, his entire passel of thoughts frozen behind an icy glare. He refused to speak of her mother, and he spurned Julie's awkward attempts to bridge the yawning gap between father and daughter.

At last Julie had fled—to Michael and Katie and the safe haven of her home in Long Beach. But she had never quite escaped the searing imprint of death on her heart. The wound still festered, infecting every facet of her life. When would she recover? Or would the rankling pain only increase now that her father was stricken?

After a restless night, Julie woke at dawn, groggy and more exhausted than when she had slipped into her uneasy slumber. As her eyes blinked against the faint streams of light seeping through the windows, she felt the oppressive heaviness of a burden she couldn't articulate at first. Something was dreadfully wrong, but she couldn't remember what it was. And then, as she raised her head and gazed perplexed around her girlhood room, she remembered with a jolt why she was here.

Her father might be dying.

Chapter Fifteen

Julie arrived at the hospital just before seven. She found her father awake, the head of his bed raised, his coloring better. He looked more like his old self. He glanced up at her without a smile and said, "What are you doing here, Julie?"

She approached his bedside, leaned over the rail and brushed a kiss on his forehead. Even his greeting put her on the defensive. "The hospital called me, Daddy. They said you had a heart attack."

"They don't know what's wrong," he muttered. "It's probably nothing. I didn't want them bothering you." He glanced around. "Get me a cup of coffee, Julie, and a packet of sugar."

She patted his arm, careful not to disturb the IV. "I can't, Daddy. That's up to the nurse." She paused. "If you're sick, you know I'd want to be here with you."

"But I'm fine," he protested. His hair looked whiter than she remembered, and thinner. It was mussed from sleeping. He wouldn't like that. He always kept his hair impeccably combed.

"The old ticker just doesn't work as well as it used to," he was saying. "I want them to finish up their tests and let me go home."

"What does the doctor say?"

"He hasn't been in yet. Should be strolling in anytime. Probably out getting in a game of golf before rounds." He stared irritably at the IV line. "Look at the slop they're feeding into me. They call this breakfast!"

"It's for your own good, Dad."

He nodded grudgingly. "That's the answer I get to every question around here." He cast her a quizzical glance. "How's everybody at home?"

She pulled over a straight-back chair and sat down, close enough to still hold her father's hand. "Everyone's okay," she replied. "Michael's busy as usual, working day and night." No use getting into the subject of Michael, she figured, and the tension between them. "Katie's doing well," she went on. "The doctor says her pregnancy is proceeding normally. She's in her sixth month now."

Her father shook his head solemnly. "I can't imagine our little Katie having a baby. You give her my love, okay?"

"Sure, Dad." And do you have any left over for me? she wanted to ask, but she bit back the question. It was foolish to feel such rivalry with her own daughter. She should be glad that at least her father had a weak spot for someone—if not for Julie herself, then for Julie's daughter. In fact, Katie was probably as close as Julie would ever get to her father.

The conversation hit a lull after that. Julie gazed idly around the room and out the window. It was crazy that she felt so tongue-tied and uncomfortable around her father—the person who had given her life, whose blood pulsed in her veins, whose very genes lived on in her every cell.

At times she sensed they were so alike they needed someone opposite them to draw them out and bring them to life, like her mother had done. Ruth Currey had been the catalyst, the vibrant spark that had quickened and animated them. Without her, they couldn't begin to connect.

The doctor arrived then, a tall, lean man striding into the room with a perfunctory, purposeful air, a noncommittal smile in place as he scanned her father's chart. He offered his hand and introduced himself to Julie as Dr. Purcell, then turned to her father and said brightly, "Well, Mr. Currey, you're looking much more chipper than you did last night. How are you feeling?"

Her father's expression remained stoic. "Like a prisoner consigned to bread and water, except there's no bread and no water, only the slop in this IV. Tell the nurse to get me some coffee."

Dr. Purcell chuckled. "No coffee. We'll put you on clear liquids today, but don't worry, the food will get better. We'll have you on semisolids tomorrow. And maybe even coffee."

"I'm not a baby, and I don't want pablum," said Alex. "How about some bacon and eggs?"

"That's probably what got you in here in the first place, Mr. Currey." He paused, his eyes moving over the chart, then said, "I have a few questions you weren't up to answering last night. Tell me, Mr. Currey, have you noticed any shortness of breath lately or a dry, hacking cough? Or trouble sleeping?"

Alex scowled. "Sure. I'm getting old. Wearing down. Aren't we all?"

"How about a loss of appetite or swelling of your lower limbs?"

Her father shrugged. "Swelling, sometimes. Appetite? Who cares about eating when it's your own lousy cooking? Coffee keeps me going."

"It could kill you, too," said the doctor.

Julie got right to the point. "Did my father have a heart attack yesterday, Dr. Purcell?"

Purcell sat down at the foot of the bed and wrote something on the chart, then looked up, from Alex to Julie. "We ran several tests last night, Mrs. Ryan. A chest X-ray and nuclear scans. An EKG. An echocardiogram that uses sound waves to look at the heart." He met her gaze. "We may do a cardiac catheterization, depending on how your father responds to treatment."

"What did you find out?" Julie pressed.

"Your father has congestive heart failure."

"Is that a heart attack?"

"Let me explain it this way," said Dr. Purcell. "A healthy heart pumps blood to all of the body in a few seconds. When it fails to do that, we call it heart failure."

"And if the heart doesn't pump right?" asked Julie.

"The blood backs up into the lungs and elsewhere, causing the lungs to fill with fluid and become congested and other body parts to swell. This strains the heart even more."

Alex broke in. "So what caused my heart to fail?"

Dr. Purcell looked directly at Alex. "In your case, Mr. Currey, our tests suggest a combination of high blood pressure, which weakened and enlarged your heart's left pumping chamber, and coronary heart disease, which causes cholesterol and fatty deposits to clog the vessels that supply the heart with blood."

"What now? How can we help my father?" asked Julie.

The doctor looked again at Alex. "It's more a question of what your father is willing to do to help himself."

Alex sighed deeply, his expression clouding. "So what do I do to stay alive?"

The physician stood up and wrote again on the chart. "We'll be prescribing several medications that should help."

"I've never taken medicine in my life," her father growled.

"The medicine isn't the hard part," said Dr. Purcell with a smile. "We'll give you drugs to relax the blood vessels and make your heart pump better. And diuretics to reduce the amount of blood to be pumped. And potassium to give you needed minerals."

"What's the hard part?" asked Julie.

"Sweeping changes in his life-style." Dr. Purcell was still smiling. "This is where your help may be needed, Mrs. Ryan. It's crucial that your father establish a whole new regimen for his life. That means taking his medicine, resting, reducing stress, limiting his fluids and eating less salt. He'll need someone close to encourage him to keep on track."

Julie stared at her father and he stared back. She knew he was thinking the same thing she was—Doctor, you're talking to the wrong people if you expect closeness and cooperation between us. We've never seen eye to eye on anything in our lives, except maybe Katie. There's no way!

Her father said it for her. "Sorry, Doc, I'm on my own here. My daughter lives in Long Beach, over two hours away with all the traffic. But I'll manage just fine alone. Just tell me when I can go home."

"Mr. Currey," Dr. Purcell said bluntly, "you're not going anywhere just yet. We want to keep you under observation for a few more days, and then you'll need someone at home to help with your care for at least the next few weeks."

"I'm not an invalid, Doc," her father said irritably. "I don't need a keeper. Don't you have those visiting nurses who drop in from time to time?"

Dr. Purcell's tone deepened. "You don't understand, Mr. Currey. You could have died last night. If you don't do what is best for your health, you could still die."

Neither Julie nor her father said much after Dr. Purcell's visit. What was there to say? Any advice she might give would be construed as nagging; any words of sympathy would be rejected as pity. For the rest of the morning her father watched his television game shows, and she flipped idly through a year-old, dog-eared magazine. She had a feeling he wished she would just go away and let him be, and she found herself wondering why she had even bothered to come visit him. If Alex Currey needed anyone at a time like this, it certainly wasn't his daughter!

After lunch, when her father was wheeled away for more tests, Julie phoned home to check on Katie. Katie answered, sounding in surprisingly high spirits. "How's Gramps?" she asked.

Julie gave her a brief report, then inquired about Katie's health.

"I'm feeling fine, Mom," Katie said brightly. "School's a drag, of course, but otherwise I'm cool."

"And the baby? Everything okay?"

"Yeah, except I'm looking more like one of those hot-air balloons every day."

"Honey, you know that's a temporary problem—"

"I know, Mom. But Jesse says I look like a snake that swallowed a rabbit or a beanpole that swallowed a watermelon. I got mad at him today for making his stupid jokes, so he made me a big platter of nachos with cheese and olives and sour cream and guacamole, and I ate every one! I probably gained another five pounds."

"Don't eat junk food, honey. Your baby needs lots of fruits and vegetables to grow strong."

"Don't worry, I know the drill, Mom. Listen, it's so amazing! When I play my music I can feel the baby kicking. She's got rhythm. She's trying to dance."

"Maybe she's just protesting your music," Julie teased.

"No, Mom, I know she likes it. I dance around my room and sing to her. I know she loves to be sung to, because that's when she kicks the most."

"Maybe you'll have a little ballerina, unless, of course, she's a *he!*"

"No, Mom," Katie declared, "my baby's a girl. I know, because we're into girl talk. When I talk to her real soft and quiet-like, she gets real still. No little boy would listen like that."

Julie relaxed a little in the straight-back hospital chair and smiled. She was glad she had called home. Katie was a breath of fresh air in a day heavy with her father's morose silences and the hospital's mordant sounds and smells.

"Listen, honey, after the nachos this afternoon, you make sure you and your dad have a nutritious dinner, okay?"

"I will, Mom. We're eating Chinese."

"Takeout?"

"No. Beth's cooking."

"Beth?" Julie's stomach clenched.

"You know. Daddy's friend from work. She volunteered to come over and fix dinner. Isn't that cool? Daddy says she's a great cook."

"Beth is coming over?"

"Yeah, she's renting some movies and spending the night. Isn't it cool someone her age would want to hang out with me?"

Julie balled her fists so tightly her fingernails dug into her palms. "Katie—your father—is he—" The word's twisted in Julie's throat.

"What's wrong, Mom? You sound weird."

"Your father—tell him to call me, okay?"

"Sure, Mom." Katie paused, then said with a tantalizing air

of mystery, "He said to tell you he'd be in touch with you later tonight."

Julie hung up the phone, shell-shocked, enraged. She couldn't believe Michael's gall. How dare he so blatantly trample their wedding vows—inviting his girlfriend over for the night the minute Julie was out of the house! And to involve her innocent Katie in the deception—that was the greatest insult of all!

Somehow Julie got through the rest of the day. Even her father's cantankerousness was beyond her now. She could think only of Michael and Beth together in her home while she carried out her lamentable mission of mercy with a father who wished she hadn't come. Even he noticed her sullen preoccupation.

"You look worse than I do," he muttered. "I'm the one with the broken ticker, not you."

"I wouldn't be so sure of that," she replied obliquely, then realized how pitiable she sounded. She reached through the metal guardrail and patted her father's mottled hand, lying limp on the sheet, fettered to its unremitting IV. "I'm sorry, Dad. I'm not very good company today."

He stared back at the television on the wall. "That makes two of us. I never asked for company anyway."

"I know, and I was thinking—maybe I'll drive home tonight—you know, just to check on Katie—and I'll drive back tomorrow."

He looked at her, one bristly eyebrow raised dubiously. "It doesn't make sense to drive home tonight, and it makes less sense to drive back tomorrow."

"I know, Dad." Why did he always make everything so difficult? And why did she constantly have to defend herself, justify her actions? "It's just—I sleep better in my own bed."

His steely gaze was unrelenting. "As I recall, that *was* your bed at my house—and your bedroom—for the first nineteen years of your life, and it suited you just fine back then."

Salty tears stung her eyes. She couldn't tell him, I can't stay, Dad. I've got to go home and save my marriage! Instead she said, "I'm not going to argue with you, Dad. You're supposed to stay calm and relaxed. So you just rest until the nurse brings your dinner tray. Meanwhile, I'm going to the house for my things and driving back to Long Beach. But I'll return tomorrow morning before you've finished breakfast.''

''I don't know why you have to risk your life on the freeway,'' he complained. ''That husband of yours should be able to hold down the fort without you for a couple of days.''

Ignoring his mutterings, Julie kissed her father goodbye and headed for the door. ''Good night, Dad. I love you.''

He was still scowling. ''I love you, too.'' Even those words he said grudgingly.

The ten-minute drive to her parents' home seemed to take forever. Her father was right. The commuter traffic was at its thickest this time of evening. At last she pulled into the driveway, got out and took long, purposeful strides up the walk to the porch. She went inside and quickly threw her things into her overnight bag.

But her mind was on Michael. She would show him who he was dealing with. If he thought he could brazenly bring that woman into their home the minute her back was turned, he had another think coming! Wouldn't he be shocked when she walked in on their little chop-suey-and-rented-flicks soiree?

Julie was checking the lock on the back door when she heard the front doorbell ringing. She heaved a sigh of exasperation. Whoever it was, she would have to hurry them off or she'd never get home tonight.

She crossed the living room and flung open the door, ready with a firm retort for any passing peddler. But the acrid words died on her lips as she stared at the tall figure in the doorway. She did a double take. Was she seeing things? ''Michael! What are you doing here?''

He stepped inside without waiting for an invitation. He was dressed in a casual shirt and slacks and carried a restaurant take-out bag in one hand and an overnight case in the other. ''Is that any way to greet your husband who's endured traffic logjam for the past two hours?'' he said with an ironic smile. He set down the bags and reached for her.

Blank with astonishment, she allowed him to gather her into his arms. ''I missed you, sweetheart,'' he said, nuzzling her hair.

"I—I didn't know you were coming," she stammered. "Katie didn't say a word—"

"I know. I told her not to. I wanted to surprise you."

"*Surprise* isn't the word," she told him. "I thought you were spending the evening with—with Beth. Katie said—"

"Listen, Jewel, I'll explain everything." Michael circled her waist and led her over to the sofa. She settled beside him, still marveling that he was there. "Here's the simple truth," he continued. "Beth offered to stay with Katie so I could drive up and spend the night with you."

Julie searched Michael's eyes, her astonishment knowing no bounds. "Why on earth would she do that?"

Michael looked genuinely puzzled. "Why not? She's a good friend. And I've helped her out in a pinch. She knew I was concerned about you facing this thing with your dad alone, so she offered to keep Katie company tonight. She's fixing Chinese—"

"I know the whole routine," said Julie dryly. "Movies and chow mein—"

"If you already knew, why did you act so surprised?"

Julie shook her head and began to laugh. The laughter began deep inside her chest and erupted in little hiccuping spasms. Michael started laughing, too, although she knew he had no idea why they were laughing. He pulled her against him, his arms strong and warm. Her earlier outrage frittered away, like scant raindrops in a vast wasteland. "It's not important, Michael. The only thing that matters is that you're here."

"*We're* here," he corrected, his sturdy fingers kneading the back of her neck. "Alone together in your parents' home." He paused meaningfully. "Talk about opportunity! You want to fool around a little?"

She slapped his cheek in jest. "Michael, you're awful!"

His face was still ruddy from their laughter, his blue eyes twinkling mischievously. "I know. Isn't that why you love me?"

She chuckled mirthfully. "Sometimes I wonder!"

His merriment receded. "How's your dad? Is he going to make it?"

"I think so, but he's got to take care of himself. He has to make some changes in his life, and I'm not sure he's willing. The doctor says he needs someone to stay with him for at least the next few weeks.''

"That long? With Katie in her condition, I don't see how you can—"

"I know," Julie agreed. "I can't stay away that long. But who else is there? It's so hard now, with Mom gone."

Michael glanced around the silent house. "Yeah, it's not the same place without her, is it?"

A sob tightened in Julie's throat. "Being here makes me miss her all the more. My dad is so lost without her. The two of us together are lost. We can't even manage a simple little conversation."

"So what's new? Your dad never was a talker," said Michael.

"But at least we had Mom as a go-between. She was the light of this house, its very soul." Julie shivered. "Now it's just an empty shell."

Michael squeezed her neck affectionately. "Maybe the two of us can put some life back into these old walls tonight. How about it?"

Julie sighed. Why did Michael see physical intimacy as the answer to every problem? She needed more from him tonight, but she had no words to express her inner yearnings.

"Did I say something wrong?" he asked. "I suppose with your dad in the hospital, you're not in the mood for—"

She slipped artfully out of his embrace and stood up. "I don't know what I'm feeling, Michael. I wish I did." Her gaze went to the takeout bag on the table. "It looks like you brought dinner. Whatever it is, it smells heavenly."

He nodded. "It's your favorite—kung pao chicken and moo goo gai pan. I figured, why should Beth and Katie have all the Oriental goodies? So I stopped at the China Garden a few blocks from here. It was one of our special places when we were dating, remember?"

"Of course I remember. Mr. Chung, the owner, always knew just what we were going to order."

"He's still there, and he still remembers. He said to give you his best."

Julie felt a heady wave of nostalgia sweep over her. She and Michael had spent countless evenings at Mr. Chung's quaint little Cantonese restaurant, gazing moonstruck into each other's eyes, deliriously in love. If only they could feel that way again! "I'll make us some tea and get out Mom's china," she said, the warmth creeping into her cheeks. "We can have a cozy little dinner right here in the living room, if you like."

He stood up and followed her into the kitchen. "I'd like that a lot," he said. As she gathered the silverware and plates, he came up behind her and wrapped his arms around her waist and pulled her close. "Being here with you in this little house brings back so many memories," he murmured. "It makes me feel like I'm twenty again and stealing a kiss, with an eagle eye out for your dad. Those were the days, huh? Nothing mattered, except the two of us."

"When did things change?" she asked softly.

His voice grew solemn. "I don't know, Jewel. You tell me."

"The real question is, can it ever be that way again?" she whispered, already terrified of Michael's answer.

"I don't know that, either," he admitted. "Life is strange. Things change and you wait for them to go back to what they were, and before you know it they change again, so if you're not careful you're always looking back, wanting something maybe you never really had in the first place."

She looked up at him. "Is that how you feel? That we never had that magical, extraordinary love in the first place?"

"No, Jewel, I didn't say that. I just think we sometimes romanticize the past. We give it a golden patina it never had. It makes the present look dull by comparison."

"Is that how you feel about our marriage?" she asked. "The rosy glow is gone?"

"Of course not, Jewel. I'm not here to criticize our marriage. If anything, I'm here to recapture a little lost romance."

But it was more than romance she wanted, Julie realized, as she and Michael sat together on the sofa, their Oriental repast spread out before them on the coffee table. She wanted that indefinable connection that was still missing in all of her relationships. Perhaps she was being too greedy, or perhaps such closeness didn't even exist. Every person was, after all, an island unto himself; the connections between people were fleeting and transitory. Just when you thought you had established a closeness you realized it had slipped away or it had never really been there in the first place.

For so many weeks Julie had been trying to build bridges—to Michael and Katie, to her father, to God, but the bridges always turned out to be walls. What was she doing wrong? Was she attempting the impossible? Had she spent too many years building protective barriers around herself to ever let anyone else in? Was she too afraid to trust anyone completely?

"You certainly look deep in thought," said Michael as he helped himself to an egg roll.

Julie looked up startled. She was mortified to realize how far her mind had strayed. "Tea?" she asked, pouring the fresh, steaming hot brew into her mother's delicate china cups.

Michael kept his gaze fastened on her. Julie could feel his eyes boring deep into her, penetrating her very thoughts. "Julie, we've got to talk," he said solemnly, "and I think this would be as good a time as any. We're here alone, without interruptions. We have the whole night to ourselves."

"Talk about what?" she asked cautiously.

"About us, our lives, our future. It feels like everything has gotten muddy between us. We're off track, Julie. Certainly you can feel it, too."

She felt the hairs on her arms prickle. This was it—the very thing she had dreaded and yet had known all along was coming. Michael was going to confess his love for Beth Chamberlin. No wonder he had come here tonight. It was the perfect setup—they were away from Katie, isolated from the entire world. What better place to dismantle a marriage than the very house where it had been launched?

"This is about Beth, isn't it?" she said solemnly.

Chapter Sixteen

"About Beth? What are you talking about, Julie?"

Julie's voice was tight, accusing. "Beth stayed with Katie so you could come here and talk to me, right?"

Michael's eyes flashed. "She stayed with Katie so you and I could have some time together. What's wrong with that?"

"Beth, of all people, staying with Katie! I couldn't believe you'd do that, Michael."

"Why not? She's a good friend. She was eager to help."

"I bet she was!"

Michael pushed his plate away and sat back, shaking his head. "Maybe it wasn't such a good idea, my coming here."

"Maybe it wasn't."

They were both silent for a long moment. Finally Michael sat forward and clasped her hand. "Talk to me, Julie. Talk to me. What's happened to us? Is it because you're still grieving your mom's death? Or is it the stress with Katie and your dad that's got you on such an emotional roller coaster?"

Tears rimmed Julie's eyes. She gazed around at the familiar pictures and mementos, everything just as it had been, as if her mother might step into the room at any moment and greet her with tender words and a warm embrace. Everywhere Julie looked she saw memories—happy memories, painful memories.

Haltingly she said, "My—my mother should be here. She shouldn't have died. Why did it have to be her?"

Softly Michael said, "You mean, why did your mother die instead of your father?"

Julie covered her mouth with her hand. "Is that what I meant? I wanted him dead instead of her? Oh, Michael, that's terrible!"

"But is that how you feel?"

Tears rolled down her cheeks. "I suppose it is," she confessed. "I feel so guilty, thinking that."

"You can't help how you feel, Jewel."

"I don't want to feel this way, Michael. I swear I don't! But you know what it was like for me growing up in this house with my father."

Michael squeezed her hand. "I know."

"He never talked to me," said Julie tremulously. "We could sit in this very room for hours and he'd never say a word. I never knew what he was thinking or feeling. I'd look at him and think, You're a stranger, coming and going in this house, and I have no idea who you are. You're worse than a stranger, because a stranger can become an acquaintance and eventually a friend."

"Julie, don't hash this out again. It doesn't help. It doesn't change anything."

"Michael, I can't help it. How can I resolve anything in my life if I can't make peace with my dad? All these years our relationship has stayed the same, never grown, never moved on past this odd discomfort we feel in each other's presence. Why? Am I that hard to talk to? Is there some flaw in my personality that keeps him from opening up to me?"

Julie stared hard at Michael, her heart jackhammering. She could see the answer written in his eyes. "It is me, isn't it?" she said incredulously. "There's something wrong with me. I can't reach out. I'm just like my father. We don't know how to open up and let other people in."

"I didn't say that, Julie."

"You don't have to say it. It's all there in your expression. You think *I'm* the problem with our marriage."

Michael released her hand and cleared his throat uneasily. "Sometimes you close me out, Jewel. Like tonight. You're holding me at arm's length. I thought you'd be excited to see me, but you act like I've done something wrong. That teed me off at first, but then we started laughing and everything was okay."

She wiped the wetness from under her eyes. "You must know why I was upset at first."

Michael brushed a wayward strand of hair back from his forehead. "You said it was Beth, but that baffles me as much as anything."

She looked at him, her eyes wide and unblinking. "I know all about Beth," she said.

He ground his jaw. "What about Beth?"

She swallowed hard over the lump in her throat. "I know there's something going on between you two." There! She'd said it. It was out in the open at last!

"Beth and me?" countered Michael. "What do you think we're doing? Having an affair?"

Her voice came out small and tenuous. "I pray it hasn't gone that far, but I know you're having some sort of dalliance."

Michael stood up and walked to the window. He slammed his palm against the wall. "You really don't trust me, do you?"

She sniffed noisily. "I want to, but you're right—I don't."

"Then it won't matter what I tell you, because you won't believe me anyway."

"Try me, Michael," she begged. "Make me understand."

He fingered the window molding, his gaze piercing the glowering darkness. "There's nothing to explain, Julie. Beth and I are friends, good friends. She's a valued colleague. I care about her and she cares about me. Can't you trust me enough to accept our friendship, and let it go at that?"

She folded her arms defensively. "How can I accept it when I'm convinced there's more?"

Michael turned from the window and looked at her, his dark

brows shadowing clear cobalt eyes. "I've never crossed the line with Beth, never! Do you believe me?"

"I want to. More than anything."

He crossed the room, sat down beside her and took her hand. "Jewel, you know Beth's scared to death of her ex-husband. He's in jail now, but who knows for how long? Beth needs friends. She's new in town. She has no one but us. She'd like to be your friend, too. I know she would, if you'd give her half a chance."

Julie averted her gaze, wrestling inwardly with a dozen conflicting emotions. Finally she looked back at Michael and asked, "Do you ever pray?"

He blinked, her question taking him by surprise. "Of course I pray. You know that. I admit my prayers are infrequent... sporadic—perhaps more lip service than heartfelt supplications. Why do you ask?"

"Because I've prayed for some things lately I'm not sure I want. I've asked God to help me know and love Him and others with His pure, selfless love, and it seems since I prayed that prayer, everything in my life has gone wrong."

"Don't blame that on God."

"I don't. Not really. But I knew I could never love the way He wants me to, in my own strength. I asked for Him to love through me, but instead of getting easier to show love, it seems to be getting harder. Now I'm wondering if God is trying to tell me I'm even supposed to love someone like Beth, who I suspect has designs on my husband."

Michael pressed Julie's hand to his lips. "She doesn't, darling. I assure you she doesn't."

"Maybe that isn't even the question."

"Then what is?"

She shrugged. "The old, eternal question. How do I love God and others the way He asks me to love?"

"Maybe you're asking too much of yourself."

"But not too much of God," she argued. "He can do it. I know He can. But how do I get hold of His love and live it in my own life?"

Michael smiled grimly. "You're getting too philosophical for me, sweetheart."

"It's not just philosophy. I'm talking about finding the answer in God that will make my life function the way it was meant to be." She ran her hand over the faint stubble of his beard. "Don't you see, Michael? I want to connect with you and Katie and even my father, but I must first have a fully realized connection with the Lord. When I feel His love, when I'm satisfied by Him, then I can love others without this desperate, all-consuming neediness that takes rather than gives."

Michael looked thoughtful. "That's a tall order, Jewel. Don't beat yourself over the head if it doesn't happen the way you think it should. Most of us are just trying to find our way through the maze, and if God gives a glimmer of light now and then, we should be grateful."

"You're saying I want a lot more than a glimmer?"

"A miracle maybe? You expect too much of yourself, Jewel, and maybe too much of others. Like me. And your dad. Loosen up a little and give us all some slack, yourself included."

"You think I'm being obsessive, don't you?"

He chuckled. "Maybe a teensy bit."

She rested her head on his shoulder as a wave of exhaustion rippled through her. "I go in these circles, Michael. I do this to myself. I know I do. I'm sorry."

He tilted her chin up to his sturdy, handsome face. The lamplight gave his skin a golden glow and silhouetted his classically chiseled features. She could smell the fresh scent of lime on his skin. "There's just one thing I want to know, Jewel."

She struggled to find her voice. "What, Michael?"

The timbre of his voice was deep, moving. "Do you believe me when I say you're the only one I love?"

"I want to believe you," she murmured dreamily.

"Believe it, Julie." Gently he moved his hand over the hollow of her throat to her earlobe, her hair. Then he bent his head to hers and sought her lips. His mouth moved hungrily over hers as he whispered, "Let me show you how much I love you, Jewel."

She returned his kiss with a bittersweet urgency. She wanted to believe him, needed to believe him. Gradually she relinquished her defenses and relaxed in his embrace, losing herself in his encompassing warmth, his masterful touch.

After a moment he stood and swept her up in his arms and nuzzled his chin against her hair. As he strode toward the bedroom, he promised, "I'll make you believe in my love again, Jewel. In your head...and in your heart!"

Julie woke as the first rays of dawn shimmered through the narrow slats of the Venetian blinds. It was the same honey-warm sun that had greeted her over a thousand growing-up mornings in this very room. She rolled over and gazed at Michael beside her, watching the rhythmic rise and fall of his chest as he slept. Last night he had tried to erase all her questions about Beth. But only time would tell whether the doubts would creep back in. For now she would think only positive thoughts.

But as quickly as she made that resolution she realized Michael would be returning home this morning, and she would have to trek back to the hospital and face her irascible father by herself. Compounding her dilemma were the pressing questions about her father's care. When would he be well enough to come home? Who would take care of him? How long before he would be able to manage by himself?

And, heaven forbid, what if he never got well enough to live alone again?

Michael stirred, opened his eyes and managed a fuzzy smile. "Good morning, honey," he mumbled thickly. "Hey, sweetheart, last night was great. The best!" He paused, studying her intently. "What's got you so deep in thought before breakfast?"

"I was thinking about my dad. Wondering what to do when he's released from the hospital. I can't stay here—there's you and Katie and my job. But what if Dad needs long-term care?"

Michael sat up and swung his legs over the side of the bed. "I've been thinking about that, too, Julie, and there's only one answer I can think of. Let him recuperate at our house."

"You'd be willing to do that?"

"Sure, but the real question is, are you willing? The lion's share of the work would fall on you."

She nodded. "It would be hard juggling my job and Katie and Dad all at once. And when the baby comes, it'll be a real circus."

"Maybe your dad will be well enough to take care of himself by the time the baby comes."

"I hope so."

"And one of these days Katie and Jesse may get married and want their own place."

She chuckled dryly. "Now you are dreaming. What we'll end up with is Noah's Ark, and we'll all be pulling out our hair."

"I'm willing to try it if you are," said Michael.

"What other choice do we have?"

"Your dad may not even be willing to come. I can't picture him giving up his independence willingly."

She nodded. "You're right. The only way he'll leave this house is kicking and screaming."

"Well, wait and hear what the doctor says before suggesting it," said Michael. "I'll drop by the hospital with you myself before driving back to Long Beach."

"Would you, Michael? I'd be very grateful if I don't have to face my father alone this morning."

An hour later, as they prepared to leave for the hospital, Michael was slipping on his sports jacket when a white envelope fell from the pocket. He picked it up and handed it to Julie. "I forgot to give you this last night. It came in the mail yesterday."

She looked at the return address. "This is from Rolland Cains, the owner of the art gallery displaying my work." She tore open the envelope and removed the contents, then uttered an exclamation of surprise. "Michael, look at this! It's a check for a—a thousand dollars!"

"You're kidding!"

"No, I'm not. This is incredible! Mr. Cains says he sold one of the paintings in my *Poverty's Children* series. He says the entire series has generated a great deal of community interest and the newspaper may want to do a feature article on them."

Michael swung her up in his arms. "That's terrific, sweetheart.

I told you you were great! Now what are you going to do with all that loot?''

She thought a moment. "I'm not going to spend it on myself or on anything frivolous. It has to be something special, something that would help poor children, because they were my inspiration. I know! Michael, it's the perfect answer! I'll donate the money to the new youth center you're building.''

He stared at her in surprise. "The youth center?''

"Sure. You were wondering where to get the funds to renovate that old warehouse.''

"You would do that, Julie? That's the first money you've earned from your painting. I would think you'd want to put it back into your artwork—buy frames or supplies or something.''

"No, Michael. This money belongs to the children who inspired the paintings. Use it to give them a place to play.''

Julie wasn't sure but she thought she saw tears glisten in Michael's eyes. "That's wonderful, Julie. Jesse and his friends will be thrilled.''

"Don't thank me, Michael,'' she insisted. "I never would have painted that series if it weren't for Jesse and the needy children in his neighborhood.''

Michael slipped his arm around Julie's shoulder as they headed for the door. "It's starting out to be a good day, Jewel. Now let's see if we can go to the hospital and cheer up your old curmudgeon of a dad.''

Chapter Seventeen

By the end of the week, Julie's father was released from the hospital with the understanding that he would receive full-time care at home for the next few weeks. Julie picked him up and drove him to the little house on Hyacinth Lane, but she knew the matter wasn't settled. There was no way she could remain in Crescent City for several weeks. She had already used all of her vacation time, and she had been away from Katie far too long already. But, whenever Julie broached the subject, Alex was adamant. There was no way he was going to leave the house he'd lived in for over half his life to stay with Michael and Julie in Long Beach.

"It's not like it would be forever, Dad," she reminded him as she served him his lunch on a TV tray. She had done her best to make the meal look attractive, using her mother's best china and a sprig of parsley to accent the chicken sandwich, cup of vegetable soup, cottage cheese and fresh strawberries. A crystal goblet held his four ounces of apple juice. "As soon as you're stronger you can come back home and have the visiting nurse check on you now and then."

Alex was sitting in his favorite rocker by the TV. "Where's

the remote control?'' he asked irritably. ''My game show's on. I've already missed ten minutes.''

She handed him the remote control. ''Don't forget your medicine, Dad. Your pills are all laid out on the table beside you in little paper cups. A cup for each meal and one for bedtime.''

''I know the drill,'' he said, reaching for the appropriate cup. ''Where's my water?''

''Take them with your juice, Dad.''

''I want water.''

''I'm sorry, Dad. No more liquids.''

''I'm thirsty.''

''You know you're on limited fluids,'' she told him, struggling for patience. ''Why do you keep fighting me on that, Dad?''

He glared at her. ''I haven't had any water all day.''

''You had coffee and yogurt this morning, and you've got soup and juice for lunch.''

''So what?''

''So the doctor wants you limiting your fluids to eight cups a day, and foods that contain liquid count, like yogurt and ice cream.''

He bent over his tray and stirred his soup. ''What's the use of living, if a body can't enjoy life anymore?'' he complained.

''I'm not trying to spoil your fun, Dad. I'm just trying to help you follow the doctor's orders.''

He swallowed a mouthful of broth, several drops trickling down his stubbled chin. ''What the docs don't know won't hurt them.''

''But it'll hurt you,'' she countered, sitting on the sofa across from him. ''If you're not careful, you'll be replacing all the fluids your water pills are getting rid of.''

''So I can't have ice cream for dessert?''

''I'll give you some sugar-free hard candy later if your mouth is dry.''

He scowled. ''You're worse than that battleship of a head nurse at the hospital.''

''I'm doing it for your own good, Dad.''

"Okay, okay, let's not talk about it anymore. I'm missing my show."

Duly rebuffed, Julie got up and went to the kitchen and turned on the spigot, filling the sink with soapy water. She was trembling slightly, anger rising in her like hot springs. "How long can I stand this," she whispered to herself, "before I go stark raving mad? That man will never appreciate a thing I do. We'll never see eye to eye on even the smallest detail. Lord, help me, or I'm going to explode!"

Somehow Julie managed not to erupt, even though the next few days were a repeat of the first day—her father ensconced before the television from morning until night, either glumly silent or complaining, while she exhausted herself trying to please him.

Meals were a nightmare. He didn't like anything she fixed him. Everything was too bland, tasteless, not enough salt, not like her mother used to fix. "Didn't your mother teach you to cook?" he snapped one evening after trying her salt-free meat loaf. "This doesn't taste like your mother used to fix. Now your mother, there was a cook. Her meat loaf was out of this world."

Julie wanted to answer back, If Mom hadn't cooked such fattening meals, maybe you wouldn't be in trouble now! But she resisted the urge, feeling guilty for even thinking such a thing, and said instead, "It's Mom's exact recipe, Dad, without the salt and fat."

"Oh," he grumped and helped himself to another mouthful.

Julie waited a moment, then decided maybe this was the time to broach another touchy subject. "Dad," she said, steeling herself for a stormy reply, "I know we sorted some of Mom's things after the funeral last year. But you still have a lot of her belongings in the closets and drawers. Do you want me to sort them and donate some of her things to a charitable organization?"

Her father glowered at her for several interminable seconds, until she wished desperately that she'd never said a word. "Forget I mentioned it," she murmured, turning her attention to the half-eaten meal on her own TV tray.

Just when she thought the subject was closed, he announced

under his breath, "This is my house. Leave things be. I'll decide what's to be done with your mother's things."

Julie kept her gaze on her plate; she didn't want her father to see the scalding tears welling in her eyes. "You're not the only one hurting," she said raggedly. "She was my mother, and I miss her with all my heart!"

They ate in uneasy silence for a while, their eyes focused on the flitting picture on the television screen. A contestant was trying to figure out a popular saying, and she kept guessing all the wrong letters. Julie knew the feeling; she was always striking out, too, it seemed, no matter how hard she tried.

She wasn't hungry, but she picked at her food, anyway. If she didn't eat it, how could she expect her father to? She had a hard time swallowing the meat loaf. It was cold now and stuck in her throat along with the sob she couldn't release. More than anything in the world she wanted to go throw her things into a suitcase and drive home. Get away from this place. Put some distance between herself and this man who inevitably managed to rend her heart.

Sometime later—perhaps a half hour—when they had both finished their dinner, she heard her father's voice amid the blare of the television set. The rancor and animosity were gone; his tone was almost tender. "I dreamed of her last night," he said softly.

"What?" she asked, thinking she hadn't heard right.

"I dreamed about your mother."

She looked at him in surprise. "You did? What'd you dream, Dad?"

He looked away and his voice was so small she hardly heard him. "I dreamed we were dancing in the rose garden to a Strauss waltz. We were both in our twenties again."

"That's a wonderful dream, Daddy," said Julie, biting back tears.

"She was the most beautiful woman on earth." He lapsed into silence after that, and when he spoke again his tone had taken on its usual edge. "Where's the remote control, Julie? Come on, hand it to me. I don't like this show."

At bedtime Julie gave him his pills and a half cup of juice. She

watched as his trembling fingers methodically raised each capsule
to his lips. When he had swallowed all his medicine, she sat down
beside him and touched his mottled hand gently. "Dad, listen to
me. In another day or two I'm going home. I can't be away from
Katie any longer. Now you can come with me if you like. I hope
you will. We'll fix up a nice room just for you. But if you won't
come, your doctor will insist that you hire a nurse or spend a few
weeks in a convalescent hospital until you're better."

"No nurse, no hospital," her father said gruffly.

Julie sighed and shook her head. "Well, that's up to you, Dad.
I've told you what I'm going to do."

The next afternoon Julie's decision to leave was settled suddenly, shockingly, when Michael telephoned, his voice tremulous,
choked with emotion. "Julie? It's me, Michael. Come home.
Now. It's Katie."

"What's wrong?" she cried.

"She—she started hemorrhaging. She's at Long Beach Memorial Hospital. Come home, Julie! She needs you."

"The baby—"

His voice broke. "She may lose the baby, Jewel."

Julie hung up the phone, dazed, her mind whirling. She
couldn't think what to do next. Pack? Make arrangements for her
father? Call his doctor and tell him she was leaving?

She looked at her father and felt any remaining composure
shatter. "It's Katie," she whimpered. "She's in the hospital."

Her father hoisted himself out of his chair and said in a take-
charge voice, "I'll get my medicine and a change of clothes. You
get the keys and pull the car out of the garage."

"You're going home with me?" she said in astonishment.

"I can't stay here alone," he replied dryly. "You've told me
that often enough. Come on, daughter. Let's go. Katie needs us."

Somehow Julie made the two-hour drive in spite of aggravating
traffic and her own tear-blinded eyes. When she entered the
sprawling lobby at Long Beach Memorial, a nurse at the information desk told her to take the elevator upstairs to the second
floor to the Labor and Delivery Suite. "May I have a wheelchair

for my father?'' Julie asked. "He's been ill and isn't supposed to do much walking."

Within moments an attendant brought a wheelchair for Alex and escorted the two of them upstairs. As soon as Julie entered the maternity waiting room, she spotted Jesse pacing the floor by the nurses' station and Michael sitting nearby on an orange vinyl couch, his head in his hands. To Julie's amazement, Beth Chamberlin was sitting beside Michael, turned his way, saying something confidentially. Julie's first inclination was to shout, What's she doing here? Resisting the urge, she ran straight to Michael and demanded breathlessly, "How's Katie?"

He stood and embraced her so tenderly she almost forgot Beth was there. "I don't know how she is," he told her brokenly. Julie had never seen him look so distraught.

Jesse shambled over in his T-shirt and jeans, his long hair tied back carelessly with a rubber band. Wiping his hand on his jeans, he greeted Julie and shook hands solemnly with Alex. His dark eyes shone with torment. "They won't tell us nothing, Mrs. Ryan! Zippo! They won't even let me see her. I should be with her. She shouldn't have to be alone."

"Michael, you don't know anything?" Julie prodded.

He rubbed the bridge of his nose. His face was wet with perspiration—and tears. "The nurse keeps saying the doctor will be out soon, but nothing so far. I'm with Jesse. I'm ready to go back there and make somebody tell me what's going on."

"She will be okay, won't she?" Julie pressed.

Michael's jaw tightened. She could read the fear in his eyes. "Like I said, I don't know anything, sweetheart, except Katie's in a whole lot of trouble."

"What happened, Michael?"

He shook his head grimly. "I'm not sure. I wasn't with her, Julie."

"You weren't with her? You mean she was alone?"

"No." Michael glanced down at Beth. "Beth was with her."

"Beth?" Julie sank down on the vinyl couch beside Beth. "You were there? What happened? Please, I need to know."

Beth nodded. Her thick ebony hair was mussed and her makeup

was smeared slightly around her eyes. She looked nervous, distracted, as if she realized Julie didn't want her here, especially during a family crisis.

Before Beth could reply, Jesse spoke up, his voice wavering with emotion. "Katie was with me this morning, Mrs. Ryan. I took her to school and picked her up and dropped her off at home. She was cool, no problem, maybe just a little tired. I swear she was okay. I wanted to stay with her, but I had to work, so I told her to call Beth and maybe have her drop by for some company."

Beth picked up the story, her voice tense, unsettled. "Katie phoned me sometime after lunch. Around two, I think. Neither of us had eaten, so I took over a pizza. She wasn't hungry, and she looked a little pale and listless. I could see she was having some discomfort, so I suggested she call her doctor, but she kept insisting she was fine."

"Just tell me," said Julie, "what happened to her?"

"I'm trying to," said Beth with a mixture of reproach and agitation. "I didn't want to leave Katie when she was feeling bad, so I stayed and we just talked awhile. Then she said she had to go to the bathroom and she got up and suddenly there was all this blood. She started to get hysterical, so I made her lie down and I called 911. The ambulance came and brought her here, and that's all I know. I phoned Michael at work and we both came right over."

"Dear Father in heaven," Julie breathed, "I should have been there for Katie. Maybe if I'd been home—"

"There's nothing more you could have done," said Michael. "Neither of us were with Katie. But the important thing is, Beth was there and did everything possible. The paramedic told her if she hadn't been there Katie could have gone into shock and—"

"Katie could have been unconscious?"

"Yes, Julie. She could have bled to death."

Julie felt faint, light-headed. "Oh, dear God, no!"

"But Beth got help right away," said Michael. "We owe her a lot, Julie."

Julie murmured a distracted thank you, but her mind was on

Katie, not Beth. The last person on earth Julie wanted to be indebted to was Beth Chamberlin.

"You don't owe me any thanks," said Beth. "I'm just glad I was there for Katie."

Julie's father spoke up from his wheelchair, his voice deep and resonant with feeling. "Don't be so modest, Miss—"

"Chamberlin," said Beth. "I work with Michael at his office."

"Beth's one of my best agents," said Michael. "And a good friend."

"You've proven your friendship, Miss Chamberlin," said Alex, more buoyant than he ever sounded with Julie. "We all owe you our thanks. Little Katie's our joy in life, and joy's not easy to come by."

"Please don't thank me. I've grown very fond of Katie, too."

Julie felt her resentment flaring. How had this woman, this outsider who had her eye on Michael, become not only part of their family circle, but a heroine to everyone, as well?

Suddenly all conversation halted as a door opened and a physician emerged wearing his surgical greens. It wasn't Dr. Russell, Katie's obstetrician, but a wiry, compact man in his late thirties, with cropped brown hair and a pencil-thin mustache. "Mr. and Mrs. Ryan?" he asked congenially, offering his hand as he approached.

Julie and Michael both stood, but before either could speak, Jesse stepped forward and said sharply, "Is Katie okay?"

"Let's sit down," the physician suggested, taking the chair across from them. "I'm Dr. Zabriskie. We have a call out to your daughter's obstetrician, and he should be in shortly."

"Tell us how she's doing," Julie urged, her palms as moist as her throat was dry.

"Your daughter's stable for the moment, Mrs. Ryan. But she's lost some blood and she's feeling a little weak and woozy right now."

"What about the baby?" asked Julie, dreading the reply.

"The baby's in some distress, but we're monitoring him closely."

Julie still wasn't getting the answers she wanted. "What's

wrong with Katie, Dr. Zabriskie? Why is she bleeding? It's too soon for the baby to come. She's just six months along.''

Dr. Zabriskie nodded. ''Yes, it is too soon. We're running tests—and doing an ultrasound.''

''Isn't there anything you can tell us now?'' prompted Michael. ''Surely you have some idea—''

The doctor looked thoughtful, obviously weighing his words carefully. ''I suspect your daughter is suffering from one of two conditions, but I'd rather wait for the ultrasound before making a diagnosis.''

''Doctor—what conditions?'' Julie demanded.

Dr. Zabriskie's tone remained restrained, professional. ''One is placenta previa...''

Julie put her hand to her mouth. ''That's very serious, isn't it?''

''It can be, if the placenta is attached to the lower half, or mouth, of the uterus.''

''Is it life threatening?'' asked Michael, slipping his arm around Julie's shoulder.

Dr. Zabriskie inhaled deeply. ''Placenta previa is a serious complication. When the placenta blocks the cervix, vaginal delivery is nearly always impossible.''

''Then you're saying Katie will have to be delivered by cesarean section,'' said Julie, shivering in spite of herself. Her daughter was too young to be facing such traumas. She should be thinking about clothes and makeup and music and dates, not whether she and her baby were going to survive childbirth.

''A C-section is a strong possibility, Mrs. Ryan.''

Jesse was pacing back and forth between the chair and the sofa. ''Am I going to lose my kid, Doc? Tell me the truth.''

''We're doing everything we can to make sure you have a healthy child—and that your child has a healthy mother.''

''But you mentioned Katie might have another condition,'' Julie persisted.

Dr. Zabriskie's brow furrowed. ''Yes, abruptio placenta.''

''Is that one as serious?''

He nodded. ''The placenta can separate from the uterus prematurely. The fact that Katie had some mild cramping and uterine tenderness leads me to believe such an abruption might be the problem.''

Julie felt her head reeling with medical gobbledygook. Would her daughter and grandchild be all right? ''Are you saying Katie and the baby are in imminent danger?''

''Mrs. Ryan, I'm saying Katie will require close medical supervision for the rest of her pregnancy.''

Jesse absently tugged on the gold ring in his left ear. Fear was etched in his dark eyes. ''You mean she'll have to stay in the hospital until the baby comes?''

''Possibly,'' said Dr. Zabriskie.

''Will she hemorrhage again?'' asked Michael, his hand absently massaging Julie's shoulder. She could feel a nervous agitation in his touch.

''We'll do all we can to lessen that possibility, Mr. Ryan,'' said the doctor. ''Now I really must get back to my patient.''

He stood and offered Michael his hand. ''Your daughter will need complete bed rest and careful monitoring. Sometimes a transfusion is necessary, but we're not anticipating that at the moment. Our goal is to give the baby time to develop and grow strong without risking your daughter's health.''

''When can we see her?'' asked Julie, the tears starting again.

''Shortly, Mrs. Ryan. For now I suggest you and your family have some juice or coffee, maybe visit the cafeteria. I'll tell your daughter you'll be in to see her soon. She's frightened and needs your reassurance. So compose yourselves. Be positive, upbeat. Believe me, Katie will feel better if she sees smiling faces instead of tears.''

Chapter Eighteen

For the next several days Julie felt as if she were wandering blindly through a wilderness or drifting aimlessly in a fog. She couldn't think straight, couldn't concentrate, couldn't make her mind function normally. She had only one compulsive, all-encompassing thought: Katie.

Would Katie be okay?

What was happening with Katie?

Katie, Katie, Katie!

And, of course, there was Katie's baby—the tiny, unseen child who could cost Katie her life or cause her enormous grief. Or, if all went well, he or she would be the source of tremendous joy in the Ryan and Dawson households. "Dear God, let all go well," Julie prayed constantly, as she drove to the hospital each morning, as she sat by Katie's bedside for hours, as she headed home each afternoon to care for her ailing father. "Take care of Katie, Lord. Give her a healthy baby. Be with us all!"

On the first Monday of October, Dr. Zabriskie entered Katie's room and announced, "Mrs. Ryan, Dr. Russell and I concur. We are sending Katie home today. She must stay in bed and have someone caring for her twenty-four hours a day, *every day,* until the baby is full term."

Julie and Katie looked at each other and broke into spontaneous grins. "You mean it, Doc?" Katie exclaimed, her arms crossed on her rounded tummy. "I can go home?"

Dr. Zabriskie wagged a finger at her, playful, yet serious. "You must obey our orders scrupulously, Miss Ryan, or you will be right back in the hospital, and none of us want that, do we?"

"No way," said Katie. She looked up questioningly at Julie. "But, Mom, who will stay with me?"

Julie flashed her brightest, most convincing smile. "Who else? Your one and only mom."

"But what about your work?"

Julie shrugged and struggled to sound indifferent, blasé. "I've missed so much work, they've probably forgotten I work there. I'll ask for an extended leave of absence."

Katie searched Julie's eyes. "Are you sure, Mom? Don't we need the money?"

Julie's smile remained carefully in place. She couldn't tell Katie she had no idea whether she would even have a job to go back to. "Don't forget, sweetheart, your mom is a professional artist now. I've been paid for my work. Who knows? Maybe I'll sell some more paintings."

"I hope so, Mom," said Katie. "Then you could stay home and paint forever."

"Let's not worry about forever. Let's just get you through the last three months of your pregnancy, okay?"

That very afternoon Julie had a hospital bed delivered to the house and set up in the family room, since her father already occupied the downstairs bedroom. Within an hour after the bed arrived, an ambulance brought Katie home. Everyone was there with presents and cards to welcome her home—Michael, Jesse, Julie's dad, even Mrs. Dawson and Jesse's brother, Scout.

"This is like a birthday party," said Katie, propped up in bed, beaming as she tore open the gaily wrapped packages. She held up a pink-and-blue quilt Mrs. Dawson had made and several paperbacks Jesse had bought her. "Look. Something for the baby and something for me," she said, pleased.

"Your dad and I figured you could use some pretty pajamas," said Julie, handing her a foil-wrapped box.

Katie rolled her eyes. "It looks like flannel will be my fashion statement for a while."

"I got you a bead kit," said Scout, helping her unwrap the small box, "'cause Grams says you'll have lots of time to make your own jewelry."

Katie squeezed his hand. "Thanks, Scout. This is totally cool."

Julie's father rolled his wheelchair over beside Katie's bed. "I can't get out to shop any more than you can, Granddaughter," he said, handing her an envelope, "but I want you to have this for the baby."

Katie tore open the envelope and removed three crisp new one-hundred-dollar bills. "Oh, Gramps, this is so rad! Thank you!"

"I've been saving that for you for a long time," said Alex. "You have Jesse go buy that baby of yours something nice."

Mrs. Dawson slipped over beside the wheelchair and placed her hand on Alex's arm. "That was so generous of you, Mr. Currey. I understand why your granddaughter thinks you are such a special man."

Julie noticed a light go on in her father's eyes. "Thank you, Mrs. Dawson," he said in his most gallant voice. "And I see why my granddaughter thinks you are such a good-hearted woman."

"And last but not least," said Jesse, leaning over the bed and brushing Katie's forehead with a kiss, "I got you this magnet frame so we can put our baby's first picture on the refrigerator door for everybody to see."

Katie studied the little floral-print magnet. "Oh, I love it, Jesse! I love everything everybody gave me. And my baby loves it, too. She's so happy to be home she's doing somersaults right now. Feel, Jes." She placed his hand on the side of her abdomen. "See? That's your daughter. She's going to be a little acrobat, just wait and see."

Later that night, as Julie lay wide awake beside her slumbering husband, she gazed up into the darkness and wondered how she was going to survive these next few months. She had never considered herself the altruistic, self-sacrificing type. She couldn't imagine herself playing full-time nursemaid to an ailing old man with a failing heart and a teenage girl with a high-risk pregnancy, even though they were her own father and daughter.

Dear God, she wondered silently, *are You trying to finish me off or show me how inadequate I am? Is this some kind of test? Am I like Job? Do I have to prove myself before You'll bless me? Do You delight in answering all of my prayers with calamities? I'm almost afraid to pray, wondering what will come next!*

Over the next few weeks Julie surprised herself by developing a fairly workable routine, thanks to some much-needed help from some unexpected sources. Each day before Michael left for work he helped Julie's father with his morning bathroom ritual—shaving, showering and dressing, thus freeing Julie to help Katie. Jesse dropped by for breakfast each morning before going to work at the garage, and while Julie cleared the dishes and put in a load of wash, Jesse kept Katie and Alex entertained and made sure they took their medicine.

Sometimes Jesse brought his grandmother over to stay with Katie and Alex while Julie ran errands or went shopping. Julie noticed her father always splashed some smelly cologne on his face when he knew Gladys Dawson was coming over. Julie had never seen her father behave like such a charmer as he did when Gladys was there, and Gladys seemed absolutely enchanted by his engagingly intrepid manner.

But Julie was most amazed by the way Beth Chamberlin stepped in to help. Several times a week, when she didn't have appointments to show houses, Beth dropped by and offered to hold down the fort while Julie grabbed a few hours for herself—to paint or have her hair done or just to take a nap. At first Julie was more than a little suspicious of Beth's overtures to help. Did she think she would get in Michael's good graces by making herself indispensable to his family? Did she assume she could allay Julie's suspicions by blithely dispensing assistance and support?

Whatever Beth's motives, Julie found herself depending on this lively, enigmatic young woman more every day. Whenever Julie felt especially harried and overwhelmed by the unrelenting demands on her time and energy, she would collapse in a chair and think, If only Beth would come over for a couple of hours so I could take a nap or finish that painting! If only Beth would bring over one of her casseroles so I wouldn't have to cook tonight! If only Beth would drop by with some of her videos or fashion magazines so Katie wouldn't exhaust me with her boredom!

One cold, rainy evening during the first week of November, Beth brought over a tossed salad and tuna casserole and, as usual, at Julie's urging, stayed for dinner. Michael was working late and Katie and Alex were playing Rook in the family room, so Julie and Beth lingered at the kitchen table, sipping hot herbal tea and enjoying the rare tranquillity.

Unthinkingly Julie asked, "Why do you do this, Beth? Why do you do so much to help us?"

"I like to," Beth said simply, without hesitation.

"But you must be giving up so much—leisure time with your friends, recreational activities, dates. You're so young and pretty. You should be out having fun."

"This is fun. For me it's fun."

"But it's not like we're family." Immediately Julie realized how her remark sounded, like a put-down. She hadn't meant it that way—had she?

Beth looked directly at her, her gaze unflinching. "But you are like family. You're the closest thing I have to a family."

Julie breathed an involuntary sigh and sipped her tea. She would never understand Beth, never know exactly how to take her. "Have you heard anything more from your ex-husband?" Julie asked. She knew as soon as she said the words, it was a stupid subject to bring up.

"No," Beth said quickly, her expression clouding. "He's still in jail."

"For a long time, I hope."

"Not long enough," said Beth. "Four months. He'll be out by the first of the year."

"The judge was much too lenient," said Julie.

Beth nodded. "He's never been a battered wife."

There was a long silence, then Julie said, "It must have been a nightmare living with a man like that."

Beth fingered her long, coal black hair nervously. Julie could see faint lines of anxiety etch themselves in her face. "The worst thing is feeling like you can never get away," Beth said quietly. "You feel like there's this invisible cord tying you to him, so you can never escape. Anytime he wants he can just reel you in, because he knows the system so well. He knows what he can get away with."

"But he didn't get away with it," said Julie. "He's in jail."

"But for how long?" said Beth solemnly. "He beat me, he terrorized me, and he knows I'm living in fear every day. And even though he's in jail he knows he's won, because it's just a matter of time and he'll be out, and he'll be back again, and it'll be worse than before."

Julie shook her head incredulously. "I had no idea—"

"Of course not," said Beth. "You have Michael."

That night, for the first time, Julie prayed without animosity for Beth Chamberlin; prayed with tears, asking God to forgive her own hard-heartedness and beseeching Him to deliver Beth from the trauma of living in the shadow of a madman. From that night on she included Beth in her daily prayers, just as she invoked God's protection on Michael and Katie and her father and even Jesse and the Dawsons. And every time she prayed she felt her connection with Jesse and Beth grow a little stronger, until one day it struck her that she no longer resented Jesse, nor saw Beth as the enemy, but as a friend.

Even so, a small part of Julie's mind recognized that Beth was in love with Michael, perhaps because Beth saw in him all that was missing in the brutal monster she had married. Perhaps because Beth had made herself so indispensable to Julie, Julie was willing to give Beth the benefit of the doubt. Surely, after all the two women had shared in recent weeks, they were beyond cattiness or feminine rivalry. The facts were incontrovertible: Julie had Michael and he was a treasure to be cherished. Julie had so much and Beth so little. Surely Julie could afford to be charitable.

For those first few weeks of autumn, even with her father and daughter bedridden and Julie their primary caregiver, she was convinced life was good and going to get better. She had a routine established, she had occasional help, and she had discovered herself to be a strong, able-bodied woman who could manage in a crisis.

But as the chill, dreary days of November slipped by and nothing changed—nobody got better, her routine failed to lighten—Julie began feeling she was using herself up. Her father and daughter would survive but she would be gone, fragmented, disintegrated, her mind scattered like confetti. It was an odd sensation, this constant chafing of the spirit, the daily abrading of her soul. Like a millstone crushing the silken lining of her heart. The relentless excoriation was eroding something deep and vital within her.

She found herself thinking, at odd moments, about running away. In her mind she played out absurd, fanciful scenarios. I'll pack an overnight bag, tell everyone I'm going to the grocery, and I'll drive to San Francisco or San Diego and check into a hotel. I'll call home and tell them I'm okay, but I won't tell them how to reach me. I'll stay locked in my room for days and sleep and sleep and sleep, and not speak to another living soul, except to order room service.

Julie played out these fantasies as she browned the roast for dinner, or stuffed her third load of clothes into the washing machine or changed the bed linens or picked up prescriptions from the pharmacy. The occasional appearance of the visiting nurse did little to alleviate the pressure. It dismayed Julie that she was feeling increasingly resentful of her father and daughter. It wasn't their fault they needed full-time care. Or was it? Katie had recklessly engaged in premarital sex and her father had stubbornly refused to take care of his health. And now Julie was suffering the consequences with both of them!

Julie knew better than to complain, for after all, family and friends were doing what they could to help. And things could have been worse. Far worse. Katie could have died. Her father could have died. But God, in His mercy, had spared them and entrusted them to Julie's care. She knew she ought to be grateful, and she was grateful, but it wasn't enough. Nothing anyone did was quite enough. The work load, the pressure, the demands were always greater than any one or two or three people could handle.

On the Tuesday before Thanksgiving, Julie managed to find a few priceless moments to steal away to her retreat and write in her journal. It had been weeks since she had written, maybe even weeks since she had offered more than paper-airplane prayers tossed to the sky with the faint hope they might hit their mark. She had the feeling she was entering the presence of One who knew her visit was long overdue and yet His silence was not condemning. He understood. He was willing to let her speak her mind, not in spiritual platitudes but in gritty, heartfelt honesty.

Lord, it's almost Thanksgiving Day and I'm anything but thankful. I know I should have a grateful heart. Katie's holding her own and so is Dad. Michael's been helpful and attentive, and even Beth has become a friend.

And yet everything within me screams against this oppressive routine I'm forced to endure. Months ago, in my innocence or ignorance, I told You I wanted to know and love You and my family better. Is this what I was asking for? If so, I've played myself for a fool, because every day I'm obliged to provide tender loving care to an extent I never anticipated. I never knew loving could be this hard. I imagined another kind of love, not this painful, grinding, exhausting existence.

Dear God, is this love?

I suppose to You it is. You, Jesus, who gladly knelt and unlatched your disciples' sandals and washed the desert grime from their feet. You who prayed with such passion You sweated great drops of blood—I suppose sacrifice is Your idea of love. You who let men nail You to a cross and then forgave them with Your dying breath, I suppose, for You, love and sacrifice go hand in hand.

But I'm not You, Lord. And I'm too soon running out of me. How can I keep giving when there's nothing left?

The irony, Lord, is that I wanted to experience real, satisfying intimacy with You and those I love, but now I'm living in such a crisis mode I can't even think about such luxuries. All I can think about is surviving from one moment to the next.

Julie put her pen down and opened her Bible to the Psalms. She read hungrily, with a neediness she had rarely felt before. "As the deer pants for the water brooks, so pants my soul for You, O God. My soul thirsts for God, for the living God...."

Julie relaxed back in her rocking chair and closed her eyes. As she rocked, she pictured herself in the ocean, lying back on a powerful wave, allowing it to carry her where it would. She let her muscles unwind, released the tautness of sinews and tendons in her arms and legs, along her neck and spine. She focused her thoughts on Jesus, her Great Comforter, her soul thirsting for the living God. His love was like a vast wave lifting her above the milieu. She could rest in Him and He would carry her through this crucible of testing.

In the silence of her room, she poured out all her complaints and frustrations. And when she could think of nothing more to say, she remained silent, savoring on some instinctive, elemental level His Spirit communing with her spirit, until Christ became her only reality and the world receded like an illusion.

When Julie returned to her household—to Katie wanting something to eat and her father wondering if he'd taken his pills—she felt strangely refreshed, as if she had been away for a time and was back now, stronger, calmer, more capable. She felt the afterglow of Christ's presence, the lingering warmth of His love; it seemed to overflow the cup of her heart and attach itself to her very words and actions. She had a new understanding of what it meant to love others with God's love. The extraordinary sensation of being cherished and valued by God was hers to savor and enjoy and share freely with others.

Even Michael noticed the difference in her that evening. "You seem so peaceful tonight, Jewel," he said as he helped her load the dishwasher. "You must have had a good day."

"I did," she replied, although she realized the routine and demands had been the same as other days. "I'm finally catching on to how God wants us to live our lives, Michael," she confided.

Playfully he snapped one of the blond curls along her cheekbone. "Sounds like something we could all use some help with."

"It is, Michael, but it's not something I can easily explain." She reached out and linked fingers with him, the way they had done in the early days of their marriage. "For now, let's just say I'm truly ready to celebrate Thanksgiving. I realize I have so much to be grateful for—starting with you."

He closed the dishwasher and drew her into his arms. His clear blue eyes glistened like warm spring waters. "Do you think we can tuck your dad and Katie into their beds a little early tonight, darling? I see a whole lot of love in your eyes and I'd like to experience it for myself."

"That's not fair, Michael," she chided. "I was talking about a spiritual experience, not what you have in mind."

He ran his finger gently over her parted lips. "Then why do I have this feeling the two go hand in hand? Whatever's got you feeling so good has got to be good for the two of us tonight."

She could feel her cheeks glowing. "Maybe you're right, Michael. Let me see what I can do about getting Dad and Katie settled in for the night. Then we'll slip upstairs before anyone even notices we've gone."

Chapter Nineteen

The day after Thanksgiving, Julie received a startling telephone call from Jerry Wiley, a reporter for the *Press-Telegram*. "Mrs. Ryan," he said in his smoothly resonant voice, "I've been talking with a friend of yours, Rolland Cains, owner of the Cains Gallery on Atlantic. He's shown me some of your work and I'm very impressed."

"Thank you," said Julie, her mind racing with excitement.

"I know art," said Wiley, "and you've managed to effectively integrate an original and provocative artistic style with a dramatic and very poignant message."

"I'm flattered you think so, Mr. Wiley."

"Mr. Cains tells me you're donating the money you receive from the sale of these paintings to a youth center your husband is building over near Signal Hill."

"That's correct," said Julie. "My husband and a number of young people in the neighborhood are renovating an old warehouse. They're doing most of the work themselves, but the center will need equipment and furnishings and at least a paid part-time staff to direct the volunteers."

"That's a very ambitious undertaking for you and your husband, Mrs. Ryan. It'd be a better world if more people would use their talents to help others.''

"It just seemed like the natural thing to do," said Julie. "We really weren't trying to make any kind of social or political statement."

"The point is, Mrs. Ryan, my newspaper would like to do a feature story on your project—a real human interest thing, you know? People today are tired of reading about violence and death and accidents. They want to read some positive news, so that's what we want to give them in this article. We want to show how a husband and wife can work together in a common cause to help downtrodden youth."

"Mr. Wiley," said Julie, "Michael and I just sort of stumbled into this project accidentally. We're just doing what we both love to do—me painting pictures and Michael renovating old buildings."

"And that's just the story I want," said the reporter. "Now when can we get together?"

Julie thought about the million and one obligations she had to tend to—laundry, shopping, cleaning, throwing together something for dinner. "Maybe sometime next week, Mr. Wiley?"

The reporter's voice ebbed with disappointment. "I was hoping to come over today, Mrs. Ryan."

"Today? You want to come here to my house? Can't I meet you at the gallery?"

"Oh, no. We want to catch you and your husband in your happy little home. We want to show the world you're real, everyday people in spite of your lofty mission."

Julie glanced around in dismay at the dirty dishes in the sink, the baskets of soiled laundry beside the washing machine, and the inch of dust on the furniture. "Maybe another time—"

"Our photographer has two hours open in his schedule this afternoon, Mrs. Ryan. He won't have another opening for some time. I'd hate to have this article fall by the wayside. It's so timely and abounding with community interest."

"All right, Mr. Wiley," she said relentingly. "If today's the only time."

"Wonderful, Mrs. Ryan. We'll be there at two."

Julie stared at the clock. It was one already. A wave of panic rolled through her stomach as she looked around the house. There was so much to do and no time to do it. Should she try to make the house presentable—or herself? Vanity won out. She ran upstairs and hurriedly put on her makeup and ran a comb through her tangled hair.

Just as the doorbell rang, Katie called from the family room. She needed Julie to help her to the bathroom. She was sure the reporter would leave before she finally flung open the door and breathlessly invited him and the photographer inside. She led them straight to the kitchen, since Katie's hospital bed occupied the family room, and her father was ensconced on the living room sofa in his robe, watching his game shows, the volume turned sky-high to compensate for the hearing problem he refused to admit he had.

Jerry Wiley glanced curiously from room to room as Julie led him and his colleague down the hallway to the kitchen. "Mr. Cains didn't mention that you also take in convalescents," he said, sitting down at the oak table that still contained her father and daughter's lunch trays. "You must have an exceptionally charitable spirit, Mrs. Ryan."

"Not always," she said dryly. She explained the circumstances that led to her caring for both her father and daughter.

Mr. Wiley shrugged, as if he preferred his own version. "Is your husband home?" he asked. "We'd like to hear his story, too."

"No, I called him, but he couldn't get away. He's with a client."

"Well, maybe the photographer should take some pictures now, since his time is limited. We'd like to snap you painting one of your exquisite pictures."

Reluctantly Julie led them upstairs to the spare room that served as her studio. Why hadn't she noticed before what a mess her house was in? She had always been such an immaculate housekeeper before her home became a—a hospital! The photographer took several shots of Julie as she pretended to be painting, but she was relieved that he took no shots of the house.

The photographer took a few closeups of Julie in the kitchen, then left Mr. Wiley to carry on his interview. No sooner had Julie started answering his questions than the phone rang. It was Jesse for Katie. Then the doorbell rang twice—the pharmacy delivering her dad's medicine and someone selling magazine subscriptions. After that came a whole onslaught of interruptions: Dad looking for the remote control—he was sitting on it; Katie wanting something to drink; Dad looking for the remote control again; and Katie needing help once more to the bathroom.

Julie could see that the reporter was feeling as beleaguered as she was. She could hear the frustration and impatience in his voice. "Maybe you were right, Mrs. Ryan. Maybe we should conduct this interview some other time at the art gallery. To tell you the truth," he confided, "I don't know how you ever managed to paint one picture, let alone a whole series."

Julie was about to tell him the situation wasn't all that bad when Katie suddenly shouted, "Mom, Mom, come quick! I'm in labor!"

Mr. Wiley was on his feet as quickly as Julie.

"I'm sorry, Mr. Wiley. You'd better go—please!"

"I'll be in touch, Mrs. Ryan," he said reluctantly as she escorted him to the door.

By the time Julie reached Katie's bedside, Katie's face was chalky with fear and her knuckles as white as the sheet she was gripping. "Mom, it's too soon for the baby. She's not due for eight weeks yet. I'm scared, Mom. Am I going to lose my baby?"

"No, darling," Julie assured her, trying to control the tremor in her own voice. "We've worked and prayed too hard to let anything happen to your baby."

"I love her already, Mom," Katie said shakily. "I haven't even seen her yet and I love her so much."

"I know, honey, I know." Julie brushed Katie's long tawny hair back from her perspiring forehead, then reached for the phone. "Listen, Katie, describe your symptoms to me, okay?"

"I can't, Mom. It just feels weird. I never felt this way before."

"Try, honey. It's important. The doctor needs to know what's happening."

"I—I feel like somebody's squeezing my tummy hard. Feel it, Mom. It's hard as a rock, like the baby's arching her back under my skin."

"I think I know what it might be," said Julie, forcing her voice to remain calm as she dialed, "but we'll check with Dr. Russell just to make sure."

The obstetrician confirmed that Katie was likely experiencing false labor, what he called Braxton-Hicks contractions. "Nothing to worry about," he assured Julie. "It just means Katie's body is practicing for the big day."

"But she'll be having a C-section," said Julie.

"Her body doesn't know that, Mrs. Ryan."

"I'd still like you to stop by and check her, Dr. Russell." Julie still hadn't stopped shaking. "I don't want to take any chances."

"All right, I'll be there about five, Mrs. Ryan."

After Julie hung up the phone, she sat by Katie's bed and massaged her shoulders and back, until she could feel Katie's tension ease. Soothingly she whispered, "It's okay, honey. Everything's going to be okay. Just relax. God is watching over you. He's watching over your baby."

"I'm sorry I freaked you out, Mom," Katie murmured. Her voice was light and soft, like a little girl's. "I was just so scared."

"No problem, honey. You had no way of knowing what was happening."

Katie turned her face to Julie's. Tears dotted her velvety lashes. "Am I going to die, Mom?" she whispered, her pale blue eyes wide and desolate in her ivory, cameo-shaped face.

Julie sat back, stunned, speechless for a moment. "Oh, sweetheart, no, of course you're not going to die. You're going to be perfectly fine, and so's your baby. You're doing everything the doctor told you to do—that's what counts."

"But what if it isn't enough, Mom? What if something goes wrong?"

Julie leaned across the bed and gathered Katie into her arms like a fragile, hand-stitched doll. "Oh, honey, God won't let anything go wrong. I just told you. He's watching over you and your baby every day.''

A large tear rolled down Katie's cheek. "I wish I had your faith, Mom."

"But you do, sweetie. Just talk to the Lord. Tell Him how you feel.''

Katie reached for Julie's hand and held it tight, her long, thin fingers interlocking Julie's, as if she were holding on for dear life. "I can't pray, Mom. You pray, okay?''

For an instant Julie's mind went blank; prayer was still such a personal thing for her. She hadn't prayed aloud with Katie since Katie was a youngster dutifully reciting her bedtime prayers. *Now I lay me down to sleep, I pray the Lord my soul to keep. If I should die before I wake, I pray the Lord my soul to take.*

Julie shuddered involuntarily. It had seemed like such a sweet, harmless prayer back then, but now its words were fraught with a dark foreboding. *Please, dear God,* she prayed silently, *don't take Katie. Don't let her die!*

Another thought struck Julie with stunning force. God had spoken to her lately with such power and love. Maybe through prayer she could communicate His closeness and enormous love to Katie. Self-consciously she began, groping for the words she had used before in her times alone with Him. "Heavenly Father, Katie and I are feeling awfully needy right now. We need You to hold us in Your arms of love and make us feel safe...."

Before long, Julie forgot that Katie was listening. Her own tears fell and her voice grew heavy with emotion as Christ's comforting Spirit surrounded her, infusing her with His love.

When she had finished praying, she noticed Katie was crying. "I want to know God that way, too," she said. "Then maybe I won't be so afraid."

"Spend time in His presence, Katie," said Julie. "Talk to Him, listen, read His Word. That's what I'm trying to do every day. He's always there, honey, waiting for us to come to Him."

At five that afternoon Dr. Russell arrived and briefly examined Katie, then called Julie into the room. His brow was furrowed as he said, "Everything looks fine right now, Mrs. Ryan, but, to be candid with you, I'm tempted to put Katie back in the hospital where we can monitor her and the baby more closely."

"Do you really think that's necessary?" Julie asked. "Katie's been so good. She's followed your instructions to the letter."

"I know. She's an exemplary patient, Mrs. Ryan." The physician wrote something down, then drew Julie aside and said confidentially, "But if your daughter should hemorrhage again, we would need to operate immediately, for her sake and the baby's."

A chill of comprehension swept over Julie. "If their lives are at risk, Doctor, by all means—"

"No!" Katie declared from her bed. "Don't make me go back to the hospital, Dr. Russell. Please, I hate it there. I'd be miserable. Let me stay home. I'll be good, I promise."

Dr. Russell sighed, his sturdy jaw working thoughtfully. "Well, let's see, young lady. Your due date is the end of January. We'll schedule your C-section about two weeks before you're due. I'd like to have you settled safely in the hospital a couple of weeks before that, just as a precaution."

"Let me stay home at least through Christmas," Katie pleaded. "I've got to be home for Christmas."

Dr. Russell's solemn expression softened at last. "All right, young lady, you're home through Christmas, as long as you remain stable and that little one doesn't insist on making an early appearance."

Katie clapped her hands excitedly. "Thanks, Doc! You're totally rad!"

The barrel-chested physician winked at Julie. "I think that's a compliment, but I'm not going to ask any questions."

Early Sunday morning, as Julie shuffled wearily into the kitchen in her robe and slippers, Michael handed her the newspaper and said in a grandiloquent tone, "Congratulations, sweetheart! Looks like you're on your way to fame and fortune."

She stared in disbelief at the full-page article and bold color photographs of her and her paintings. The headline read, Local

Artist With A Mission. "Oh, Michael," she exclaimed, taking the paper, "I never imagined!"

Her father was already at the table, sipping his coffee. "Does this mean—if you get famous—you're going to raise my rent?" he inquired slyly.

"Oh, Dad," she scoffed, "you don't pay rent. You're living here for free!"

He flashed a small, sardonic smile. "In that case, I guess I don't have to worry."

"What do you think, Dad?" Julie cried, riding a heady crest of euphoria. "They must like my work. Isn't this great?"

Alex looked at her, his coffee cup poised near his lips, and murmured, "Your mother would be proud."

She wanted to ask, What about you, Dad? Aren't you proud? but she couldn't bring herself to say the words.

"Read the article, Julie," urged Michael. "It sounds, as Katie would say, totally rad."

Julie began reading, a bit self-consciously. "'Local resident and artist Julie Ryan, a determined, gifted woman with a mission, is on a crusade the city council and police commission would do well to note. With the help of her successful Realtor husband Michael Ryan, Ms. Ryan is attempting to offer local teenagers and gang wannabes a viable alternative to the crime-and-violence syndrome decimating so many of today's youths.

"'The couple, combining their substantial talents in art and construction, launched their courageous enterprise by purchasing a warehouse formerly owned by the Apex Furniture Company. The Ryans have solicited local teens to help them transform the abandoned structure into a neighborhood youth center. Funds to equip and staff the center will come from the proceeds of a fund-raiser auction to be sponsored by the Rolland Cains Gallery on Atlantic on the third Saturday of December.

"'For the auction, Ms. Ryan has donated a collection of her watercolor paintings titled *Poverty's Children,* inspired by the very young people the center will serve. Ms. Ryan's work, presently on display at the Cains Gallery, has already generated considerable interest among members of the Southern California art community...."'

Julie read the rest of the article in silent amazement, then handed the paper back to Michael. "It's wonderful, isn't it? The reporter understood just what we're trying to do! And he talked about you, too, Michael. This isn't just about me, you know that, it's about the two of us and our mutual goal."

She sat down at the table, light-headed with pleasure. "The article is so inspiring, Michael, it makes me want to get up and—and do something right now to help those kids."

Michael laughed. "That's the purpose of the article, sweet-heart—to get people inspired and motivated. Besides, you are doing something. You're donating your paintings. They'll fetch a handsome price, thanks to your talent—and this article!"

Julie reached for Michael's hand. "The article will make a difference, won't it? I feel it already."

Michael took both her hands in his and pulled her up into his arms. "You bet it'll make a difference, Jewel. Now it's not just us and the kids pulling for this project. I have a feeling we'll have the whole city of Long Beach behind us!"

Chapter Twenty

The week after the article appeared, everywhere Julie went people came up to her and said, "Aren't you the lady in the newspaper?" Some were merely curious and went on their way, but others shook her hand heartily and wished her well. A few even had tears in their eyes as they handed her a check for the youth center.

Julie felt overwhelmed by all the attention. Was this what it felt like to be a celebrity? She fleetingly considered wearing dark glasses and a scarf when she went out, but then she realized she was enjoying the attention. She was wise enough to realize her modicum of fame would be over in a few days when her article was modestly lining people's garbage cans.

It occurred to Julie that she would trade every compliment she had received for one genuine word of praise from her father. Again and again she replayed his Sunday-morning comment, wringing it for all it was worth. "Your mother would be proud." That was a fact Julie knew already. Her mother had been proud of her atrocious kindergarten scribblings. Her mother had dared to hang Julie's horrible paint-by-number fiascos like original Rembrandts all over the house. They were still there, looking like the disasters they truly were now that her mother's eyes of love no longer viewed them.

On Wednesday morning, the first day of December, Rolland Cains phoned with more good news. "Julie, your fund-raiser is shaping up very well," he told her, his voice buoyant. "I'm sending out invitations for a special reception for you just before the auction. I wanted you to know I'm inviting some important names in the art world, including a few New York agents who regularly scout California galleries for new talent. Of course, I can help establish your name locally, but *they* can give you the kind of national exposure I can't provide. So bring in some of your recent work—a variety of subjects and mediums—oils, watercolors, acrylics, portraits, still-lifes, landscapes."

"But you already have my *Poverty's Children* series on display. Won't that be enough to show the agents?"

"The series will certainly prove how talented you are, but a variety of work will show them your versatility and range. It'll give you an edge. Believe me, I know what I'm talking about."

"But I've poured all my energies into the series. I don't have much else."

"Well, see what you can do, Julie. You have nearly three weeks."

Three weeks! There was no way Julie could create a body of quality work that would impress an agent in three weeks, even if she had nothing to do but paint! With Christmas coming and her dad and Katie to care for, she had no idea how she'd even find time to shop for gifts, send out cards or decorate a tree.

At dinner that evening Julie told Michael and her father about Rolland Cains's phone call—the reception he was planning and the New York agents he had invited. "He wants me to bring in more work," Julie lamented, "but he might as well be asking for the moon."

"Maybe you can juggle your schedule and find a little time here and there to work on your paintings," said Michael.

"Sure, I can see it now!" Julie said, her voice heavy with sarcasm. "Like I'm going to have time to pack up, drive somewhere, find the perfect scene, set up my palette and easel, paint, clean up, then pack up and drive home in time to fix dinner or help Katie to the bathroom?''

"All right, I'll try to get home more often and help out so you can paint," said Michael. "And you know Beth is always glad to come over and give you a break."

"I don't want you and Beth holding down the fort while I'm off somewhere painting," she said through clenched teeth. I already feel like I'm sharing you too much with Beth. "I'll just tell Rolland I can't do it."

"You can do it," said her father, poking gravely at his meat loaf. "Just don't leave the house."

"You mean, just don't paint?" said Julie, puzzled.

"No. Paint stuff around here," said Alex, his attention still on his plate.

"Paint stuff around here?" she repeated, trying not to let her irritation show. "What stuff, Dad? Cluttered furniture, baskets of laundry, still-lifes of medicine bottles and dirty dishes?"

"Anything you see," said her father, ignoring her sarcasm.

"Oh, great! Anything I see!" countered Julie.

"What's so hard about that?" her father shot back.

"Just this, Dad. In case you missed my meaning just now, all I see is dirty laundry and cluttered rooms and crusty dishes in the sink. Not exactly aesthetically pleasing, is it!"

"Then look harder," he said solemnly. "Paint Katie and me playing Rook. Sketch Katie singing lullabies to a baby not even born yet. Draw Michael sitting in his chair talking to a client on the phone. For crying out loud, daughter, look in the mirror and paint the face looking back at you. Use your imagination. That's what an artist does."

Julie was about to inquire truculently how her father had the slightest idea what an artist did. But suddenly his words took root like a sapling in fertile soil. "I could do it, couldn't I? They would have to be hurried sketches or very spontaneous paintings on the run," she said, warming to the idea. "Maybe even some pen and ink drawings or acrylics or oil pastels."

"Stop babbling about it," said her father, "and just do it."

She searched his eyes. "You would really let me paint you?"

He cleared his throat noisily. "As long as you don't tell me to sit still like a statue or wear some outlandish costume."

"That's a promise, Dad."

In the days that followed, Julie did just as her father had suggested. She painted Katie crooning to her unseen baby, her father perched before the TV working the remote control like a weapon, and Michael poring over the morning newspaper in his tank top and running shorts. She even sketched Beth and Jesse bent over the kitchen table decorating Christmas cookies, and Michael, Jesse and Beth trimming the enormous blue spruce Michael brought home one week into December.

Julie felt as if she were not participating in Christmas this year so much as she was keenly observing it from a distance. When she wasn't painting, she was carrying out her caregiving duties as usual, with the help of Jesse, Beth and Gladys Dawson. And Michael, of course, when he wasn't at the office or working on the youth center renovation.

The days of December possessed a strange, surreal quality, as if life were almost normal and yet not quite. One evening as Julie lay in bed next to Michael, she said, "Someday I want our lives to return to normal."

"What's normal?" he asked.

"I've forgotten," she said.

It was nearly Christmas and the whole world was gearing up for the celebration. In a haphazard fashion the Ryan household was gearing up, too. They had a tree now, nicely decorated and Christmas cookies in pretty tins and a wreath on the door and even a few packages under the tree. Julie had put no cards in the mail, but people would understand when she scrawled an apology on next year's cards: "Sorry you didn't hear from us last year. Our family was in a state of crisis, but we're fine now."

She prayed that would be true, that next year at this time they would all look back on this year and smile wistfully and say,

"Boy, that was quite a time we had, but, thank God, everything came out okay."

Lord, please let everything turn out okay, she prayed every morning when she slipped away to her bedroom retreat for her time alone with God. Usually she was able to snatch only ten minutes or twenty or sometimes an entire half hour to read the Scriptures, talk with God and savor Christ's comforting presence. She had discovered, by hard experience, that this was the only way she could survive. When the days came crashing in on her, she literally fled to her room and threw herself on God's mercy. "Help me, God, before I come unglued.... God, take this anger, this frustration...keep my lips sealed before I say the wrong thing.... Dear Jesus, rock me in Your arms because I'm so tired I could die!"

It occurred to her one day that she was actually living the prayer she had uttered in blissful innocence so many months ago. She was growing to know and love God and others in ways she had never anticipated. If she had known how hard the process would be, that in a sense it would require a dying to self, that truly knowing and loving always exacted a price, she might have had second thoughts and selfishly counted the cost. But she was glad now she hadn't known, for she wouldn't trade what God was doing in her life for anything in the world.

But that didn't mean life was a picnic now—far from it—a circus maybe, a bad movie, at times a horror show. The Tuesday before the Cains Gallery auction and reception, both Katie and Julie's father experienced minor crises that had Julie beside herself with fear, worry and exhaustion.

After lunch, her father complained of dizziness and shortness of breath, and nothing seemed to help. Julie phoned Michael, who promptly came home and drove Alex to the emergency room. The doctor changed his medication, prescribed a breath inhaler and warned him to stick religiously to his diet. According to Michael, her father snapped back, "There's nothing religious about that diet. It's straight from hades!"

Katie was feeling an unusual amount of distress, as well. Off and on all day she called Julie to her bedside with countless anxieties and complaints. "Mom, I'm having those strange, gripping pains again, worse than before. Are you sure I'm not in labor?... Mom, I can't stand just lying here in this bed. If I have to stay here another hour I'll freak out.... What can I do, Mom? I'm so bored. I've seen all the TV shows a dozen times."

At last, in desperation, Julie called Beth and asked her to stop by for dinner and then spend some time with Katie. "I'm afraid my daughter gets rather tired of my company," Julie explained, "and right now I'm sick and tired of hers. If someone doesn't give us a break soon, we'll both go bonkers."

Beth was glad to oblige. She even brought a cheesecake for dessert. While Julie and Michael helped get her father settled for the night, Beth played Scrabble with Katie. When Katie had fallen asleep, Beth joined Julie and Michael in the kitchen for a slice of creamy cheesecake. It was an odd, yet cozy moment, the three of them sitting together around the table, the lamplight low and what Katie would call "elevator music" playing on the stereo.

"Thanks for coming over," Michael told Beth.

"I'm glad to, anytime," said Beth in a tone that sent flags waving in Julie's mind. Would Julie ever get past the feeling there was a subtext between these two that she would never be able to read?

"I hope we didn't take you away from anything important," said Julie. *Or anyone!* she wanted to add.

"No, I wasn't doing much," said Beth in a small, tentative voice. "Just reading my mail."

There was something odd in the way she said *mail*, so Julie asked, "Anything interesting?"

Beth was silent for a long moment before replying softly, "I received a letter from the warden at the prison. He was notifying me Roger, my ex-husband, will be released in less than ten days. A free man, just like that."

"I'm sorry, Beth," said Julie. "I can see how upset you are."

"There's more," said Beth. "He wrote me a letter."

"Who?" asked Michael. "Your ex-husband?"

Beth nodded, tears gathering in her eyes. "He said things."

"Threats?" inquired Michael. "If he threatened you, you can file a complaint with the police."

"Not threats exactly. More like little insinuations. He said, 'I'm really looking forward to seeing you...we have a lot to talk about...and things to settle, once and for all.' I think I know what he means, and it's not good."

Michael sat forward and stared hard at Beth. "Do you think your life is in danger?"

Beth reached for her purse and pulled out a tissue. "I—I'm probably being overly melodramatic."

"Once your ex-husband's on the loose again, you shouldn't be staying alone, Beth," said Michael. "Isn't there somewhere you can go where he can't find you? You must have family, friends, someone—"

Beth shook her head. "My parents have been dead since I was a teenager. They were killed in a car crash by a drunk driver. I have a great-aunt, but she's in a nursing home in Ohio. As for friends, when I married Roger he made me give up all my friends. He was so jealous he checked the phone bill every month to make sure I hadn't called someone he didn't approve of."

"That's incredible," said Julie. "Why did you marry a man like that?"

Beth twisted a strand of shiny ink black hair around her finger. "I ask myself that question every day. I was very young, not quite eighteen, and my parents had just died. I was a basket case. We had always been so close, my folks and I. I was a real mess. I didn't know what I was doing or where I was going.

"Then I met Roger. He worked in the law office that handled my parents' estate. We began dating almost immediately. He was studying to be a lawyer, but he never passed the bar exam. Every time he failed, it made him more angry and unreasonable. Several times when we were dating he struck me, and each time I broke up with him. Then he would make impossible promises and beg me to take him back. I always did. Finally he told me he would change and not be so insecure if I just married him. I resisted the impulse at first, but five years ago I gave in and we were married."

"Obviously things didn't improve," said Julie.

"No," Beth replied. "I knew marriage was a mistake right from the start. Roger's temper tantrums got worse; he wouldn't let me finish college or go to work or even have a friend over. After five years I filed for divorce, moved to Southern California, went back to school and got my Realtor's license. I worked for a small firm for a while, but it was a dead-end job. Then, thank God, Michael gave me a position in his office. I've never been happier. I know I never would have made it this far without his help."

Julie sipped her coffee. "I never realized how hard your life has been."

Beth shrugged self-consciously. "Everyone has trials—"

"We know that for a fact." Julie paused for a long moment. "I don't know how you'll feel about this, but I've been praying for you, and if there's one thing I know, it's that prayer works."

"No one has ever told me they were praying for me."

Julie looked over at Michael and said impulsively, "Why don't you pray for Beth's safety right now, before she goes?"

Michael stared at Julie in surprise, then nodded uncertainly, and the three of them joined hands around the table. His prayer was simple and abbreviated—a heartfelt petition for Beth's protection.

Later, as Beth was leaving, Julie stood with her for a moment on the porch. The December air was invigorating—a chilly mixture of ocean salt, fresh rain and pure, clean, smog-free air tinged with the pine scent of Christmas.

"Thanks for everything, Julie," Beth said softly. "You have no idea how much it means to me to have you and Michael as friends."

"I think I do," said Julie. "Everyone needs a friend, and God has been reminding me I need to let people know He's available for the job."

Beth stepped close and gave Julie a brief, spontaneous embrace. "God has already shown me His love through you and Michael. Thank you."

Julie smiled, speechless for a moment. She felt a surprising, unexpected bond with this woman she didn't quite trust. Beth was a survivor, stubborn, proud, and resilient—the kind of person Julie admired, in spite of herself.

I can't believe I'm feeling as protective toward Beth as Michael does, Julie acknowledged silently. It's almost as if we were sisters. Is this what sisters feel—an overriding sense of caring in spite of the petty bickering and jealousies?

Chapter Twenty-One

On Saturday evening, Julie's heart pounded with excitement and misgivings as Michael, looking elegant in his tuxedo, escorted her into the sleek, modern, glass-and-stucco Cains Gallery for her reception. From the vestibule she could hear the echoing strains of a string quartet playing a concerto from Mozart or Brahms. "Oh, Michael, I'm so nervous," she confided. "What if they don't like me?"

"Relax," he whispered, squeezing her hand. "This is your night. You'll knock 'em dead."

"Dead isn't exactly what I had in mind," she replied, taking a deep breath.

"Okay, then you'll dazzle them, Jewel. You're as beautiful as your paintings."

She smiled gratefully, hoping her form-flattering, green velvet gown with its scalloped neck and cap sleeves conveyed the proper balance of femininity and professionalism. She reminded herself she was as ready as she'd ever be for this evening. Her makeup was flawless, her jade jewelry exquisite, and her blond hair had been styled in an elegant, upswept twist, giving her a rare and delicious feeling of sophistication. Now if she could just carry it off!

The gallery's spacious, tastefully decorated reception room was already crowded with people in their evening finery—women in cocktail dresses or shimmering gowns, men looking dapper in their dark suits or tuxedos. Julie recognized no one, except Rolland Cains, who came striding over to greet her, smiling, looking proud. "Julie, welcome! You look stunning! Everyone is so eager to meet you! And you, too, Mr. Ryan. Please come with me."

As he led Julie and Michael through the milling throng, he said confidentially, "Our show has attracted many local patrons of the arts and several people from the media. Look, even a reporter and cameraman from Channel 5 News. They don't usually cover art shows, but I think they're approaching it from the community angle—the idea of selling paintings to raise money for that youth center of yours, Mr. Ryan. Perhaps both of you could give them an interview."

"Sure," said Michael. "We'd be glad to."

Cains lowered his voice another notch. "Julie, I especially want you to meet John Adler, a contributing editor with *American Artist* Magazine. He could give your career a real boost."

"You mean he's going to do an article on the show?"

Cains's eyes twinkled. "That's why he's here. So be sure to spend some time with him, answer his questions, tell him what he wants to know."

"I'll do my best."

The introductions began in earnest as Cains steered them deftly from one cluster of art devotees to another. A waiter offered Julie a tray of stuffed mushrooms, shrimp egg rolls, Buffalo wings and smoked salmon. She grabbed an egg roll as Rolland whisked her off to meet still another art fancier.

Later, just before the auction, Sam Woods, the television reporter, collared Julie and Michael by the punch bowl and requested an interview. When they agreed, he signaled his cameraman, and suddenly Julie realized whatever they said could appear on the eleven o'clock news!

"Tell me, Mrs. Ryan," intoned the reporter, "how you got the idea of auctioning your paintings to finance your husband's youth center."

"I don't know," she admitted. "One thing led to another. Both Michael and I wanted to use our talents to help young people. It seemed natural for me to paint and him to build."

"Were you inspired by General Colin Powell's challenge to corporate America some time back to volunteer to save our country's fifteen million at-risk kids by bringing caring adults into their lives?"

"We weren't consciously thinking about General Powell's challenge," said Michael, "but we certainly agree with his assessment of the need for volunteers to work one-on-one with kids."

"And that's what you're doing now, Mr. Ryan?"

Michael looked impassioned as he said, "Yes, I am. For months now I've been working shoulder to shoulder with neighborhood youngsters to build the youth center, and every day I'm discovering what a difference a caring adult can make in a kid's life. I'm hoping we'll have a lot of dedicated volunteers when the center opens next month."

The reporter turned to Julie. "Mrs. Ryan, the auction is about to begin. What sort of response do you expect to see to your work?"

She shook her head, flustered, her cheeks flushing. "I have no idea, Mr. Woods. I'll be happy if we make enough money to equip the youth center and hire a part-time staff for six months or a year."

On the drive home that evening, Julie and Michael both laughed at her humble reply to the reporter. "Man, who would have guessed!" trumpeted Michael, his fingers doing a victory dance on the steering wheel. "Not only did your paintings bring in enough money to equip the center, we've got enough to pay a small staff for the next three years. That's quite a Christmas present for those kids, Jewel."

"I never dreamed my paintings could bring in that kind of money," said Julie. "And did you hear what that art agent told me—that round, bald man, Salvatore Calucci—about representing my work on the East Coast? It's like a dream come true, Michael. I'm still pinching myself!''

Michael reached across the seat and playfully pinched her thigh. "Let me do all the pinching, okay, darling?"

She closed her fingers around his and said with a coy little sigh, "Really, Michael, is that all you think about?"

He looked over and winked, his face silhouetted by ribbons of darkness and moonlight. "You bet, and I'll prove it when I get you home."

She laughed. "You sound like one of those teenage boys with raging hormones."

He pressed her hand to his lips. "And don't you forget it, my darling!"

"I feel a bit reckless myself," she confessed. "And giddy. I can't believe how giddy I feel, Michael. And I swear I drank nothing stronger than sparkling cider."

"Maybe it was the stuffed mushrooms. I've heard they can be quite an aphrodisiac."

"I said I feel giddy, Michael, not—"

"No, it's not mushrooms, is it? It's something else. Seafood. Clams?"

"Not clams, Michael. Oysters."

"I hate oysters."

"Me, too," she agreed.

He released her hand. "We'll forget the oysters."

"We don't need oysters, Michael," she said engagingly, her fingertips tracing his powerful jaw. "We just need each other."

He looked at her, his eyes glinting like stars. "And we have that, don't we, Jewel? Each other."

She studied his sturdy profile as he turned his gaze back to the road. "Yes, Michael," she murmured thoughtfully. "It's strange. I feel closer to you tonight than I've ever felt."

"Same here, Jewel."

"We could be nineteen again," she said, her voice light and breathless. "In a way I'm tired, but inside I feel so upbeat and full of energy, I could paint an entire canvas tonight."

He chuckled dryly. "Oh, no, you don't, sweetheart. We're cele-

brating together, just the two of us in our private retreat. A little
music—our old Neil Diamond favorites—a few flaming candles
and kisses, and who knows where the night will lead?''

She snuggled her head against his shoulder and said softly,
''No mystery to it, Michael. I know exactly where it will lead.''

On Sunday morning Julie woke, sweet dreams of last night
lingering like the fragrance of rose petals. She stretched luxuriously, basking not in the afterglow of the auction's rousing success but in the remarkable closeness she had shared with Michael.
She had waited for so long to feel this way about him again.

She looked over at his side of the bed; it was empty, but she
could see where his head had creased the pillow. She pulled the
pillow over against her face and breathed in the lime scent of
Michael's aftershave. *Thank You, Lord,* she prayed silently, *for
giving me such a wonderful husband and for drawing us closer
than we've ever been before.*

She sat up, still hugging Michael's pillow, and glanced around.
Where was Michael? He wasn't in the shower or she would hear
the water running. He was probably helping her father with his
morning routine. Sunday mornings were always a hassle, trying
to get Dad and Katie settled so she and Michael could slip off to
church for a couple of hours.

Her thoughts were broken by the sound of footsteps in the hall.
Suddenly Michael appeared in the doorway with a tray of orange
juice, coffee and a muffin. ''I was going to do the breakfast-in-
bed routine,'' he said, placing the tray on her lap, ''but this is the
extent of my culinary skills.''

''This is wonderful, Michael. I feel pampered. Thank you!''

He sat beside her on the bed. ''Enjoy it fast, Jewel. Your dad's
out of sorts because he can't find his breath inhaler, and Katie's
upset over some fight she had with Jesse last night. And Beth
phoned at the crack of dawn, sounding hysterical. A problem with
her ex-husband. I told her I'd come over as soon as you were up
to take care of Katie and your dad.''

''You're going to Beth's? Now?''

''She's in trouble, Julie. What can I do?''

Suddenly last night was slipping through Julie's fingers. "Beth's always in trouble, Michael."

"I know. But she doesn't have anybody else to turn to."

"She doesn't want anybody else."

Michael heaved a disgruntled sigh. "We can't let her down, Julie. She's done a lot for us lately. We owe her."

"Did you ever think maybe she wants us feeling indebted to her?"

Michael stood and looked in the dresser mirror, straightening his tie. "You hold down the fort here," he said, tension tightening his voice. "I'll be back as soon as I can. Maybe we can still make the late service."

"No," she said glumly, "we might as well forget church today. With Beth, Katie and Dad all needing us, we'll never get away."

Michael leaned down and brushed a kiss on her forehead. "Think about last night and you'll feel better."

She shook her head. "Suddenly last night feels like a million years away."

After Michael left, Julie showered and dressed, lamenting how quickly the real world intruded on her dreams and burst the fragile enchantment of romance. How fleetingly she had been Cinderella at the ball. Now she was back as the scullery maid with a dozen chores demanding her attention.

Even as Julie approached the family room—now Katie's domain—she could hear Katie shouting urgently for her. "I'm coming," Julie called, resolving not to let her daughter see her own simmering irritation.

Katie was sitting propped up on several pillows, her favorite stuffed bear lying on her rounded tummy, her milk white face framed by flowing amber tresses. Her aqua eyes were wide and beseeching. "Mom, where were you? I thought you'd never come!"

Julie sat down on the side of the bed and massaged Katie's arm. "I'm sorry, sweetie. I can't be everywhere at once. What's wrong?"

"I don't feel good, Mom." She rubbed both sides of her abdomen with her fingertips. "I keep having those funny pains. I just feel yucky all over. I hate this, Mom. I'm so tired of staying in bed. All the kids are out now for Christmas break. They're going to the mountains to ski and hang out together while I have to stay in bed forever like an invalid."

"It won't be forever, honey, I promise. Just another six weeks and you'll have your sweet little baby to hold in your arms. Don't you look forward to seeing your baby?"

"I guess." Katie's pale lips settled into a pout. "Jesse and I had a fight last night, Mom."

"A fight? About what?"

"After the baby's born, he wants me and the baby to go live at his house with him and his grandma."

Julie stiffened. "Really? When did he decide that?"

"I don't know. He says he's the man and he should take care of his family. I think it's a macho thing."

"What did you say, honey?" Julie asked guardedly.

"I told him no," said Katie, jutting out her chin. "I said I'm staying here." She looked imploringly at Julie. "Mom, I couldn't stand living in that little dinky house in that awful neighborhood. I want to stay here in my own room with all my things."

"But someday, if you should marry Jesse—"

"I don't want to get married, Mom. I want life to be like it used to be. I want to have friends over and go to school and ball games and parties. I want to stay up late listening to music and talking on the phone and doing my hair and having fun like I used to do."

"Oh, darling, I wanted all of that for you, too!" said Julie, caressing Katie's cheek. "But you can't go back."

Katie was sobbing now. "Why can't I, Mom? Why can't I be the girl I was before? I just want to be a kid again. I don't want to be old and settled like you!"

Julie blinked away her own tears. "I wish I could give you back your old life, Katie, but I can't. You've got to accept the life you have now and make the best of it."

"But what will I do if Jesse and the baby take up all my time? What if I become someone I don't even like? Oh, Mom, what if

I start hating Jesse? What if everything's so hard I even hate my baby?''

Julie stroked Katie's arm. ''It—it's not too late to consider giving up your baby for adoption.''

Katie's eyes widened with alarm. ''Oh, Mom, how could I ever do that? You didn't give me up.''

''But what was right for me isn't necessarily right for you.''

Katie lowered her gaze, her long lashes brushing her cheeks. ''Jesse mentioned that last night. He said maybe we're not ready to be parents.''

''It's something to think about, honey. You and Jesse still have time to make your decision.''

Katie looked up intently. ''No, I want my baby. I want her more than anything in the world. But I just want my old life back, too!''

''We can't change what is, sweetheart, but we can ask God to give us the strength to get through it.''

Katie clasped her mother's hand. ''Pray for me, Mom. God listens to you.''

''He listens to you, too, Katie, if you just share what's in your heart.''

''I do, Mom. Sometimes I do. But right now, you pray, okay?''

Julie nodded reluctantly. With her anger at Beth still smoldering, praying was the last thing she felt like doing. But she prayed aloud anyway, and felt better afterward. She could see that Katie felt better, too. ''God is watching over you, honey. Everything will work out okay,'' Julie told her, going to the doorway. ''Would you like me to fix you some hot cocoa and toast like I made when you were little?''

Katie nodded, managing the wisp of a smile. ''And don't forget; cut the toast in three strips so they're easy to dunk.''

''I'd never forget that,'' Julie assured her.

After fixing Katie's cocoa and toast, Julie checked on her father in the living room. He was sitting in his favorite recliner by the TV, one hand on the remote control as always. He was ''channel surfing,'' as Katie put it, and he seemed in no better sorts than the rest of the family this morning.

"I'm not hungry," he told Julie when she offered to fix him some oatmeal and toast. He raised one shaggy eyebrow and gave her a scrutinizing glance. "But if you were going to fix me some sausage and eggs or pancakes with heaps of butter and syrup—"

"Dad, you know you're not allowed to have those things," said Julie in exasperation. Why did he insist on pushing the limits like this? Why did she always have to be the bad guy, telling him what he couldn't have?

"At my age I should be able to eat what I enjoy," he complained. "If it kills me off a year or two sooner, so what? With your mom gone, what have I got to live for?"

Julie sank down on the sofa across from him and shook her head wearily. "Dad, why do you say things like that? Are you just trying to get me riled up this morning? If so, you've already accomplished your purpose."

"I'm not trying to rile anybody. I'm just speaking the truth."

"Well, it's not the truth. You have a lot to live for—the rest of your family—me, Katie, and soon a new great-grandchild you'll want to spend time with. We want you to stay healthy."

He refused to budge. "A couple of fried eggs and a sausage link or two won't make a hill-of-beans difference."

Julie stood, hands on hips, and stared down at him. "No, Dad. If you want sausage and eggs, fix them yourself."

His brows formed a menacing vee over dark, flashing eyes. "I just may do that! In fact, I just may go home!"

"Home? Now where's that coming from?"

He stared back at the television screen. "I'm doing better. I could get by on my own at home. Besides, I've worn out my welcome around here."

"No, Dad," said Julie, her patience thinning, "you haven't worn out your welcome. We're glad to have you here, but we all have to work at getting along."

He looked back up at her. "You have enough on your hands with Katie. You don't need an old man to wait on and pick up after."

"If you're afraid you're too much trouble, Dad, you're not," Julie assured him. "You've been wonderful for Katie—the two of you playing games together and joking and laughing. You've been good medicine for her.''

His voice softened. ''She's been good medicine for me, too.''

''So it's settled,'' Julie said with more conviction than she felt. ''You're staying here. Next week is Christmas, and we're all going to have a wonderful time. After that, we can talk about your going home.''

Her father aimed the remote control at the TV set and flipped through the channels, one after another, too fast to have the slightest idea what was playing. ''I'll have that oatmeal now,'' he said under his breath.

Julie was about to go to the kitchen when she heard the front door open and close. It would be Michael, of course, and it was a good sign that he was home already from Beth's. Eagerly Julie strode across the living room to the foyer and was about to give her husband a warm greeting, when she stared in surprise at the doorway. There stood Michael with Beth beside him, and he had her luggage in his hands. Seeing Julie, he flashed a sheepish grin and asked, ''Got room for one more house guest, Jewel?''

Chapter Twenty-Two

For a long minute Julie didn't know what to say. She felt like laughing at the absurdity of the moment, then like crying. Either way, Beth stood in the entryway waiting, her raven hair tousled around her tear-streaked, porcelain face, her amber eyes sad as a puppy's. She was wearing a robin's egg blue silk blouse and tight jeans. "I'm sorry to barge in on you like this, Julie," she said as Michael set down her suitcases. "I told Michael I could go to a hotel or a women's shelter, but he insisted I come home with him."

"You'll feel the same way, Julie, when you hear what happened," said Michael, leading Beth over to the sofa. Beth sat in one corner, her elbow on the tufted arm, her legs curled under her, looking graceful and limber as a model.

Julie took the armchair across from them, but she didn't feel like sitting down. She sat forward, her back stiff, waiting for an explanation that would make sense. Please, Michael, come up with something good, because the last thing on earth I want is Beth Chamberlin living here with us! A sudden nervous energy coursed through Julie's limbs, making her feel as if she'd had too much coffee when she'd had no coffee at all. No matter what Beth's story, Julie didn't want her moving in with them, and she was ready to say so. "So what's wrong?" she asked woodenly, hiding her skepticism.

"It's her ex-husband," said Michael. "He's out of jail—"

"He came to my apartment," said Beth shakily.

"When?" asked Julie.

"Last night," Beth replied. "I wasn't there. I had stopped by here for a couple of hours. You were both at the reception, and I figured your dad and Katie could use some company."

"Jesse was here to keep an eye on things," said Julie.

"Yes, that's what I discovered, but he and Katie insisted I stay, so we played Rook for a while, then I went home." She drew in a deep breath, then said unevenly, "When I got home, I could see someone had broken in. I was terrified. I didn't know what to do. I went to a neighbor's and called the police. They came right away and checked the apartment to make sure the intruder was gone."

"Are you saying your ex-husband broke in?" asked Julie.

"Yes." Beth wrung her hands, twisting her gold watch band. "He must have been drunk. The place smelled like a brewery."

"Did he hurt you?"

"No, I never even saw Roger. But my apartment was ransacked. I never saw such a mess in my life—my clothes thrown everywhere, my jewelry and CD collection scattered around, drawers emptied out on the floor."

Julie shook her head. "Why would he do such a thing?"

"He's crazy...and he wants me back. He wrote messages with my own lipstick on my mirror. They were horrible!"

Michael spoke up, his tone somber. "He wrote, 'You're dead, Beth, unless we get back together! It's just a matter of time!' So you see, she couldn't stay there, Julie. That lunatic could come back and try to harm her."

"But what if he comes here?" cried Julie.

"He has no reason to connect me to you," said Beth, brushing back her shiny hair. "I'm sure he wouldn't track me here."

"Hon, Beth's just going to stay for a few days until she can find another apartment. We have that spare room upstairs where you paint, Jewel. The couch makes into a bed. I'll take her luggage upstairs and get things set up. You won't have to do a thing.''

Julie nodded uncertainly. Overriding her sympathy for Beth was a sense of amazement at the way this needy young woman constantly managed to insinuate herself into their lives. Now Beth would actually be living in the same house with them!

"I won't be any trouble, I promise," Beth assured her. "And someday I'll find a way to thank you and Michael."

"That's really not necessary," said Julie distractedly. Everything was happening so fast she couldn't think straight. How had her life and Michael's become so inexorably connected with Beth's? Where would it all end?

Michael paused on the stairs, Beth's suitcases in hand, and called back, "I'll be going with Beth to the police station, Julie. It may take a while, so we'd better plan a late dinner."

"The police station?"

"I have to file a complaint against Roger for breaking and entering," said Beth.

Julie frowned at Michael. "Why do *you* have to go?"

"Beth shouldn't have to go through something like this alone. She's been through enough already."

"I don't mind going alone," Beth said quickly.

"No," Michael replied. "I said I'm going, and that's final."

After Beth and Michael left for the police station, Julie hurriedly fixed her father's breakfast, checked on Katie, then fled to her bedroom retreat and wrote with trembling fingers in her journal.

Heavenly Father,

Sometimes I think I'm going crazy, and other times I feel like everyone's crazy but me. Today I feel like Alice in Wonderland confronting raving Mad Hatters and crazed queens shouting, "Off with their heads!" I'm trying so hard to be loving and patient, but inside I feel like climbing the walls or running away. I have turned myself inside out for this family of mine, and I have nothing left to give.

I yearn to feel Your love and comfort, Lord. I need Your healing touch right now, or I'll never make it through the day. I'm bur-

dened for Katie, frustrated with Dad, angry with Michael and suspicious of Beth. Forgive me, Lord, for falling so far short of Your love. Help me to sort out all these negative feelings and show me what to do, because I'm at my wit's end.... And, Father, thanks for always being here for me, no matter how needy and broken I am.

By the time Beth and Michael returned from the police station, Julie was feeling more in control. Dad and Katie were napping, Christmas carols played on the stereo, and a ham and scalloped potatoes were baking in the oven. Julie was even feeling philosophical about Beth's temporary sojourn with them. After all, Beth was already a frequent visitor in their household. What did a few more days matter?

Beth seemed in better spirits, too. "The police don't think Roger will make any more trouble for me. They figure he probably skipped town and is long gone."

"He could be in another state by now," Michael agreed. "He knows the police will have an all-points-bulletin out for his arrest. So I think we can relax a little."

"That's good news," said Julie, setting the linen-draped table with her holiday china. "Now we can all sit down, have a pleasant Sunday dinner and cultivate a little Christmas spirit around here."

But shortly after midnight, the peace and calm Julie had prayed for was shattered by a horrific scream. At first Julie wasn't sure what had awakened her. A scream, yes. But was it part of her dream, or was it real? And where did it come from? Beth's room? Katie's room downstairs?

Julie clambered out of bed, her mind still shrouded in dreams, and awkwardly pulled on her robe and scuffed downstairs to the family room. She quietly peeked in just as Katie screamed again. Immediately Julie threw on the light switch and rushed to Katie's bed. Katie was sitting in a pool of blood, hysterical.

"Call an ambulance!" Julie shrieked, gathering her daughter into her arms and holding her close. Katie was cold and trembled so fiercely Julie could hardly hold her.

The household sprang alive, everyone running and speaking at once. Michael phoned 911 while Beth brought a blanket and wrapped it around Katie. "Elevate her legs," she told Julie. Together they rolled up several blankets and tucked them under Katie's legs and lower back.

Katie looked like a wispy, white ghost as she clutched Julie's hand and shrilled, "Don't let me die, Mom! Don't let my baby die!"

"You're both going to be fine," Julie told her shakily, praying with a raw, racking urgency that God would make it so.

Within minutes Julie's father shambled into the room, his face pasty with alarm. "You'll be okay, Katie, my girl," he said, emotion coloring his voice. He remained stoically by the bed holding Katie's hand, waiting for the ambulance to arrive.

For Julie, it all felt like a dream, the stuff of nightmares—Katie hemorrhaging, Michael on the phone demanding an ambulance be sent immediately, Beth urging everyone to remain calm, Dad looking so feeble and frail, yet insisting on staying by Katie's side, and Julie, frantic, shell-shocked, her mind spinning off in every direction at once as she tried desperately to reassure both Katie and herself.

But Julie's mind was bordering on hysteria as the paramedics arrived and rushed to Katie, surrounding her like birds of prey, examining her, checking her vital signs, starting an IV. Even Julie could see how quickly Katie was deteriorating—growing lethargic, nearly lapsing into unconsciousness, her eyes glazed, her skin a translucent pearl white. *We're losing her!* Julie thought wildly as the attendants lifted Katie on a gurney and wheeled her out to the ambulance. *Not my little girl! God, please don't let me lose her!*

"Please, let me ride with her in the ambulance," Julie begged the paramedic.

"Sorry, ma'am, you'll have to follow in your car. Every minute counts." And with that he went striding out the door.

Julie started after him, choking on a sob, but her father stopped her, clasping both her arms in his stubborn hands. His salt-and-pepper hair was mussed, his moss brown eyes as dark and deep as ocean brine. "Julie!" His commanding tone spoke volumes. She stopped and stared mutely at him. He held her firm, his eyes locked on hers, the lines in his face shifting in ways she'd never seen before. His chin puckered and his eyes glistened with a rare tenderness. "She'll be okay, Julie, I'm sure of it. Now go get dressed and ride with your husband."

"Oh, Daddy!" She sank against him and let his arms surround her. She couldn't recall him ever holding her like this before. She felt like a child in his embrace, safe, protected, cherished. "I love you, Daddy," she whispered against his stubbled cheek.

"I love you too, darling." The words erupted with pent-up anguish, raw, resonant with feeling. She had never heard him speak with greater conviction. "Hold on to your faith, Julie."

"I'm trying, Daddy."

Michael was suddenly at her side, urging her toward the stairs. "Come on, Julie. Get dressed. Beth will stay here with your dad."

For Julie, the drive to the hospital was pure torture—not knowing how Katie was, not being able to comfort her, not knowing what would confront them when they reached the hospital. Julie's stomach churned with nausea, as if a fist were pummeling her from the inside out. "We can't lose our little girl, Michael," she whispered over and over. "God, please, please don't take her!"

Michael said nothing, his jaw like steel, his eyes on the freeway, his hands white-knuckled on the steering wheel.

After an interminable silence, Julie asked in a small, pained voice, "Do you think God is trying to punish us, Michael?"

"Punish us? What for?"

"I don't know. For our sin."

"Which sin?"

"You know." She fished in her purse for a tissue and blew her nose. "For getting pregnant with Katie before we were married? And now He's punishing her for the same thing, the same sin we committed. It's like that verse you quoted once, 'The sins of the fathers are visited unto the next generation.'"

Michael cast her a piercing glance. "Listen to yourself, Julie. You don't know what you're saying."

"Yes, I do. I've never gotten over the guilt of it, Michael. Have you? Isn't it always there between us? Even now? I still don't know if you would have married me if I hadn't gotten pregnant."

He looked at her again, in astonishment. "What are you talking about?"

"The reason you married me—you had to. You had no choice."

"There's always a choice, Julie."

She gazed at his strong profile through teary eyes. "Are you saying you would have married me even if I wasn't pregnant with Katie?"

He gave her a look that sent an electrifying ripple through her. "I married you because I loved you, Jewel, pregnant or not."

Tears streamed down her cheeks. "I never knew for sure."

"Well, you know now. And as for God punishing us, you know the answer to that, too."

She nodded. "Christ paid the price for our sins. But sometimes I don't feel forgiven."

"Maybe you haven't forgiven yourself."

"Maybe not."

As Michael turned into the parking lot at Long Beach Memorial, he said, "Katie's going to be okay, Jewel." He pulled into a space and turned off the ignition. "We've got to believe that."

"I'm trying to, Michael," she said, her hand on the door handle.

Once inside the hospital, they went directly to Obstetrics on the second floor. At the information desk the nurse told them only that the ambulance had arrived and Katie was being prepped for surgery. She had no information on Katie's condition or the baby's. "But Dr. Russell, your daughter's obstetrician, has been notified, and he's on the way," she assured them.

"Can we see her?" pressed Julie. "Just for a minute?"

"I'm sorry, Mrs. Ryan. You'll have to wait for the doctor."

"Let's go sit down, Julie," Michael urged.

"We need to call Jesse. He should be here."

"I'll phone him," said Michael.

Ten minutes later Dr. Russell came striding across the waiting room, his expression grave. "Mr. and Mrs. Ryan," he said, his tone clipped, formal, "we've taken Katie to the operating room. It looks like the placenta has separated from the uterine wall, so I'll be doing an emergency C-section. The baby's in some distress, and Katie's lost a lot of blood."

"Will they be all right?" asked Julie urgently.

"Katie's a trooper, Mrs. Ryan. She'll fight hard for this baby. And you can be sure we'll do everything humanly possible for her and your grandchild. Say a prayer, because the rest is in the hands of God."

Julie brushed away a tear. "I haven't stopped praying."

A smile flickered in Dr. Russell's eyes. "Neither have I, Mrs. Ryan." He nodded at Michael and said, "I'll see you both in about an hour."

Jesse arrived within minutes after Dr. Russell disappeared into the surgical suite. Jesse was full of questions and moved around the room with a restless agitation, muttering to himself, taking deep breaths, shaking his long hair back from his head and tapping the wall nervously with his fist. "If anything happens to Katie and the baby, I'll never forgive myself," he said under his breath. Several minutes later he said haltingly, "I did this to her...it's my fault. Man, I love her! She's gotta live. She's gotta!"

For the next twenty minutes both Jesse and Michael paced the room, the two of them drifting back and forth to the water cooler, then to the window and reception desk, and back again, as if they were marking off steps in a strange tribal dance. When nearly a half hour had passed, Jesse marched over to Julie, his thumbs hooked on his jeans and said, as if Julie were the one deciding things, "Katie's gotta be okay. And the baby—Katie loves that baby. They both gotta make it!"

Julie nodded, her throat tight with unshed tears, and whispered, "Pray, Jesse. That's all we can do."

Jesse lifted his shoulders in a helpless gesture, then slumped down on the vinyl couch beside Julie. His voice was heavy with discouragement. "I've been praying, but I don't know if anybody's listening."

"Someone is," said Michael, going over, squeezing Jesse's shoulder.

"We should pray together," said Julie, her gaze moving beseechingly between the boy and the man.

Michael nodded and sat down beside her. He drew her against him until their heads nearly touched. She could see the emotion working in his face; he was trying hard not to break down. He looked over at Jesse and started to speak, but the sound wouldn't come. He cleared his throat and sniffed noisily, then rubbed his nose with his handkerchief. Finally he managed to rasp, "God loves Katie—more than we do. No matter what happens, He loves her!" He clutched Julie's hand firmly in his and lowered his head. "God, bring Katie and the baby through this. Please, God! Don't let her—" His voice broke. He tried once more, then buried his face in his hands.

Julie pressed her head against his shoulder and stroked his arm soothingly. "It's okay, Michael," she whispered. They were all silent for a long time after that.

Another half hour passed before Dr. Russell finally emerged from the operating suite, still in his scrub greens, his surgical mask hanging around his neck, his brow furrowed. As he approached, Julie noticed he looked older than she remembered, as if he had been to war and back and was here to tell the tale.

She shivered involuntarily and stood up. Michael and Jesse stood, too. Michael clasped her hand tightly, as if they were about to take the dizzying plunge on a roller coaster ride. No one spoke; no one moved; no one breathed.

"Katie came through the surgery," he said. "We've moved her to Intensive Care, where they'll be monitoring her closely."

"Is she okay?" asked Jesse.

"She's very weak, son. She lost a lot of blood. We transfused her and tied off the major artery in the uterus. Our concern now is postpartum hemorrhage. If the bleeding continues we may have to go back in and remove the uterus."

"The uterus?" Alarm tightened in Julie's chest. "Then Katie wouldn't be able to have more children."

"I'm afraid not, Mrs. Ryan, but that's an extreme measure. Let's not anticipate the worst."

"What about the baby?" asked Michael.

Dr. Russell inhaled deeply and nodded. "Your granddaughter lost blood, too and suffered some fetal distress, but she's alive. She's small. About five pounds. She's in an incubator in the neonatal intensive care."

"A girl! Katie wanted a girl," said Julie softly. "She'll be okay, won't she?"

"I won't mislead you by painting a rosy picture, Mrs. Ryan. Katie and the baby both have a fight on their hands. The next twenty-four hours will tell the story."

"They better not die!" said Jesse fiercely. "Tell me, Doc. They won't die, will they?"

Dr. Russell clasped Jesse's shoulder and smiled faintly. "Not if I have anything to say about it, son."

"When can I see Katie?" asked Julie.

"Let's give her a couple of hours to recover from the anesthetic. Meanwhile, you may want to take a little walk to the neonatal intensive care nursery and sneak a peek at your new granddaughter."

Minutes later Julie felt a flutter of excitement as she entered the neonatal nursery and gazed at the row of incubators looking like little glass boxes on wheels, some empty, but many occupied by miniature beings that seemed extremely old rather than precariously young—their faces pinched and wrinkled, their limbs mottled and frail, the adversities of the ancients in their puckered expressions.

The nurse led them to Katie's baby in the far corner—the newest arrival. Julie stared intently through the glass, fearful of what she might see. The infant lay motionless, except for its tiny chest rising and falling as it struggled to breathe. The baby was connected to an assortment of tubes and monitors that spewed out data about heart rate, blood pressure and urine output. Julie studied the round rosebud face and the tiny, grasping fingers. She was small, but still a well-proportioned baby—and very pretty, with black curly hair and half-closed, smoky gray eyes.

"Look at her, Michael," said Julie. "Isn't she the most beautiful baby in the world?"

He managed a wistful smile. "Next to Katie."

Julie stepped aside so Jesse could get closer to the incubator. At first he seemed reluctant, as if he wasn't sure how safe it would be. But after a moment he moved over and stared in silence at the fragile infant in the box. "Man alive," he exclaimed with pride and astonishment, "that's my kid!"

Chapter Twenty-Three

Nearly forty-eight hours after Katie had been rushed to the hospital for an emergency C-section, Dr. Russell told Julie and Michael he had good news. Drawing them aside as they approached Katie's room during visiting hours, he said with a twinkle in his shrewd eyes, "Your daughter is doing so well we'll be releasing her from the hospital in three or four days."

Julie's heart soared. "Thank God!"

"More good news," said Dr. Russell with a smile. "Your granddaughter—I believe Katie has named her Brianna—little Miss Brianna is doing very well and will be able to go home in about a week. Don't tell Katie, but I may even release Brianna on Christmas Day if her progress continues the way it has."

"That would be a wonderful Christmas gift for all of us," said Julie.

Michael nodded. "We're ready for both our girls to come home."

"And the young man, Jesse?" the doctor asked. "Will he be going home with you?"

Julie glanced from Michael back to the doctor. "Right now Katie and Jesse are only friends."

"And too young for marriage?" Dr. Russell asked gently.

"Perhaps in time," Michael said. "We'll be there for them, whatever they decide."

Dr. Russell smiled pensively. "With the C-section, your Katie will still need rest and visits from a home nurse for the next two or three weeks."

"I'll see that Katie follows your instructions to the letter," Julie assured him.

"Katie's fortunate to have two very supportive parents. Now you two go on in and have a fine visit with my star patient."

Entering Katie's room, Julie was pleased to see her daughter sitting up in bed brushing her hair. Her cheeks had a rosy glow and she was wearing a little makeup and a pink flannel nightgown Julie had bought her. Julie smiled. If Katie's vanity had returned, she had to be feeling better.

"You're looking good," she told Katie.

"I'm feeling pretty good, except for my incision," Katie replied, gingerly touching her abdomen. "Jesse was here earlier, and he brought me some magazines and a new CD, but he had to go to work."

She looked at her father. "He likes working for you, Dad, even better than his work at the gas station. He says you're a slave driver, but he doesn't mind."

"And he's turning into quite a responsible young man," said Michael.

"I know, Daddy. And he's determined to support our baby." She yanked her brush through a tangle of honey brown hair, then looked up expectantly. "Have you seen the baby today, Dad?"

"Not yet. We'll stop by the nursery after our visit with you."

Katie beamed a radiant smile. "They took me in a wheelchair to see her. She's so little and so pretty. Like a china doll. I sat and memorized how she looked, and talked to her and sang to her. I wanted to hold her so bad. They said maybe tomorrow."

"Just think, in a few days you'll both be coming home," said Julie. "You'll be back in your own room for Christmas, Katie."

"I can't wait. I'm going stir crazy in this place. And the food is gross—so bland and totally yucky. I'm dying for a pizza or a burrito or a chili dog."

Julie shuddered. "The baby will do better on more wholesome food."

"Don't preach, Mom. I'll do the best I can. But I can't go home without my baby. Don't let them send me home without her, Mom."

"It's not up to me, sweetheart, but I have a feeling you'll be getting just the Christmas present you want."

For the next three days Julie spent every possible hour at the hospital visiting Katie and the baby. It was an exhausting schedule, but she was the only one free, although Michael managed to slip away from the office for an hour or two each day, and Jesse came by whenever he wasn't working. Even Beth came by several times between showing houses.

Two days before Christmas, as Julie served a hurried breakfast of oatmeal and toast so she could leave for the hospital, her father tapped his spoon on his plate and groused, "How come I can't go see my granddaughter and new great-granddaughter?"

Julie looked at him in surprise as she buttered the toast. "I didn't know you wanted to, Dad."

"Of course I want to. Why doesn't anybody think to ask?"

"We figured you wanted to stay pretty close to home, Alex," said Michael, sipping his coffee. "We don't want you getting too tired."

"You're all afraid I'm going to drop dead, but I have no intention of checking out just yet. I've still got things to do."

"I could drive you over this afternoon for a couple of hours, Mr. Currey," offered Beth. She looked at Michael and added with a wink, "If my boss will give me some time off."

He smiled. "Your boss suggests you take all the time you need. Our appointment schedule is light today, anyway. No one wants to look at houses two days before Christmas. Everybody's out doing last-minute shopping. In fact, I plan to spend some time at the hospital later this afternoon myself."

"Then it's settled," Alex told Beth. "I'm going with you to see Katie and that little baby of hers."

Julie wiped her hands on a dish towel and said, "While you all finish eating, I'm going on to the hospital. I want to be with

Katie when they take little Brianna out of the incubator this morning and transfer her to the regular nursery.''

"Wait for me," said Michael, wiping his mouth with his napkin. "I want to be among the first to hold that little gal in my arms, too."

An hour later the three of them—Julie, Michael and Katie in a wheelchair—waited in the nursery as the nurse wrapped Brianna snugly in a receiving blanket and placed her in Katie's arms. Julie felt tears gathering behind her eyes as she gazed at her child and grandchild.

Katie looked so young in her lacy pink nightgown and matching robe, her burnished hair cascading around her shoulders, her face clean-scrubbed and beatific as an angel's as she smiled down at her tiny daughter.

Julie couldn't help thinking of the young mother Mary rocking the baby Jesus in her arms and marveling over His tiny fingers and toes. Mary couldn't have been much more than a child herself when she cradled the Savior of the world against her bosom.

Katie looked up at Julie and said, "Mom, you have tears in your eyes."

"Happy tears, sweetheart. Tears full of love." Julie reached out and smoothed back Katie's hair. "How does it feel to hold your baby at last?"

Katie beamed. "Oh, Mom, I love her so much! She's lighter than my dolls. And smaller, too. I can't believe she's real."

"She's a perfect little doll," said Julie.

After a while, Katie asked, "Do you want to hold her, Mom?"

"Let me help," said the nurse. She carefully lifted the bundle from Katie's arms to Julie's.

"You're right, she is light, Katie. I don't remember you being this tiny."

"I wasn't. Didn't you say I weighed eight pounds?"

"Whatever you weighed, you were just as gorgeous as your little daughter," said Michael.

After a minute Julie laid the baby in Michael's arms. "Hold her head, honey. That's it," she instructed. "Oh, darling, the two of you look so cute together. If only we had a camera."

Michael chuckled. "We do. At home in the closet."

"Bring it next time," said Katie. "The video camera, too."

"Look," said Michael, sounding pleased, "she's holding my finger. What a grip this girl's got. I have a feeling she's going to be a star athlete. Or maybe a mountain climber."

"No way," said Katie. "She's going to study ballet and be an artist like Mom and design all her own clothes. Or maybe she'll be a fashion model with her picture on all the magazines."

"I have a feeling she'll be anything she wants to be," said Michael.

"I won't let her do like I did," said Katie solemnly. "I don't want her to miss out on being a kid. And I want her to go to college and travel and have a wonderful career."

Julie squeezed Katie's shoulder. "We all want the best for our children, honey. But some things they have to decide for themselves."

Katie looked up earnestly at Julie. "Will you help me raise her to love God the way you do, so she'll make the right choices?"

Julie nodded, blinking away a tear. "I'll do everything I can to help, sweetheart."

"Hey, look at this," said Michael. "She's opening her eyes. She wants to know what's going on."

"She's looking right at you, Michael," said Julie, gently stroking the infant's rosy cheek. "Look at her studying you so intently, like she knows you're her grandfather. She's saying, 'Come play with me, Grandpa.'"

"Well, I think she's going to have to get a little bigger before I take her to the zoo or out for ice cream."

Brianna's rosebud mouth puckered and she made a soft mewling sound. "Oh, oh," said Michael, promptly handing her back to the nurse, "I think she wants her mother."

"She's probably hungry," said the nurse. As she placed the baby back in Katie's lap, she told Julie, "I'm taking them back to her room. Katie wants to try nursing."

Katie reached for her mother's hand. "Come with me, Mom. I'm scared I won't do it right."

"You'll be fine, honey. It just takes patience and practice."

Michael leaned over and gave each of his girls a quick kiss.

"While you girls do the 'mommy' thing, I'm going to work. I'll be back later."

While Katie was making her first valiant attempt to nurse her tiny daughter, Beth and Julie's father arrived. Julie met them outside the door of Katie's room and told them, "It's feeding time, so it'll be a few minutes before you can see the baby."

"That's fine. I'll go to the cafeteria and get us all some coffee," said Beth.

"Make mine strong, with two packets of sugar," said Alex.

Julie pulled a chair over beside her father's wheelchair. He was wearing his best blue suit and a pinstripe tie. His graying hair was neatly combed, and his freshly shaved skin smelled sweetly of cologne.

"You look great, Dad. How are you feeling?"

"Fine. Beth drives a little fast, but she got us here in one piece. But I'm already hungry after that light breakfast."

"We could have lunch here at the cafeteria after you see Katie and the baby."

"No, thanks. I had enough hospital food in Crescent City. But we passed a nice-looking steak house on our way here."

"No, Daddy. No steaks. Maybe some chicken?"

"Yeah, maybe chicken." His voice trailed off, then he said, "Your mom never treated me like this, fussing over every morsel I put in my mouth."

"Mom didn't know you had a bad heart, Dad."

"Well, I'm going home after Christmas. That's decided."

"Only if the doctor says you can live on your own again."

"I'll get one of those visiting nurses, if I have to."

Julie nodded. "That may work out just fine, Daddy."

"I miss my home," he said, staring down at his hands.

"I know, Daddy. I'm sure you miss all the things that remind you of Mom."

He nodded. "That and more. I miss the smell of my own house. And the sound of my own clocks. I know where the floor creaks and where to find things in the icebox and where things go in the drawers. It's an old house, not new-smelling and shiny and big like yours, but I like it just fine."

"I like it too, Dad." Julie patted his hand and smiled. "You know, Daddy, anytime you want, you can get rid of my paint-by-number paintings Mom hung years ago."

He looked sharply at her. "Why would I want to do that?"

"Because they're ugly as sin. I know you only left them up because Mom loved them so much."

He massaged his wrist, as if his arthritis was bothering him. "Your mother was going to take them down a long time ago."

"Really? Why didn't she?"

"I wouldn't let her."

Julie stared at her father in amazement. "Why not, Dad?"

Her father kneaded his knuckles with his thumb, his gaze lowered, his voice low and gravelly. "They were part of you. I liked them."

A lump swelled in Julie's throat, filled with tears from all the years of yearning for her father's love. "I can give you some new paintings, Daddy. Beautiful paintings. My best ones."

He nodded. "Fine. I'll hang them by the old ones."

Chapter Twenty-Four

When Beth returned from the cafeteria with coffee for everyone, the fragile ambiance of closeness between Julie and her father slipped away like sand through the fingers. But, as Julie sipped her coffee, she knew she would savor the memory of those moments always. And whenever she looked at her childish number paintings on her father's walls, she would know he loved her in his own private way.

"I hope you wanted your coffee black," said Beth, breaking into her thoughts.

Julie looked up, startled, and smiled. "Yes, this is fine. I needed something to wake me up. With the schedule I've been keeping lately, I never get enough sleep."

"Then why don't you go on home and take a nap," said Beth.

"Oh, no, I couldn't."

"Sure, you can. I'll stay with your father while he visits with Katie and the baby. Then I'll take him somewhere for lunch and bring him home."

"There's a nice steak house not far from here," said Alex spiritedly.

"Great! I love a good steak," said Beth.

"This really isn't necessary, Beth," Julie protested.

"Sure it is," said Alex. "You look tired, daughter. Go home and get some rest."

"Maybe a nap would be good." Julie stood and slung her purse strap over her shoulder. "Thanks, Beth. And, Dad, don't get too tired. And don't eat too much steak, you hear?"

"We won't be late," Beth promised.

On her drive home Julie mused with a note of irony, "Beth's not only trying to charm Michael, now she's charming Dad, as well. I guess, if I admit it, she's managed to charm the whole lot of us."

At home—with the rare luxury of the entire house to herself—Julie decided to take a leisurely bath before her nap. She put a Christmas tape on the stereo and lit several pine-scented candles around the oval tub. She emptied lavender bubble bath into the rushing lukewarm water, then stepped gingerly into a shimmering cloud of opalescent bubbles. She could already feel the tension easing in her taut muscles as she sank down into the fragrant, lulling warmth.

She soaked for nearly a half hour, listening to the melodic strains of "White Christmas" and "Oh, Little Town of Bethlehem." She inhaled the fragrant bouquets of flickering candles and diaphanous bubbles and whispered a prayer of gratitude for God's innumerable blessings.

As she towel dried her hair after her bath, Julie heard the doorbell, sounding distant, yet insistent. Usually there were leisurely spaces between the echoing chimes, but this time they were crowded together, one after another, frantic and demanding.

Julie hurried downstairs in her terry-cloth caftan, her hair still damp and tousled, the fragrance of her dusting powder surrounding her like a perfumed haze. In the living room the redolence mingled with the pine scent of the towering blue spruce, bountiful with Christmas tinsel and garlands—all seeming to promise a joyous holiday after a season of trials and uncertainty.

The ringing persisted as Julie crossed the living room to the foyer. It must be Michael, she mused. He must have misplaced his key. Or maybe it's Beth, home already with Dad.

Julie threw open the door without thinking, expecting to see a familiar face. Instead, her eyes settled on a stranger—a florid, rangy man in a corduroy jacket and rumpled jeans, his shirt open carelessly at the neck, his cropped brown hair flaring back from a high forehead. He had the face of a fighter—solid and irregular, with pronounced cheekbones, a prominent nose, narrow, compressed lips and a rock-hard jaw. He might have been attractive if his features weren't somehow off center, skewed, like a photograph taken at the wrong angle.

"May I help you?" Julie asked uneasily, already wishing she had looked to see who was there before opening the door.

"Where's Beth?" said the man, his tone heavy, clipped.

"Beth?" A tremor of fear fluttered through Julie's chest.

"Beth Chamberlin. I know she's staying here. I've seen her come and go."

"I'm sorry. She's not here," said Julie firmly. She stepped back and started to close the door, but the man sprang forward and caught the door with the flat of his hand. With the stunning swiftness of a jackal, he darted inside the foyer and slammed the door behind him.

"Get Beth," he demanded, his thick brows crouching over steely, ball-bearing eyes.

Panic mushroomed up into Julie's throat. For an instant she couldn't speak. Struggling to salvage a semblance of propriety, she said politely, "You—you must be Beth's husband—Roger, isn't it?"

He ignored her faltering attempt at hospitality. "Tell Beth to get her fanny down here—and make it quick!"

Julie crossed her arms defensively. Her robe covered her, but she still felt exposed, vulnerable. It startled her to realize she was trembling. "I told you, Beth's not here."

The man took a menacing step toward her, his hand on something in his jacket pocket. "And I say she is here. Do I have to tear this place apart to find her?"

Julie stiffened her spine and squared her shoulders. With all the boldness she could summon, she said, "I think you'd better leave now. I'll tell Beth you were here."

The intruder lurched forward and seized her wrist. Pain shot up her arm. "You get her down here, lady!" he snarled, his expression fierce, malignant. His face loomed so close to hers she could smell the sweet, noxious odor of liquor on his breath. His free hand moved in his pocket and he produced a gun—a shiny metallic gray: a pistol, a revolver, real or a toy, Julie had no idea. She didn't want to find out. "Get Beth," he growled, "or there'll be more than one corpse in this place today."

Julie's mouth turned to sand. "I—I told you, she's not here."

The man released her wrist and glanced around, brandishing his weapon in the air. "Beth? You here? I'm not playing games, Beth. You get down here!" He looked back stonily at Julie. His eyes had the red-rimmed, bloodshot glaze of an alcoholic. "She's out with him, isn't she—the two of them fooling around?"

"Who?"

"The man in the real estate office. I know all about him. I followed her to the place where she works. He's there, too. I've seen them together—talking, laughing. I've followed them to this house. I've seen them come in together. Who is he? Your husband?"

"I don't know who you mean," she whispered, terror filling the pores of her flesh.

"Sure you know. He's your husband, isn't he? What a stooge you must be! They're doing it right under your roof!" He nudged her throat with the cold, hard nozzle of his gun. "Maybe the two of us should fool around, too," he taunted, his lips curling into a sinister smile. "You know what they say. What goes around comes around."

Julie recoiled from his touch, her heart hammering, her legs wobbly as gelatin. "I—I'll go look for Beth," she whispered, the words riding a deep, shuddering sigh.

The man's shoulders relaxed; he stepped back slightly and grinned, as if he knew he had won. "I figured you'd see it my way, lady."

Julie pivoted sharply and took quick, breathless strides across the living room to the staircase. Without looking back, she bolted up the stairs, praying he wouldn't follow her. At the top of the stairs she hesitated. Where to go? It would be only seconds before the man realized she was pretending to get Beth. He would be outraged that she had tricked him. She might even become his target instead of Beth.

With no time to think, Julie raced blindly down the hallway to her bedroom. But even as she darted inside and locked the door she heard the man lumbering up the stairs, shouting, "Beth! Where in blazes are you!"

Julie ran to the nightstand for her cordless phone and stared in shock at its empty base. She stared frantically around the room. *In the name of heaven, where's the phone?* With its spacious retreat and cozy powder room, the master suite was the size of a small apartment. The phone could be anywhere.

She checked among the bed and sofa pillows. No phone. *Michael, Michael, where did you put the phone?* She hurried over to the tall cherry-wood entertainment center with its TV, VCR and stereo. Christmas carols were still playing sweetly in a jarring counterpoint to her terror. The candles were still lit around the tub and sweet floral scents lingered in the air.

But the phone that could provide her a lifeline was missing. And for all its roominess, her bedroom offered nowhere to hide and nothing with which to defend herself. "God, help me!" she whispered as she extinguished the candles. Pungent wisps of smoke spiraled in the air like whirling shadow dancers.

Julie sank down weakly on the velvet chair by her dressing table. She was panting so hard she was light-headed and her wrists felt prickly and weak. She stared at her reflection in the mirror and for an instant didn't recognize herself. Her face was chalky with fear, her lips pale as moonlight. Stay calm, she admonished herself. The phone is here somewhere. Keep your mind clear and focused; your life may depend on it.

"Beth! You in there?"

Julie jumped up, her heart lurching with alarm at the sound of the intruder's slurred voice outside her door.

Over and over he banged on the door, the walls vibrating with every blow. "Beth! Open the door!"

In desperation Julie paced her room, looking for something, anything, to use as a weapon. There was a large ceramic vase on the bureau. She had seen people in the movies break such vases over the heads of their attackers, but she couldn't imagine herself doing such a thing. She would surely drop it or miss. And one wrong move would spell disaster.

The pounding increased, the shattering noise boomeranging through the house. The door shuddered on its hinges. Julie could hear the door frame splintering with each explosive impact. Amid the blasts she could hear the man's crazed voice. "Beth, you're a dead woman, you hear me? So help me, dead!"

Julie hugged herself and rocked on the balls of her heels. She couldn't swallow, couldn't speak, couldn't pry her thickened tongue from the roof of her mouth. She was caught, trapped like an animal with nowhere to run.

Dear God, there had to be a way out.

Her desperate gaze swept over the room again. Her heart leapt as she caught a glimpse of the cordless telephone on the bureau behind the ceramic vase. She must have set it there unthinkingly. She seized it and clasped it to her breast. *Don't let it be too late to call for help!* she thought wildly.

Was there time even to dial, to speak?

One more strike and the door could burst open, and he'd have her.

Nowhere to run.

Or was there?

She hastened through the powder room and slipped into the cool, compressed darkness of her walk-in closet, knowing it could be her salvation or a death trap. As she closed the closet door, she heard her bedroom door crash open and slam against the wall, shaking the entire house.

A sob tore through her throat as she pushed a heavy cardboard box of art books against the light paneled door. It wouldn't keep him out, but it might buy her a few precious seconds. Her breathing ragged, she grabbed another box from the shelf and placed it on the first box, then another, until she managed to wedge the boxes against the doorknob.

Her fingers trembling, she felt in the darkness for the phone and moved her hands blindly over the smooth, raised buttons.

Where was the nine? The one? She pressed the buttons, praying they were the right ones and listened for the operator. A female voice came on the line, inquiring, "What's your emergency, please?"

"A man with a gun is in my house," Julie whispered thinly, cupping her hand around the mouthpiece. "He's going to kill me."

The operator's tone remained controlled and professional as she confirmed Julie's address, then said, "I've dispatched a squad car and backups to your house. They're only blocks away. They'll be approaching without sirens. How can they enter your house? And exactly where is the man at this moment?"

"My front door is unlocked," Julie whispered. "Tell them to come upstairs. He's in my bedroom, on the right."

"What is he doing right now, ma'am?"

"I don't know. I don't hear him. He broke down the door. He must be in my room. He may be in the retreat off the bedroom or on the balcony."

"Listen and see if you can hear him."

Julie removed the phone from her ear and listened. She heard a loud, steady pounding sound, then realized it was her own heartbeat. There was no other sound. "I don't hear anything. Maybe he's gone."

"Don't hang up," said the operator. "Stay where you are until the police arrive."

Julie waited, the silence deafening, the darkness nearly palpable. After a moment she heard lumbering footsteps in the powder room. "He's coming," she whispered, her pulse rate skyrocketing.

"Stay with me," said the operator. "The police are on your street now. In moments they'll be surrounding the house."

Just outside the closet, a deep, raw, venomous voice broke the stillness. "Beth, you in there?" A fist slammed against the hollow-paneled door. "Let me in, you two-timer!"

"He's found me," Julie whispered into the phone. She crouched down on the floor and leaned her weight against the boxes, every nerve electrified.

"Mrs. Ryan, officers are entering your house. Where's the man now?"

"Upstairs in my powder room, just off the master bedroom."

"Beth, open up!" came the bellowing voice. "You hear me?"

"I hear the man now," said the operator. "Stay on the line with me, Mrs. Ryan, until officers have apprehended the suspect."

A splintering sound ricocheted through the paneled wood. "He's breaking down the door," Julie cried shrilly.

The thick, frenzied voice roared, "Beth, open the door or I'll shoot right through it!"

In the heavy, suffocating darkness Julie drew her legs up against her chest and circled her knees with her arms. She pressed her forehead against her knees and imagined herself in a cocoon, safe, far away, in the hands of God. *Jesus, hold me in Your arms, keep me safe in Your arms.*

She heard a commotion outside the closet—scuffling sounds, footsteps heavy on the carpeted floorboards, a man's startled, protesting voice, then several masculine voices shouting at once, barking orders. She held her breath, waiting, listening. After a moment there was silence, dead silence. She waited some more.

A muffled voice came from the phone. "Mrs. Ryan, are you all right?"

"Yes," Julie told the operator shakily, "but I don't know what's happening."

"Officers have the suspect in custody."

"Thank God!" Julie flexed her legs and tried to stand, but her ankles wouldn't hold her yet. She leaned against the boxes and sucked the scant air into her lungs.

She jumped when a gentle rap came on the closet door. "Mrs. Ryan? It's Detective Whitcomb. Are you all right?"

Awkwardly she pushed the boxes aside, opened the door and sank with relief into the officer's arms. He held her as she broke into convulsive sobs. "It's okay," he told her, patting her back like a kindly uncle. "The man's gone. You're safe."

She couldn't stop shaking. She was trembling like a leaf in a rainstorm, shivering like a puppy after a cold bath. Through chattering teeth, she stammered, "I—I thought I was going to die!"

After the officers had gone, Julie—still trembling, her voice unsteady—telephoned Michael at the office.

"I'm sorry, Mrs. Ryan," replied his secretary, Rose. "Beth Chamberlin picked him up and they went out to lunch with your father."

"Michael went with them?"

"Yes, Mrs. Ryan. The three of them went out together."

Julie felt a flood of resentment. How was it possible—Beth and Michael having a pleasant lunch while she fought for her life against Beth's ex-husband!

"Mrs. Ryan, if it's an emergency, I'm sure you could reach Mr. Ryan at the steak house by the hospital. Would you like me to get the number for you?"

"Yes—I mean, no!" Julie hesitated. The last thing she wanted to do was frighten her father. "No, thank you. I—I'll see Michael when he gets home."

Julie heard the phone click and then the dial tone, but she still held the receiver, her emotions clashing like thunderbolts. How dare Michael be out with Beth when she needed him so desperately! How was it possible everyone she cared about was elsewhere, absorbed in other interests, when she had nearly died!

With trembling fingers Julie dialed Katie's hospital room, just to hear the sound of her daughter's voice and to remind herself that somewhere life was still normal and unchanged.

She heard it ring once, twice, but she slammed down the receiver before Katie answered. She couldn't let Katie hear the tremor in her voice. She would know something was wrong. I can't upset Katie. She has enough to think about with the baby. I'll just have to wait for Michael to come home.

Julie sat down on the edge of her bed and ran her hands over the billowy comforter. Try to relax, she told herself. Unwind, regain your composure. She stretched out on the satiny spread and fluffed the pillows under her head. She was safe, she reminded herself. God had protected her. The nightmare was over. Now if only she could convince her mind.

On the screen of her imagination Julie replayed every harrowing detail of the past hour, beginning with the ringing doorbell and concluding with the officer holding and consoling her in his arms. In between were the horrifying images of the drunken intruder pursuing her, his rough fingers gripping her wrist, his odious breath hot on her face, the diabolic look in his eyes as he waved his gun at her.

After a while weariness got the best of her. Julie drifted into slumber, taking the nightmarish images into her dreams. She slept restlessly for a time, then woke with a start when she heard a noise downstairs—the front door opening and shutting and footsteps resounding in the marble foyer.

She sat bolt upright, her heart pounding like a jackhammer. Someone was in the house with her again!

Chapter Twenty-Five

Slipping out of her room, Julie stole to the landing. She was still in her terry caftan, barefoot, her blond curls tousled, uncombed. She stood in a spot where she couldn't be seen from downstairs. Holding her breath, she listened, then sighed with enormous relief when she recognized the wonderfully familiar voices of her father, Michael and Beth. She heard Beth tell Michael, "I'll help your father get settled in his room. Then I'll be right back."

Her father's voice came back stubborn and inflexible as iron. "I can get myself to my room. I'm not a cripple yet."

"Okay, Mr. Currey," said Beth sweetly, "but if you need any help, you give me a call."

As Alex shuffled down the hall to his room, Julie heard Michael say, "I wonder where Julie is. She must be home. Her car's in the driveway."

I'm here, Michael! The words were on Julie's lips when it occurred to her to wait until her father was safely in his room. No reason for him to know the harrowing events that had just transpired in this house.

"Julie's probably upstairs showering or resting," said Beth.

"Then I think I'll run upstairs and change. Julie will probably want to go back over to the hospital. You can go with us or stay here with Alex, if you like.''

Beth's voice lowered confidentially. ''Michael, before you go upstairs, we need to talk.''

''Sure, Beth. What's up?''

''Not here. In the living room, okay?''

''Sure.''

Julie heard their footsteps fading as they left the foyer. She shrank back, not wanting to be seen. Something in Beth's tone sounded an alert in Julie's mind. She wanted to hear the rest of their conversation, and yet she wasn't one to eavesdrop. Still, this was her house and her husband, and she had something urgent to tell him, regardless of what Beth had to say.

Julie slipped quietly down the stairs and padded across the foyer, but paused just short of the living room. Perhaps she should give Beth a chance to tell Michael what was on her mind before breaking in with her disturbing news.

Beth was speaking in a confidential tone. ''We've needed to have this talk for a long time, Michael.''

''I'm not sure this is a good time, Beth. So much is going on.''

''No, Michael. It's exactly the right time. Now that Katie and the baby are going to be okay, it's the perfect time—''

''The perfect time?''

''You know. Time to tell Julie...about us.''

''About us? What about us?''

''You know. Julie needs to know how we feel about each other...that we'll be together eventually.''

No, this isn't happening! thought Julie, outside the door. She leaned back against the wall and closed her eyes. *No, God, please, no!*

''Hold on a minute, Beth.'' Michael sounded agitated.

''I know. I feel the same way you do, Michael,'' Beth rushed on, her voice light and breathless. ''I don't want to hurt Julie, either. I've honestly come to care about her. Like a sister. I love your whole family like they're mine. I'd do anything for them.''

''I appreciate that, Beth. Julie does, too.''

Beth's voice was soft, persuasive. Julie had to strain to hear the words. "But we can't go on pretending like nothing's happening between us, Michael. Julie's a good person. She won't stand in our way once she knows how much we love each other."

Beth's quiet words blasted into Julie's consciousness like exploding dynamite. Julie pivoted sharply, reeling from the shattering impact and covered her mouth as a sour taste rose in her throat. She pattered quickly back down the hall, hurried up the stairs and fled to her bedroom. She quickly shut the door, rushed to her retreat and flung herself on the tufted sofa.

Julie thought she had endured the worst assault of her life earlier today, but that was nothing compared with this. She wanted to cry; she wanted to scream; she wanted to throw something against the wall, break something and see it shatter in a million pieces, the way her heart was breaking now. She wanted to hurl something at Michael and make him hurt like he was making her hurt. But her anguish was too deep to reach with tears. She tried to cry, but her chest heaved with a dry, racking spasm. No tears would come; the sob remained locked in her throat.

She sat up and hugged herself and rocked back and forth. Her mind struggled to make the words she had heard seem real. Nothing about this day was real. Surely Beth's husband hadn't come stumbling into her home threatening her with a gun, chasing her through her own house, cornering her in her closet. Surely she hadn't believed with all her heart she was about to be murdered in her own home. Surely she hadn't just heard Beth and Michael standing in her living room declaring their love for each other.

"Dear God, what are You doing to me?" she cried aloud. "How can these things be happening after all we've gone through with Katie and the baby? Just when I thought life was going to be good again, You're taking away the most important man in my life. How can I go on without Michael?"

From deep within her consciousness she heard a voice, not audible, but as real as any voice she had ever heard. *Trust Me. I love you. I am working all things for your good.*

At last the tears came, freely, washing over the deep hurt. "Dear Jesus, help me," she prayed with a raw desperation. "I need You. I have no words, only pain. Please help me!"

Julie lost track of time. Ten or fifteen minutes passed when she heard a click at the door. Someone was trying the handle. She slipped off the sofa, combed her fingers through her hair and went to the door. She heard Michael's voice. "Julie, it's locked. Let me in."

She opened the door and stared up at him, her cheeks still damp with tears. He gazed down at her, the lines around his forehead and mouth deep, troubled. She had never seen him look so wretched. He had the face of a man about to ask for a divorce.

She brushed away her tears, but she couldn't bring herself to say anything but his name. "Michael."

The furrows in his brow deepened. "Are you okay, Jewel? You've been crying."

She nodded. "I—I guess everything finally got to me."

"I know. It's been a trying time for all of us." He paused meaningfully. "But I think everything's going to work out now, at last."

He's talking about him and Beth, she realized. Everything's going to work out for the two of them now that the crisis is over with Katie.

"Where's Beth?" she asked thickly.

"In her room, packing. That's what I want to talk to you about, Julie. Beth's decided she can't stay here any longer."

Julie wanted to ask, Does that mean you're packing and leaving now, too, Michael? Are you going away with the woman you love?

Julie ran her hand over the smooth surface of the bureau. "Before she goes, Michael, tell Beth her ex-husband was here to visit her earlier."

"Her ex-husband? Here? He came to our house?"

"I let him in," said Julie, her voice trembling again at the memory. "I thought it was you or Beth at the door." She crossed her arms against her chest. Even thinking about that madman make her feel weak and nauseous again.

Michael reached out for her. "Dear God in heaven, Julie, did he hurt you?"

"I'm okay," she said tremulously, backing away. "I'm all right now. But he ranted and raved and waved a gun."

"A gun?"

"I called the police. They came and took him away. It's over, Michael." Everything is over, she thought darkly. "You can tell Beth she doesn't have to be afraid anymore. Her ex is back in jail, and I don't think he'll be out for a long time."

"Thank God he didn't hurt you!" Michael came and embraced her, a comforting gesture, but she broke away. He drew her back into his arms more forcefully, his warmth and closeness making her pain all the more acute.

Now that she was losing him, she realized how utterly and intensely she loved him. It overrode everything, even the seething anger she felt over his betrayal. She was probably even foolish enough to take him back if he changed his mind about Beth. Surely this was the ultimate humiliation. All her life she had felt rejected by her father, and now she was being rejected by the husband she had adored and trusted.

And yet she hadn't been rejected by God. Even now, He was whispering His comfort in the silence of her heart, assuring her that all things would ultimately work out for her good. If only she could believe that. If the worst could happen and she could still believe God meant it for her good, then she could face anything life threw at her without being afraid.

"Julie, did you hear me?" It was Michael, sounding concerned, impatient. "I was talking to you. Did you hear anything I said?"

She looked at him as if she were seeing a stranger—a handsome, virile man who over the years had become part of the very fabric of her being. Sometimes she wasn't sure where she left off and he began. They complemented each other in so many ways—each was strong where the other was weak.

Only none of that mattered now because he was ready to walk out of her life for another woman, a woman who didn't really seem like the enemy, because Julie had come to know and care for her, flaws and all. Beth wasn't an evil person. She was, like Julie, a flawed human being—a very needy, wounded young woman whom Michael apparently loved.

"Julie, what's wrong with you?" Michael again. "You look so preoccupied, almost dazed, like you're in shock. No wonder, after that madman came storming in here. Maybe I should call the doctor. Are you sure you're okay?"

She looked up at him and studied his earnest, chiseled features, so perfectly honed that women couldn't help noticing him. Julie wanted to lash out at him, hurl a thousand accusations at him, but God's consoling love seemed to act as a buffer. It was as if she were responding emotionally to God's love rather than to Michael's betrayal. It was a mystery, baffling, that the stunning impact of Michael's actions were being filtered through Christ's presence. Jesus was in this room with her, giving her His strength and comfort even as Michael stood here ready to shatter their marriage vows.

So this is what it's like, she thought, to sense God's Spirit buoying and strengthening me even when my world is crumbling! "Michael," she said firmly, "you said you have something to tell me. Tell me now. Get it over with."

He paced the room, raking his fingers through his hair. "I don't know how to tell you this, Jewel. I know it's going to come as a shock, and the last thing I want to do is hurt you after what you faced with that lunatic and all we've been through with Katie and the baby."

"Just tell me, Michael. What is it?"

"It's about the suspicions you've always had about Beth—you know, how she felt about me. You were right all along."

A chill knifed through Julie. "I know."

"You know?"

"I was downstairs a little while ago. I heard you and Beth talking in the living room."

"You heard? Then why didn't you say something? Why did you let me go on like this?"

She hugged herself again, protectively. "I don't know, Michael. I guess I need to hear it from your own lips. I can't make myself believe this is happening. I don't even know what to say to you. I thought I'd feel angry, outraged—and maybe I do—

maybe it's too soon for it all to sink in. Right now I just feel numb inside.''

Michael reached out and ran his hand lightly over her bare arm. ''That's how I feel too, Jewel. I'm so sorry—''

She pulled away from his touch. ''It's a little late to be sorry, Michael.''

''I know. You were right all along. I should have listened to you.''

She looked blankly at him. ''Listened to me? What are you talking about?''

''About Beth. You were right about her. I should have believed you.''

Julie shook her head, bewildered. ''I don't understand—''

''I'm talking about Beth,'' said Michael, ''about her outburst, her confession, her crazy idea about the two of us—''

''You're not making any sense, Michael.''

He arched one brow quizzically. ''You said you heard everything, Jewel. Then you heard Beth say she and I had a future together—''

''Yes.'' Julie's voice tightened. ''I heard her say the two of you are in love and it's time to let me know you plan to be together.'' Her hands felt cold, clammy. She massaged the back of one, then the other. ''Every word is seared in my head, in my heart. Are you happy, Michael? I hope so, because I feel like I'm dying inside.''

Michael seized her hands and said fiercely, ''Julie, if you heard our conversation, you must have heard me tell Beth there's nothing between us because it's you I love—you I'll always love.''

''Me?''

''Yes, you.''

''But Beth said the two of you are in love—''

''It's what she wanted to believe, Julie.'' Michael released her hands and rubbed the bridge of his nose. ''I have to accept some of the blame for this, Julie. I admit I was flattered by Beth's attentions. A part of me was attracted to her, but I never meant to lead her on. I told her so. We were never more than friends.''

''Just friends?'' Julie touched the hollow of her throat, an unconscious gesture, her mind still trying to grasp the truth. "You must have done something, Michael, to make Beth believe you loved her. She's not a stupid woman. And you're not a stupid man. You must have sensed how she felt about you. Even I saw it."

"I know. You warned me." Michael loosened his tie. "I just wasn't thinking straight. For a time after your mother died, things weren't going well between us, Julie. You remember. I felt like you were shutting me out. And then Katie got pregnant, and I felt like I was losing my little girl. When Beth started acting so kind and sympathetic, it just seemed natural to turn to her. But I swear I was never unfaithful to you."

"Not even in your heart?" she challenged.

Michael sat down on the bed and pulled his tie from around his neck. "I can't answer that, Julie. On some level I suppose I enjoyed Beth's flirtations and maybe I flirted back. Maybe I wanted it both ways. Beth needed me, and I liked feeling needed. That was something you and I never had. I never felt like you really needed me. You always held back a part of yourself. You always had to be strong and self-reliant. It was like you were afraid to be vulnerable."

She sat down beside him on the bed and twisted the gold wedding band on her finger. "I was afraid of being rejected, the way my father rejected me when I was a child. I thought if I wasn't vulnerable, I wouldn't be hurt. If I hid behind a wall, no one could wound me. But that doesn't excuse you, Michael, for leading Beth on."

"I know. I was wrong. I apologized to her."

"What will she do now?"

"I'm not sure. She's hurt and embarrassed. I have a feeling she'll look for another job, although I told her she's welcome to stay with our office."

He paused for a long moment, his expression solemn. "One more thing, Julie. After our talk, Beth realized she's been using our family as a sanctuary or a safety net after her divorce, so she wouldn't have to face the real world. She admitted she's got to carve out a new life for herself, that she can't live her life vicariously through us. I hope today will be the first step in a happy future for her.''

''I hope so too, Michael. I cared about her, you know that. And Dad and Katie are crazy about her. In spite of everything, I wish her well.''

''I know,'' said Michael. ''That's what I love about you.'' He touched her hair, clasped her curls in his hand. ''I'm sorry, Julie, for hurting you. I was wrong. Will you forgive me?''

She pressed her cheek against his palm. ''I want to, Michael. Right now I still feel hurt. But I forgive you. I do. Because I love you with all my heart.''

Michael moved his fingertips gently over her cheekbone and traced the outline of her lips. ''And, Jewel, my priceless Jewel, I love you beyond words.''

She didn't resist as he pulled her against him and brought his mouth down tenderly on hers. It was a kiss of many paradoxes, filled with passion and pain, sorrow and joy, disenchantment and hope. And, for Julie, with the kiss came the confidence that her marriage would be stronger for all the trials they had endured. And maybe that was the lesson God had been trying to teach them all along.

Epilogue

Memories.

Precious memories.

Dear Lord, we've been building so many memories these past two years, my heart overflows with reminiscing. Right now, as I write, I'm sitting at the kitchen table watching two-year-old Brianna in her high chair, playing with her birthday cake. She has managed to smear chocolate frosting all over her chubby pink cheeks and through her chestnut brown curls. She utters shouts of glee as her round fingers sink deliciously into the mounded cake, as if it were a wet and gooey mud pie.

Jesse is busy snapping pictures while Michael captures the entire hilarious event on videotape. Katie stands poised with a washcloth, shaking her head and rolling her eyes and trying not to laugh. Laughter will only encourage Brianna to new heights of mayhem and misadventure, like the times she bathed her teddy bear in the toilet and emptied a box of corn flakes into the fish tank. "Fishes eat breakfast, Gramma," she explained with perfect logic.

As I watch Michael and Katie and Jesse swoop and prance around Brianna, urging her to smile and wave and clap, I think about how far we've come as a family. These past two years haven't been easy, but we've been blessed in so many ways.

Katie's eighteen now and still living at home, attending junior college when she's not caring for Brianna. She hopes to be a teacher someday. But she's the first to admit she's not quite ready yet for marriage.

Jesse still works for Michael and has become a skilled carpenter. He also helps out at the youth center, which, thanks to so many dedicated volunteers, is a rousing success. Jesse is proud he's able to support his daughter, and he hopes one day he and Katie will be married. But for now they're good friends—and devoted parents—who still have some growing up to do.

Michael and I have done some growing ourselves. He's taken the lead in having an occasional family time to talk and pray and read from the Scriptures. These special times have drawn us closer to God and to each other. Sometimes Katie and Brianna join us and we all sing "Jesus Loves Me" and jubilantly clap our hands like foot-stomping, old-time Gospel singers.

Occasionally we hear from Beth—a Christmas card, an announcement about the new real estate office she opened in Santa Barbara, and, last summer, an engraved wedding invitation with a note scrawled across the bottom: "This time I've really met Mr. Right. Hope you all can come and meet him, too! Love, Beth."

Michael and I drove up for the wedding, and Mr. Right turned out to be a really nice guy. I admit Beth and I had a few awkward moments, but the spark of friendship was still there, too. I wished her well, and I have a feeling the next time we hear from Beth, it'll be a baby announcement.

Michael and I don't talk much about Beth anymore. We're both too busy to brood over the past. He's still running his real-estate office, renovating houses, with Jesse's help, and volunteering at the youth center. I'm busy painting, and now that I have a New York agent, I'm swamped with commissions. Several local galleries are displaying my work, and I'm hoping to be accepted soon by one of the national watercolor exhibitions.

No matter how busy we are, Michael and I make a point of

visiting Dad a couple of times a month to check on his health and make sure he's following doctor's orders. Dad's still living alone and managing on his own, stubborn and proud as always. He still doesn't say much, but that's okay, because I've learned to hear love in the silences. And I noticed he's hung the new watercolors I gave him right beside my old, artless paint-by-numbers.

Lord, I'd love to write more, but I'm sitting in the midst of a blissful, wall-to-wall chocolate hullabaloo. Little Brianna, crowing with delight, has just pushed her entire fudge cake on the floor, and everyone's rushing about, shrieking and laughing at once, while Michael dutifully videotapes the uproarious pandemonium.

I sit where I am, ignoring the mess, watching, smiling, scratching these words in my journal and tracing gossamer memories like spinning reels of videotape, to savor with Michael through all the cherished and variegated years of our marriage.

* * * * *

Dear Reader,

As I was writing Julie's story, I wanted to show her struggling with the same issues that I—and most Christians—struggle with. How do I come to know and love God with all my heart, mind, soul and strength, the way He commands us? And how do I learn to love others as myself?

This is a favorite theme of mine as I write my novels and speak to women's groups across the country. How can we become authentic, joyous women of passion who consistently experience God's love and in turn share that loving intimacy with our husbands, children and those in our circle of love? The "good news" is that we can indeed develop an intimate, moment-by-moment "walk and talk" with Christ that will see us through our trials and heartaches and make us the loving, fulfilled women we want to be. In *Decidedly Married,* I tried to portray Julie's day-by-day journey of love and faith as she learned to experience God's presence and discovered a more abundant love for her husband and family.

In the book, Julie's pastor touched on the secret to such a life: "Fall in love with Jesus. Get to know Him as you would your most intimate friend.... Don't leave Him in the pages of your Bible or in the walls of your church. Let Him come alive in your heart. Let His Spirit breathe and speak in the hidden rooms of your mind. Let Him move in you and change the very landscape of your soul."

Dear reader, I pray that you are experiencing the joy and delight God has for you. Remember, Christ spread His arms and died on a cross for you. His arms are still open to welcome and forgive you and enfold you in His all-encompassing love. And remember that I love you, too!

Warmly,

Carole Gift Page

Continuing in April from
Love Inspired...

FAITH, HOPE
& CHARITY

a series by

LOIS RICHER

**Faith, Hope & Charity: Three close friends
who find joy in doing the Lord's work...and
playing matchmaker to members of this
close-knit North Dakota town.**

You enjoyed the romantic surprises in:

FAITHFULLY YOURS
January '98

Now the matchmaking fun continues in:

A HOPEFUL HEART
April '98

Faith, Hope and Charity are up to the challenge when
a headstrong heroine clashes with an impossibly
handsome lawyer. Could love be on the horizon?

And coming soon, a dedicated nurse falls for the
town's newest doctor in:

SWEET CHARITY
July '98

Love Inspired™

IFHC2

Welcome to *Love Inspired*™

A brand-new series of contemporary inspirational love stories.

Join men and women as they learn valuable lessons about facing the challenges of today's world and about life, love and faith.

**Look for the following May 1998
Love Inspired™ titles:**

A FAMILY TO CALL HER OWN
by Irene Hannon

LOGAN'S CHILD
by Lenora Worth

THERE COMES A SEASON
by Carol Steward

Available in retail outlets in April 1998.

LIFT YOUR SPIRITS AND GLADDEN YOUR HEART
with *Love Inspired!*™

**Steeple
Hill**™

I598

Concluding in May from

 ™ *Love Inspired* ™

VOWS

a series by
Irene Hannon

Don't miss the conclusion to this deeply emotional
series about three close friends....

*Each has a secret hidden in their past.
Each will experience the love of their own special
man. But will they be able to conquer the shadows
which still plague them...and look to the
future with renewed faith?*

The series began in October with...
HOME FOR THE HOLIDAYS

Continued in February with...
A GROOM OF HER OWN

And concludes in May with...
A FAMILY TO CALL HER OWN

When Rebecca Matthews fell for dashing Zach Wright,
he offered her a glimpse of happily-ever-after.
However, a traumatic incident in her past warned her
not to dream of a family of her own. But then Zach
became the guardian of a precious little girl, and
Rebecca knew the Lord wouldn't want to turn away
from this man and child....

Only from *Love Inspired.*